THE SENTINEL

A NOVEL

T.M. HAVILAND

**DARK SPACE
PRESSWORKS**

CONTENTS

THE
SENTINEL

Millions of years before life sprang forth on Earth, life got a head start in another star system, far from Earth. That lead was roughly the time it took for the human force to push forth through primates to modern, intelligent mankind. In their remote corner of space, the life form understood nature's competitive design, that it transcended the universe, and shrewdly used their head start to their advantage. Regardless of why they had been granted a head start other intelligent life had to live with the *consequences*.

ONE

Year 2124, Endurance Site, Northern Antarctica

One hundred and sixty-eight kilometers inland from the northern coast of Antarctica, on top of the glacier of ice blanketing the continent, Nick Standish and his team of master mining engineers hit earth at the bottom of their ice shaft. This was a special dig, unlike any of the others. They'd dug other mineshafts, deep holes on other continents for mining companies to extract Earth's riches. None compared to this one, through ice, in the last frontier on Earth.

Nick waited for Hammer—the crew's nickname for the demolition robot—as the machine grabbed the last chunk of ancient ice with its claw, rotated its torso, and heaved it into the container on the platform. He then touched the control panel and watched the lift take off, gliding up the track and heading two-thousand six-hundred meters to the top of the shaft he and his crew had dug. It was a hole big enough to house two industrial lifts, the next phase of their project.

At the top, a crane machine would pick up the large bucket of ice and discard its contents onto a growing mountain of rubble. Head cocked back nearly ninety degrees, Nick squinted as he gazed up at the top—where they had started nearly a year earlier—at the glowing ring of sunlight reflecting off the blue ice. He smiled and was content, satisfied they had hit bottom. He loved digging deep in the Earth, hunting for hard-to-find resources; he loved the physical challenge. It wasn't just a new hole. It was also the start of a new hunt, in a part of the world that still remained very much a mystery.

Nick removed his gloves, popped the latch on his clear-domed helmet, and raised it from the seal of his thermal suit. Slowly, he breathed in the arctic air, cringing at the burn in his nose and throat. He scratched his long beard and looked around at his comrades and grinned. "Boys..." he said with some gusto. "We fucking did it!" With bare hands and feeling some hard-earned success, the men shook hands and grabbed each other's shoulders.

Nick knelt and touched the surface—soil that hadn't felt air in over fifteen million years. He wondered what rare elements the mining project would uncover. Iridium? Dysprosium? New elements to add to the periodic table? Fossils of creatures never seen before? What else? *Well, Jonathan and Ellie... we're here now*, he thought to himself. *Time to explore.*

"Let's do a full sweep before we wrap it up for the day," Nick called to his crew.

Francisco, one of the engineers, picked up a penetrating scanner and walked over to their marked starting point. He turned on the device, pointed it at the wall of ice, and walked around the perimeter of the shaft. A quarter of the way, he stopped.

"What's wrong?" asked Nick.

Francisco frowned. "Man, the display just freaked out." He powered the device off and back on.

A moment later, the earth beneath the men's boots rumbled. Instinctively, they put their helmets back on and looked up as they backed against the walls of the shaft. Ice flakes fell, but no ice—nothing big. Nick sighed. "Just a small one," he relayed into his helmet's com unit. The vibrating earth slowly died out. They removed their helmets again and breathed.

That night, in the most remote spot on Earth, the hardened men celebrated the raw grit of the doing. Jonathan De Clare, their employer, would celebrate their hole through the ice as a doorway to the vast untapped riches deep in the frozen continent. Scientists would celebrate their achievement as a giant step towards finding answers to many questions about evolution of life on Earth. The world would remember their efforts as a historic point in time, an awakening to what was out there in the universe.

———

Sitting in his conference room at JDC Resources Group headquarters in Lucerne, Switzerland, Jonathan De Clare and a few of his investors and board members met to hear the great news from the Endurance team. Eager to hear from Nick, Jonathan leaned forward and pressed a button on the control unit laying on his conference table. The entire wall slid sideways, revealing a large screen. A moment later, Nick and his crew appeared on the wall-screen, sitting around a planning table inside the Endurance main station. Behind the crew, a curved glass wall framed a scene with a crane, snow crawlers, a vertical-takeoff aircraft, and—in the distance—ice-covered mountains jutting up through the Antarctic glacier.

"Hello men!" said Jonathan. "I understand you have news for us."

Nick rocked forward, resting his forearms on the table. "We have some significant news, Chief!" Tattoos meandered out of his shirt sleeve around his bicep. "We hit bottom! Twenty-six hundred meters of ice." He smiled and winked. "Takes some real cojones to do, Boss. We hit some roadblocks along the way. Even a minor tremor at the very end when we were wrapping it up at the bottom of the shaft. But we did it!"

"Very exciting news team!" Out of the corners of his eyes, Jonathan caught the slight movements of a couple men at his conference table, sitting up straighter and pushing their chests out. They didn't see big rugged men like Nick and his crew too often.

"See this, Jonathan?" said Nick with his hand wrapped around a glass jar. "It's full of dirt. Dirt that's been preserved for twenty million years. It's some old ass Mesozoic dirt. Hell, it could have gold in it. I haven't yet run it through an analyzer. At any rate, it took a lot to get that dirt. It's a little souvenir for you."

Jonathan and his group laughed. The engineers on the screen cracked grins.

"Thanks, team. I'm proud of you guys. I'll be there soon to pick it up." Jonathan looked over at his investors realizing a couple were still new to this game. "Next phase is to build the structure to house the dual lifts that will run up and down between the surface and the bedrock level." After seeing a few nods he turned back to the screen. "So, what's the schedule for constructing the lifts, Nick?"

"We begin assembling the framework immediately. All the components for phase one have been flown in."

"Can you show us the shaft? I just want to admire you and your team's hard work."

Nick looked across the table at another engineer. He was already working the controls. Jonathan recognized Sergey Kalashnikov—his company's top roboticist and the project's head machine engineer.

Sergey accessed one of the drones docked outside the main station and transmitted to it instructions. "Here we go."

The wall-display in Jonathan's conference room switched to split screen. On the left were Nick and team, and on the right was a view from a drone staring at a parked snow crawler. The drone lifted off its charging station, ascended straight up above the site, and rotated its camera downward. The bird's-eye view of the Endurance site was clear. The sun glistened off the metal surface of the disk-shaped main station. A vertical-takeoff cargo aircraft sat parked on a nearby landing pad. Rows of heavy metal structures to the elevator framework lay near the shaft. A robotic tower crane stood tall over the site.

The drone hovered over to the opening of the vertical shaft through the glacier, and slowly descended. Its lights illuminated the walls of ancient ice. Minutes later, as the craft approached the bottom, it slowed and levitated while its engines blew air across the frozen floor. A flag planted in the earth wafted back and forth with the letters *JDC* emblazoned on both sides.

Jonathan's eyes widened; his heart rate picked up. "Team... seeing that flag just gets my blood pumping. In all seriousness, I am impressed. *This* is a major milestone." With a forced calm, he leaned back in his chair. His thick black and grey hair, longish beard, and regal demeanor denoted a confidence that rested on many years in the business, experience gained by skillfully building his empire himself, stone by stone. Jonathan applauded his team.

The engineers cracked smiles through their beards. They appreciated their boss's sincerity. But mostly, they didn't give a shit. They knew how hard they had worked; what they had achieved. They were now ready for a bit of celebration.

With his eyes fixated on the flag on screen, Jonathan thought for a moment about the empire he had built over the past fifty years. He knew he was the world's largest global supplier of natural resources. His hundred and forty-five thousand employees and over a hundred and fifty mines were spread across every continent in the world. His operating capital, AI scanning technology, robotic machinery, smelters, refineries, and ships brought raw metals, rare earth elements, and other of Earth's riches to the demanding markets of the world. He was single-handedly pushing to open up Antarctica and mine the treasure waiting under all that ice. He knew he could do it and he had the know-how and, most importantly, the capital.

While watching the flag float back and forth, Jonathan longed for someone to share the thrill with, to enjoy the rewards of his success along the path of empire building. He had searched for that woman, but the relationships always ended. The closeness never developed. Nevertheless, even staring the age of seventy-two squarely in the eyes, he still yearned for that one.

Jonathan exited his office to meet Aleksander—his first and most trusted investor. It was a clear day in Lucerne. *A rarity*, he thought. He could see the top of Mount Rigi off in the distance at the far end of the clear glistening lake. Lake Lucerne's tree-lined path, dotted with boat docks, espresso stands, and manicured gardens, had not changed in hundreds of years. Mothers on benches talked while sipping their cappuccinos. Children rode scooters and chased each other. Jonathan found Aleksander in his usual spot—sitting on a bench, breaking bread and tossing it to a pair of ducks he had befriended.

After their usual business-handshake and tactful greeting, the two men ambled slowly along the lake front, their private conversation unfolding at the pace of their walk like many merchant bankers and their clients—old monied families, oligarchs, and monarchs—had done for hundreds of years. They retraced the same path they had walked for many of their talks and negotiations.

Jonathan was in selling mode. "It's the space industry. These advanced materials and technology used in off-planet exploration are sucking up Earth's reserves quicker than anyone had ever thought possible. Every time scientists fill in the periodic table with a new, rarer element, we find some highly valued use for it in materials, energy production, or computing technology."

Aleksander glanced at Jonathan. "I agree, Jonathan," he replied in a thick Russian accent. "I understand the dwindling global supplies and the challenges that lay ahead. That's why I'm onboard with Endurance. Or, let's say, I am cautiously on board. I see the potential advantage it could give us. It's the Treaty that concerns me, as well as all your other investors. It still doesn't allow mining. It is a significant risk. It could impede us for a long time. What are you hearing from the board and our other sources?"

Jonathan had built JDC on the back of high-risk frontier projects and learned early how to mitigate risk through information, knowing as much as possible about an issue. High quality information came through contacts into powerful governments. To get that information, he paid premium fees to his board of directors—all former CEOs of the world's leading banks, former heads of state and other former higher-ups who knew the value of their contacts. Many board members' villas along the Amalfi Coast and other exotic locations had long been paid for by simply sitting on his board.

"Leaders are being pushed to face the coming global supply situation. I understand the topic is on the agenda more often at the G-X meetings." Jonathan cast a glance at Aleksander. "I call them G-X because every year or two other countries get invited and then some get booted from the club."

Aleksander raised an eyebrow. "Yes, and my country is always going through the revolving door."

They both chuckled as they slowly paced along.

Jonathan had other sources as well. Not on his payroll, but well compensated. Some were his eyes and ears inside his competitors. He looked at Aleksander. "I also know our competitors are testing the Treaty in other parts of the continent and they are getting away with it for longer than in the past."

"My contacts are... how do you say it... singing a similar tune? They spoke of this last G-X meeting. Closed-door sessions of smaller groups had discussed the topic. Evidently, things got a little heated."

"If bigger governments start throwing their weight into the discussions, I am sure tensions will rise," said Jonathan, looking off in the distance.

Aleksander had put a lot of trust in Jonathan's skills at executing and understanding the risks, the main reasons he had parked so much money with him. His money was patient. He wasn't driven purely by returns and short-term gains. He sought multi-generational growth. Yet, he had real scars from time and too much patience in other investments.

They reached the espresso stand by the boat dock, their normal turnaround spot.

Aleksander stopped. "What's the biggest challenge you see?"

Jonathan reflected for a moment with his hands behind his back. He knew his agreement with the Norwegians on mining rights in their claimed territory in Antarctica was rock solid. Once the Antarctic Treaty fell apart, they would stake out their claim and then his agreement would go into effect. That was no longer a significant risk. His eyebrows raised. "Global unrest," he sighed. "Countries want access to the resources there. They will want their share of the pie, so to speak. Our forecasts tell us global supplies of metal resources will diminish, prices will rise enough that countries will turn to aggression, as they have often done in the past."

Aleksander finished breaking the bread and dropping the crumbs. The two ducks had caught up, realized there was no more bread, and wandered off towards the water. He looked at Jonathan and held his gaze. "You know, my friend, I have learned some hard lessons from other investments where the rewards were there, but the risks exceeded our ability to influence and control. My gut tells me this one is going to require a lot of attention, and a lot of capital. Your other investors share my concerns, Jonathan."

Jonathan listened. He knew what Aleksander was saying, without saying it. If the project started looking like a sinkhole for money, with no end in sight to the regulations, they would all pull the plug.

Jonathan smiled as he patted Aleksander on the shoulder. "How about an espresso for the walk back? I'm buying."

TWO

Year 2124, Mars

A formation of aerial drones traced slowly over a quadrant along the dry, featureless equator of Mars, two thousand kilometers west of Station Athena. The penetrating scanners probed under the Red Planet's surface, hunting for signs of natural resources—H_2O, Silicon, Iron, rare elements. A third of the way through their job, three of the fifty drones flinched. Each wobbled in space, banking left and right erratically, as if something had briefly disconnected their thinking parts from their control parts. Within a few seconds, the three regained control of themselves and resumed their positions in the formation.

The drones progressed methodically, slowly, heading northwest towards their destination; a charging outpost between stations Athena and Chronos. Four hours into their day's work, they completed scanning the quadrant, powered down their scanners and sped up to a cruising velocity. They each had just enough reserve power to manage through any unanticipated weather and to comfortably reach their rest stop just over the distant ridge.

Docked at the charging station, the drones uploaded their data, where it was relayed on to Mars Space Station. The information was then forwarded to Earth, and onto its final destination, ADESA—short for Adaptive Deep Earth Scanning and Analysis technology. The thinking machine processed its queue of jobs in a *FIFO* order—first in, first out. Its purpose was to recognize patterns in data, like identifying human faces in a picture, to identify natural resources and signs of underground deposits that could be mined and used to help achieve self-sustainment, and, eventually, profit. Each job's data was pumped through complex algorithms, transforming it, massaging it into useful forms. These visual images showed what dense materials lay beneath a surface; graphs and concentrations of potential elements, sizing estimates of potential veins of raw metal. At the conclusion of the analysis for each job, ADESA compiled reports, detailing what it believed might be present under the surface.

Heading eastward from Station Athena along the Mars equator, Gabriele Rousseau, senior section leader for IMTEC—the International Mars Terraforming and Exploration Corporation—walked a brisk pace along the well-worn path that meandered out, around an outcropping, and then back to the station. Over decades, many engineers, scientists, and workers based at Athena formed the trails around the station from their outdoor excursions to help clear their heads during the typical year-long rotations.

"Gabriele." The virtual assistant in her helmet suddenly crackled to life, jolting Gabriele from her focus on the trail. "A message has come in from Michael. Shall I play it?"

Winded from the walk she breathed out and replied, "yes... play it." The assistant retrieved the message from Station Athena where it had just arrived from Earth.

She started walking again, but slower. In the center of her face shield, a transparent video message played, overlaying the Mars terrain in front of her. Michael was on his sailboat. Against the white of the cockpit, he looked more tanned than usual. She smiled as she thought about the many adventures they had on that boat since they had started dating.

"Look at that sunset," he said, pointing towards the bow of the cruiser. The drone videoing the scene rotated ninety degrees. A brush of orange painted the horizon. Gabriele caught a glimpse of Mount Olympus and knew exactly where Michael was when he recorded the message. "Can't wait for you to get back, sweetheart. I want to go south. I was thinking, after this lengthy stay on Mars, you would be ready for more sunshine and warm weather. I know it will be a short stay this time, but we'll make the best of it."

You're reading my mind, Michael, she thought as she picked up her pace while watching the footpath.

"How are things? I know you're loving it there, with the expansion work and everything, but I can imagine you're also getting tired." He took a drink from his glass. She could see he was steering with his foot and smiled. "I loved the video you sent of the greenhouse and the range of plants being grown there. I showed it around the lab. Everyone thought it was cool."

After the video finished, Gabriele gazed around and grinned, knowing what Michael would be thinking if he were there looking at that scene. *No trees? No ocean? No animals? Just kill me now.* She knew he loved his research at IMTEC—countering effects of space travel on humans—but at the same time he was clear, he had zero interest in leaving Earth. She missed him. Over the long stretches of time away, she had learned to turn off the *missing everyone* emotion. But with Michael, turning it off wasn't easy.

"Gabriele," came the assistant's voice over her helmet's audio. "Enrico is calling."

"Okay, put him through."

Enrico fizzled in on her face shield. "Hey, are we still on for the team meeting?" he asked in his thick Italian accent. "We have a few ADESA reports to work on."

She glanced at the time in the upper right corner of her shield. "I'll be back in time," she panted. "Just out for a walk. I needed a little outside time."

"Okay. I'll keep to the schedule and see you in a while."

Enrico faded out. Gabriele picked up her pace again. Her breathing increased in lockstep as the weighted suit—to simulate more gravity—created more of a workout. Ahead, the path turned around the cliff outcropping and from there she knew it was just forty-five minutes back to the station.

Gabriele walked into her section and looked at Enrico—feet propped up on the desk, tablet in hand. "Team meeting?"

Startled, he looked up. "Hey, Chief. Right on time."

The two walked along Station Athena's main corridor to their section's planning room. At around 4 o'clock, the Sun shone through the glass dome ceiling of the passageway, illuminating the changing scenes from Earth which lined the walls. Gabriele felt her arms swaying more than usual while walking along. Simulated gravity and her weighted clothes were less of a restriction than the space suit she had been in for the past two hours. She thought about the upcoming departure and dreaded the first weeks back on Earth—when real gravity would kick in.

"Looks like everyone is here," said Gabriele, rolling her chair up to the table.

"I'm hurt," announced Jordan—one of Gabriele's machine engineers—walking through the entry, cup of something in her hand.

The team chuckled.

Gabriele cracked a smile while continuing to review the agenda items on her tablet. A moment later, she looked up at her team—those in charge of the terrestrial scanning and analysis program. "We have quite a laundry list to knock out before we return home next week. Jordan? How's that pack progressing that's returning from section Whiskey-16?"

"The recharging rover reported back just a few minutes ago," replied Jordan. "The drones are docked and almost fully recharged. They'll have enough juice to complete half of the last grid block and get back to base. Then they'll need to come in for maintenance."

"We need to get those guys back out as soon as we can."

"I know, Boss," replied Jordan. "You know I'm the best mech here."

Enrico cleared his throat without looking up from his tablet.

"Okay team, next item. New scanners and drones," said Gabriele.

"Given our procurement cycle, we should order those soon," responded Enrico. "These will be the next gen models. We'll need ample time to harden them for Mars and get all the gear tested properly before the next rotation."

"Send the request to HQ," ordered Gabriele. "I'll sign the order and get it moving." She then looked up as if she were looking over the top of reading glasses.

"Anyone not returning that I don't know about?" She paused. No one said anything. "No one wants to earn any OT?"

"We've all been here too long already," retorted an engineer. "And we only have six months of shore leave this time."

"Just asking," replied Gabriele calmly. "Alright. Let's press on with these reports."

Enrico slid the control pad towards him, powered up the main display in the room, and navigated to the team's data. He opened the top report from the previous day's surface scans.

One by one, they reviewed the details from ADESA. When signs of potential natural resources looked strong enough, they created new work orders—directions for land rovers with deep scanners to visit the sites and probe under the surface to verify and quantify the findings. Once their confidence level reached a certain point, they sent engineering teams to take boring samples. Positive samples led to excavation plans.

As the team worked through the list of reports, Jordan suddenly sat up straighter.

"Hey, stop there," she exclaimed. She scanned the flight details section in the next report. "Looks like two...no, three drones malfunctioned."

"Three? Must have been some bad weather," said an engineer.

"Let's see the details on that line item," said Jordan.

Enrico navigated deeper into the report.

"None of them reported anything," said Jordan, scanning the data.

"Let's check the weather for that quadrant and time stamp," said Gabriele. "Just to be sure."

Enrico pulled up the weather map of the planet and input the coordinates where the drones malfunctioned. He slid the time meter backwards and stopped a half-hour before the event, then slowly moved the meter forward over a one-hour window. "Looks like a clear sunny day on Mars, guys."

"Should we bring that pack in?" asked Gabriele.

Puzzled, Jordan replied, "Maybe. I'll get a dump of their internal logs today. If I don't find anything I suggest letting

17

them complete their run. I'll schedule full 'rectal-oscopies' for next time they're in for maintenance."

Gabriele smiled with a shake of her head.

Others laughed.

Enrico pressed on to the next section—scanning results for the quadrant. Near the end of the section, he stopped. A block within the quadrant was flagged. The descriptor read *Anomaly*.

"Interesting," said Gabriele. "What's *that* time marker?"

Enrico opened the details.

"Anyone recall the time those drones malfunctioned?" asked Gabriele, looking around at her team.

Enrico navigated back through the report to the flight details. "Close," he noted. "Looks like they were near the block when it happened."

Gabriele rocked back in her chair. "Their malfunctioning must have thrown off ADESA. That's what caused it to report an anomaly."

"Maybe," replied Enrico.

"You're not buying it?"

"Maybe there's something there and the malfunction was just a coincidence," said Enrico.

Gabriele nodded. "A possibility. Put it in the research queue with all the other anomalies. We'll get to it. Next report."

"There's a third possibility we're all forgetting," said Jordan with a frown.

"What? That there's something there and *that something* caused the drones to malfunction?" asked an engineer.

"Exactly," replied Jordan.

"Like what?" asked Enrico.

"I don't know," replied Jordan, raising her hands. "An alien ship buried out there waiting to gut us all."

The group laughed.

"Three drones flipped out in the same area. I think we should look into it; sooner, rather than later."

Gabriele leaned back slightly, tapping her finger on the armrest of her chair. This was an economic versus curiosity decision. She knew IMTEC's objectives backwards and forwards; self-sustainment, yield, production, in situ resource utilization. She also knew they were way behind on all fronts. A few changes in the project queues added up to schedule impacts. Her job at these points was crystal clear; align the decision with IMTEC's plans. But, like most everyone on Mars, Gabriele was part explorer. At heart, she was really there for another, more personal aim—answers to burning questions, discovery, hunting for signs of life.

She stopped tapping her fingers and nodded. "Okay. Put it in the priority queue to re-scan that part of the quadrant. Next report."

THREE

Year 2126, Endurance Compound, Northern Antarctica

Eight hours after leaving JDC facilities at the private airport in Melbourne, and the last hour spent pushing through a powerful storm, the aircraft approached the Endurance site. It was a heavy cargo transporter, but no match for the powerful arctic winds that had tossed it up and down for the past hour.

You're just grinning at this old plunderer, aren't you? thought Jonathan, gazing out of his window at the endless, undulating sheet of white. He loved coming back to this site—Antarctica, a massive block of ice bigger than the United States and Mexico combined, tucked away on the bottom of the planet, quietly keeping vast reserves of natural resources hidden away.

Through the bands of snow, Jonathan spotted the Endurance main station in the distance, resting above the ice on top of a grid of hefty metal legs. Occasional rays of Sun broke through the clouds and flashed off the round metallic structure, and the clear domes covering the subterranean passageways connecting it to the rest of the compound. The subway station —as the team called the thick-walled building that housed the lifts servicing the tunneling work twenty-six hundred meters below the surface of the glacier—stood taller than the other structures. A big snow cat was just pulling back into the warehouse after clearing the landing pad for the approaching plane.

Three-and-a-half years had passed since the Endurance venture began. It took one year to set up the site, another to dig the elevator shaft, and the rest to build out the bedrock level and begin tunneling. After so much time without any financial returns, Jonathan's short-sighted investors were beginning to lose interest. Their expectations never aligned with the long-term nature of resource extraction, so he had to resell them on it—a soft-skill he had long mastered.

The machine tossed in the high winds as it approached, rotating its engines into a hovering pattern, then beginning a slow vertical descent to the landing pad. Resting firmly on the ground, everyone took a few deep breaths before suiting up in thermal gear.

Peering out the side portal, Jonathan saw the main station's cargo lift gate lower from underneath its belly onto the ice sheet. Nick stepped off the platform and leaned against the wind as he pressed towards the craft. Jonathan rotated the side door latch and rocked it open, allowing a wave of frigid air to wash through the cabin.

Nick stepped through the door into the belly of the craft, looked around for a moment at the visitors, then announced

21

through his long beard in a thick Australian accent, "Welcome to Endurance! Let's get inside where it's heaps warmer."

The group of investors held their bags tight in the pounding wind as they made their way across the ice. After they all had stepped on the palette, Nick pressed the *Up* button. The electric lift rose into the station, jarring to a stop at the top as the air seal cinched tight.

After a late night catch-up with Nick and Sergey and just four hours of sleep, Jonathan woke, still feeling uneasy from the turbulent flight. He sat up, rubbed his face and eyes, then pushed his fingers through his hair and peered out of the tinted glass wall of his room. A silhouette of the sun was faintly visible in the sky through the opaque state of the glass —the station's environment was still in nighttime mode— blocking the near twenty-four hours of sunlight at that time of the year.

With a mug of coffee in his hand, Jonathan strode into the control room.

The front wall of glass stretched from floor to ceiling, revealing a panorama of the ice world outside. Screens on the side walls displayed maps of the site, maps of the tunnels, and status of all the control systems. Nick sat in front of a screen, still wearing workout gear from what Jonathan assumed must have been an extremely early morning workout.

Slightly startled, Nick turned around. "Hey, Jonathan."

"Morning. How's everything?"

"I'm just running through all the system checks. No issues."

Jonathan drifted over to the glass wall, now transitioning to a morning setting. "Weather doesn't look bad out."

"It'll be nice for the first half of the day," replied Nick. "But then later it's going to turn nasty again."

"What's the schedule for these investors?" asked Jonathan as he walked along the wall, studying the outside.

"We'll start by showing them around the compound, as soon as we can, while the weather is working for us. Take them on some rides in the snow-cats, tracing over where the tunnels run." Nick rocked back in his chair. "That will help get them better acclimated. Then in the afternoon we'll suit up and take them down below. Show them around the tunnels. Wearing space suits and trotting around on the bedrock level under this glacier should get them excited about the project. We'll show them all the automation, Atlas digging away, and some recent boring samples. I've got it all ready to roll."

Pleased, Jonathan cracked a slight smile as he panned the wide-open span of ice. Yet, he felt the familiar nervousness bubble up in his gut—something that surfaced with all his risky frontier projects. And Endurance had become the riskiest. He gritted his teeth slightly and buried the feeling.

After two venturous days at Endurance, it was time for the scheduled update with his full investor base and board members. Jonathan's team back in his office had planned this remote meeting for maximum effect. The tower crane, small mountain of rubble, warehouse, and white mountain peaks off in the distance all provided the perfect backdrop behind him and the visiting investors.

Jonathan leaned forward and touched a control on the device laying on the table in the engineering room of the Endurance main station. A minute later, faces of all twenty-four investors and board members from around the world filled in the grid on the display in front of him and his on-site guests.

With his hands crossed and resting on the table, he started the meeting. "Thanks everyone for joining this somewhat unorthodox project update."

"This is actually very orthodox for you, Jonathan," opined one of his long-time investors. "Are you ever not at one of your project sites?"

Everyone chuckled.

"Looks like Endurance, if I'm not mistaken."

Jonathan cracked a smile. "Hence, why I've put Endurance at the top of our agenda." He then pointed to the table with both his forefingers. "*This*, everyone, is our most ambitious project to date. And given the progress Nick and his team have made here, I believe it's time to pull this project back to front and center."

Jonathan glanced from face to face on the screen. "Those of you who have been with me long enough know it takes years to develop assets to a profitable state. There are no shortcuts around laws, governments, treaties, militias, corruption, or wars." He turned and pointed out the window. "Let alone Mother Nature. Operating in hostile parts of the world is simply part and parcel of this business. Look out there. Geological scientists have known for decades Antarctica is rich in resources. Possibly the biggest trove the world has ever seen. The challenge is digging up the trove without breaking the bank, so to say."

He stretched his arms out to the side and said proudly, "Now we can dig here. And now, with this fully automated site, the numbers work. All tunneling, scanning, and excavation work is carried out by robotic machinery as these gentlemen here have experienced over the past couple days."

Jonathan leaned forward on his elbows. "What truly makes this now possible is a thinking machine. All the robots are under the guidance of an intelligent system. With this technology, it takes a crew of less than ten people to operate this site." He tapped his finger on the table. "*This* is the future of mining. AI managed, fully autonomous operations. With the Endurance Project, we are going to bring the vast natural resources of Antarctica to the world's markets." He glanced down at the console and touched an icon of a photo on the screen. The wall-display split into two sections. One side showed the investors and board members, the other displayed an image of another key player in his plans. "Just a little refresher of how we got here. This is Dr. Eleanor Mayfield." He paused for a moment to let the investors take in the picture of Ellie Mayfield now on their screens. "I stumbled on the idea for this project years ago after reading an article by Dr. Mayfield. In it she described the ancient ecosystem of Antarctica and its connection with eastern Africa; how the giant creatures that once roamed Africa roamed Antarctica as well."

On the display, Ellie was standing in front of a large cave opening in a jungle setting with her cowboy hat on and wearing dirt-covered field dress. Jonathan grinned. He remembered her cowgirl, hard-working, get-in-the-dirt attitude from the first time they met. She was attractive and smart. He liked her and was thrilled she agreed to work with him on Endurance.

"She grew up in South Africa, top of her class, now a well-known field paleontologist and distinguished professor at Witwatersrand," said Jonathan. "I approached Dr. Mayfield and showed her our technology and skills and how we could access the time-locked earth in Antarctica and hunt for fossilized remains of the world she had described in her writings. After some time and collaboration, I set up and funded Endurance as a scientific exploration project and brought Dr. Mayfield onboard as a consultant and as our lead paleontologist."

He turned his gaze to the investors at the table. "With this scientific endeavor, we gained access to what many geophysicists and geologists believe is home to possibly the largest remaining reserves on Earth. With the technology you've now witnessed, we are going to find ancient relics and fossils that help science understand the life that once existed here." He lifted a finger and raised his eyebrows. "And at the same time, we are going to discover, identify, and map out the rich mineral reserves we know are here."

He leaned forward and folded his hands together. "Soon, when the Antarctic Treaty is dissolved, and the opposition to mining here subsides, we will be ready. Antarctica is where mining is headed. We have to be here; building our expertise and learning how to operate in these harsh conditions."

Endurance was risky. With the Antarctic Treaty still in place; major governments still opposing mining there; environmental groups watching him with a magnifying glass; Jonathan knew he was walking a political tightrope with this project. Until they made some big scientific discovery, something to satisfy the skeptics, it was a risk he had to manage.

"Jonathan, to date, what have you found there? What has your AI scanning technology found?" asked an investor on the screen.

With the control pad on the table, Jonathan navigated to a project folder and opened an image onto everyone's screens. "These are concentrations from boring samples taken in the main line and in the new tunnel we just visited." At the bottom of the graph were the names of elements: gold, platinum, titanium, molybdenum, palladium. Bars representing concentrations stretched up vertically.

"The resources are here," he said calmly. "This land once connected to eastern Africa; Australia; South America. We all know the large folds of gold, copper, platinum, silver, and rare elements in those countries that had supplied the world for hundreds of years. Those rich veins continued into Antarctica. The goal of Endurance is to be here; learning, mapping, operating, biding our time until the restrictions are relaxed and deep mining is permitted. Endurance, the *scientific exploratory project,* makes this possible. However, until we make a big scientific discovery, this project will continue to be viewed with skepticism."

Sitting down the table from Jonathan, chair rolled back, hands resting on his crossed legs, the new investor spoke up. "Jonathan, I don't doubt the resources are here. Enough credible science seems to support it. I've just seen the operation. It is very impressive. Nick and the team here are absolutely top notch. That said, speaking for myself and my backers, we are most concerned about the restrictions on mining. In over two hundred years they've barely changed."

Jonathan nodded as he met the man's steady gaze. "You're right!" he replied, and then paused. "But you and your partners and everyone in this meeting know they must change, or there will be unrest in the world. Reality is sinking in for governments. They're starting to understand reserves in the Arctic and Greenland are drying up. They are seeing the accelerating demand the space industry is creating." He cracked a slight smile. "And from what I understand, we have yet to strike gold on the Moon or Mars."

"I don't agree with your optimism," replied the investor tersely. "The Treaty still stands and doesn't look like it's going anywhere. You're operating and burning through capital as if its demise is imminent."

Jonathan's smile faded. "*We...* are showing the world this can be done. Our discoveries here will further catalyze the global rethink of this continent, and the Treaty. Once the world sees what is here, Antarctica will be divided up and mined for its resources. And we're leading the way."

FOUR

Months later. Under the Antarctic glacier, down the main line tunnel, Atlas—a tunnel boring machine—had been forging a new tunnel: T11. The tunnel was not straight. None of the tunnels were straight. They followed paths dictated by the thinking machine ADESA in its quest to find large veins of highly valued natural resources, and to discover fossilized skeletons of living creatures long forgotten. With ease, ADESA ingested and analyzed mounds of data streamed to it from deep surface scans. The set of things it could recognize buried underground grew as it was fed more data from different mining and excavation sites around the world.

A small fleet of drones and rovers equipped with precision scanners provided ADESA's eyes and other senses. It orchestrated its team of machines at the Endurance site to map and scan every square centimeter of every tunnel floor, wall, and ceiling.

Along the new tunnel, rover ER4 was hard at work, making its way along the earthen floor. Midway down the tunnel, while scanning a section, ER4 stopped. It backed up and re-scanned the wall while moving slowly forward towards the next section. Four meters further along, it stopped again. The machine began to jolt back and forth. Quickly. Erratically. Like something was shaking it. A minute later, it stopped. Three minutes later, ER4's secondary control system powered up and engaged its maintenance protocol. It drove itself back down the main line tunnel and into the service elevator. At the top of the lift, it exited and motored itself down the passageway to the warehouse.

Inside the main station, on the three-dimensional site map covering a wall in the control room, a red alert bubble appeared above ER4 as ADESA updated the site activity log on the screen.

[17:52] - ER4 offline
[18:21] - ER4 in maintenance - data recovery in progress
[18:29] - Sending ERD2 to perform deep scans
[19:16] - Analyzing ERD2 data
[19:20] - Possible fossil embedded in wall section T11G4B23
[19:23] - Floor section temperature deviation from surrounding sections - significant
[19:27] - Retrieving specimen from wall section at T11G4B23

ADESA dispatched a robot to the location and gave it precise instructions. After reaching the spot, the machine carefully removed a chunk of ice from the wall containing a rock formation and loaded it on a transporter. The block was then delivered to the lab where a technician de-iced it and inspected what had been found. The technician noticed what he thought might be a bone fragment in the rock's face. He had the rock imaged and scanned for analysis and recording. Within seconds, the Endurance team had received an alert of the fossil discovery.

[19:47] - *ER4 data recovery complete*
[19:47] - *ER4 data corruption detected*
[19:48] - *ER4 ERD2 data cross verification in progress*
[19:50] - *ANOMALY discovered in floor section*

Dr. Rachel Dibaba was an expert in AGI—Artificial General Intelligence. After completing her advanced studies in the sciences, she started with Z-Scan Technologies—a firm now owned by Jonathan—as a scientist in their Algorithms Group. Within two years, she was leading all research and development for the firm. Three years later, she and her team had created ADESA. Used extensively on Earth to sniff out veins of metals, other natural resources, and even fossils buried deep under the surface, the technology had found a new use; exploration on Mars.

The walls of Rachel's office were covered with equations, formulas, and pseudo-code of algorithms. Space on the wall behind her computer screens was reserved for pictures— photos of her and colleagues at metal mines and fossil excavation sites in Africa and on other continents where ADESA was hard at work. There were pictures of her in Antarctica at the Endurance site riding snowmobiles, and group photos of her with the team standing in front of the main station. In the center hung a photo of her and Nick, gearing up in thermal suits.

Okay, let's figure this one out, she told herself, as she put her headphones on and selected a music collection she had titled *Bug Tracking*. She then turned her chair back to her screens, to the three-dimensional terrain-map of Mars. Using the joystick control on her desk, she rotated her view in the map, like navigating a drone across the planet's surface. She stopped at a large caldera and navigated around the edge of the crater. A geological scientist on her team had told her the once active volcano on the planet could have created the veins of ferrous metals discovered nearby. After getting sidetracked sightseeing around the Mars terrain, she made some notes, then tracked twelve-hundred meters to the location of the issue she was researching. ADESA had flagged another *anomaly*.

At the site, Rachel engaged the terrain-map's auto-navigator to retrace the surface in the same pattern the drones had followed when they had first scanned the quadrant. She was looking for clues as to why ADESA didn't identify the small vein of ferrous metals under the surface. ADESA had found the vein but didn't identify the metals within it. Instead, she had labelled it an *anomaly*. It took boring samples to figure out what it was.

Over time, ADESA had become unmatched in her skills at identifying things and pointing out matches to other past findings. Rachel was even amazed at ADESA's abilities. Yet occasionally, something small could throw off her senses. Sometimes it was something obvious and other times it wasn't. Atmosphere, gravity, material density, and other natural factors all played a role and had some effect on ADESA's analysis. And on Mars, all those factors were different.

Rachel selected a large rock lying on the surface, almost directly over the vein. A small window appeared on her screen, listing the traces of ferrous and non-ferrous materials the scanners had detected in the rock. *Nothing unusual,* she noted.

After inspecting a few more rocks, she rotated her view downwards and flew into the surface, descending slowly through the subterranean map created from the deep-scanner data. She looked around for obstructions that could have thrown off ADESA's analysis. Reaching the small vein that had stumped ADESA, Rachel looked at the location data panel on the right side of her screen. The depth read fifteen and a half meters. She rubbed her eyes and yawned. *Nothing too unusual here,* she thought. Frustrated, she kept digging while thinking over ADESA's algorithms. She had to figure this one out and move onto the next one.

As the scanning program expanded on Mars, the backlog of anomalies continued to pile up. The one on her screen had surfaced nearly two years earlier. She was hoping the software upgrades she and her team were wrapping up, and the next generation scanners in testing would fix many of these issues.

Rachel rotated her chair and looked out her window that framed Munich, and watched the locals and tourists walking on the stone streets that wound through the capital of Bavaria. She loved the old-world look of the city, the low-rise buildings still made from cut stone. So different from the tiny village in South Africa where she grew up. Even after being in the city for years, she still delighted in watching it.

A soft tone resonated from her computer. She turned and looked at her screen.

A message window appeared.

? About ADESA

The text was next to Nick's picture. She smiled, then closed the door to her office and touched the *Call* button. *Locating Nick Standish...* faded in and out on her screen. A moment later, he appeared.

"Hey, that was fast." Nick's beard lifted as he grinned.

Rachel felt an involuntary smile spread over her face. "I'm in my office working on some issues with ADESA on Mars and your message popped up."

"Do you have a date yet for coming back to Endurance?"

She looked back at him. She never imagined she would fall for a guy like Nick; rugged with no interest in office work. *Kind of the polar opposite of what mom had in mind*, she thought. But under all that hair and tattoos was a very intelligent guy, one who was fun to be with. She felt herself blushing as she smiled. "Why, do you miss me?"

"I do."

"Real soon," she replied. "We have a new generation of scanners I want to integrate out there."

"This time, plan to arrive in Melbourne a few days early, if you can. I would love to spend some time together there before we head off to Endurance. There are some descent spots around Victoria. Bell's Beach still rocks. Sound interesting?"

She leaned towards her screen. "You know I love surfing."

Nick grinned.

"Since you're working on issues with ADESA, did you see the alerts here?"

"No, not yet. Is it something interesting?" asked Rachel, curiously.

"Interesting and weird, really. First, it looks like ADESA might have found something fossilized in this new tunnel, T11. That's the cool part. But there's something else—it also reported an anomaly in a section near where the potential fossils were flagged."

"Give me a second." Rachel turned to her other screen, to another ADESA dashboard, and selected the Endurance site.

"Do you see the log?"

"I see it..."

"What does that mean? I haven't seen that before."

She read through the data, then turned back to Nick. "Looks like one of the grid blocks that were scanned is warm. Warmer than the other surrounding ones. The temperature differential between the one block and the others is significant."

He thought for a while. This was something new. "But why would that cause ADESA to call it an anomaly?"

Rachel kept reading through the log entries. "There's something there, Nick. ADESA attempted to create images from the scanner data. Did you see those?"

"Yeah, I saw those images, but I couldn't make out anything. If it's some type of mineral deposit then ADESA would know, right?"

Rachel thought for a moment. "Yes... she should... *but* something is throwing off her analysis. Without getting closer, it's hard to say what the issue is."

"I always wondered whether ADESA was a dude or a gal. Now I know."

"She's a smart girl," replied Rachel as she continued to read through the data.

"Definitely looks like something large is buried there," Nick said excitedly. "I'm going to excavate that wall to get closer to it."

Rachel had been focusing on the logs. She turned back to Nick. "Oh, that sounds great. The rover, ER4, went offline midway while scanning that block. Have you figured out what happened?"

"We checked out the little guy. Ran end-to-end diagnostics on him. Sergey was stumped. He said two subsystems had malfunctioned. One was the drivetrain. Looks like the program that runs its controller was corrupted. But he said those systems are embedded and shielded and they don't just get corrupted."

"He's right," she replied. "The shielding protects against low grade radiation but it's not really effective against anything high-energy." Frowning, she turned back to her other screen—to the Endurance dashboard—and drilled down in the data. She scrolled through logs from each component.

"What are you thinking?"

"Something—"

"What?"

"Give me a minute." A moment later, her eyebrows raised.

"What'd you find?" Nick saw the surprise on her face.

"It looks like the primary MEMS gyroscope was jolted. And then, after a while, it returned to its equilibrium state."

"The device that tells the rover the direction it's facing?"

"Exactly," replied Rachel. "Whether it's tilted over, or headed up a steep grade. Old-school tech that's survived the times. Something knocked it way out of whack. And I am guessing what did that is what cooked its controllers."

"I can tell from the look on your face, you have an idea."

"I do," she replied. "But it doesn't make—" She gazed off to the side for a moment.

"Rachel?"

She looked back at him and hesitated, knowing it was impossible given where this happened. "Nick. It doesn't make sense. But this seems like the work of some type of focused energy pulse. It almost looks like something meant to do this."

FIVE

In a lecture room on the first floor of the social sciences building of Witwatersrand University, Ellie stood in front of her class—her red hair pinned back in a bun, classroom glasses on—and gave her last lesson for the semester; an under-grad-uate class titled *The Evolution of East African Terrestrial Ecosystems.* Through her glasses, she saw all thirty-two students in shorts and t-shirts, both the local ones physically present and the ones attending virtually. A drone cleaner washed the tall windows that looked out onto the busy urban campus. Thick, leaf-filled trees dotted the lawn between the buildings beyond.

On the main wall behind Ellie an image of a large blue Earth with one landmass in the middle filled the screen. The title at the top of the slide read *GONDWANA.* The subtopic read *The Relationship between Antarctica, East Africa and post K-Pg (Cretaceous-Paleogene) Evolution.* Lines were drawn across the face of the landmass like marking off pieces in a puzzle. If split apart, each piece would be one of the modern-day continents. Antarctica connected into southeastern Africa almost perfectly. On the bottom of the image, a timeline stretched from the left, $180\ Ma$, to the far right ending at $15\ Ma$.

Standing off to the side at the podium, Ellie touched an image on the room control pad. The landmass on the screen enlarged and filled the entire wall. She looked back at her students. "Geologists named this ancient continent Gondwana. This image resembles what we believe it looked like some one-hundred and eighty-million years ago." Ellie touched another button on the control pad. The image of Earth evolved as time moved forward a few million years per tick. Slowly, as the time arrow progressed to the right, continents broke away from Antarctica. After Africa separated, the Indian subcontinent broke off and slowly drifted away. When the time marker reached the $66\ Ma$ point, Australia and Antarctica were still connected and still had a subtropical climate and flora. Images of exotic plants appeared.

Ellie paused the presentation and looked around the curved, theater-style room at her students. "Can anyone name the extinction event that occurred at this point?"

A hand went up.

"Yes, Juliana."

"It's the Cretaceous-Paleogene event."

"That's right. And what happened during this period?"

"A bolide impact caused mass extinction of all living creatures."

"Correct!" replied Ellie. "It was a catastrophic event! Imagine... a million nuclear explosions going off simultaneously. Boom!" she shouted. She glanced around the room and smiled as students sat up and laughed. "Not much was left, aside from small crocodile-type species. Understanding how life and the environment evolved after that event provides the stage for human evolution. It's the most studied extinction event in history."

Ellie strolled back to the podium and continued her presentation. When the time marker reached 40 *Ma* Australia separated from Antarctica. She stepped towards the wall and slid her hand across the lower part of the image. "Notice, after the separation with Australia and as the continents drift apart, the latitudinal ocean currents started flowing, isolating Antarctica. When we near the twenty-three-million-year point, South America fully separates. From that point forward, the Antarctic Circumpolar Current flowed, fully isolating the continent."

She drifted away from the screen towards the front row of students. "When that happened, warmer air and ocean currents stopped flowing that far south. Antarctica started cooling. Ice formed and started spreading, replacing forests." The time marker continued to move to the right. On the screen, white replaced the green of Antarctica. At 15 *Ma* the marker stopped. Antarctica was now covered in white.

Ellie drummed her fingers on the student's desk in front of her as she skipped her gaze around to different students. "From this point forward, Antarctica was frozen over. Parked down at the South Pole, *far* away from all other landmasses, it remained unknown to us until recent times."

She walked down the row of students, tapping lightly on their desks. "Yet, as we just saw, it was alive and flourishing with life up to the K-Pg event. And then after K-Pg, for millions of years, until it was uninhabitable, it played a major role in the evolution of new life. As scientists discover more about Antarctica, our picture of the evolution of life on Earth will grow significantly. It's the last undiscovered landmass on Earth and it has been frozen under kilometers of ice for millions of years. It's just waiting to be discovered."

Ellie turned around and walked back to the center desk. "I will stop there. Our plan was to use the last half of today's lecture to answer questions about the material before the final." She looked around the room. "Does anyone have a topic they would like to review?"

A hand went up.

"Yes, Dewa."

The student spoke excitedly. "Professor, I read an article you wrote a few years ago on Antarctica. The possibilities you brought up were fascinating; how it's possible a separate line of early primates might have developed in Antarctica after the continental breakup. Have you found any signs of primates there?"

Ellie smiled. "That article was more an exercise in possibilities, bordering on fiction really, but it was fun writing. I am glad you liked it but to answer your question, unfortunately, we haven't found any signs of primates."

Another student raised their hand.

"Yes, Stephan."

"Professor, do you think speciation would have possibly continued there, leading up to a different line of Homo sapien?"

Ellie paused. "Interesting question. But no... I don't believe so. Once the continent fully separated and the Antarctic Circumpolar Current began to flow, the cooling process on the continent likely picked up significantly. As is generally believed today, Antarctica started rapidly cooling around twenty to twenty-three million years ago. Current estimates indicate it was completely frozen over by ten million years ago. Life would have become very challenged."

Another student spoke up, "Could the rapid cooling have created an evolutionary pressure that caused an acceleration of speciation?"

"Sounds like an interesting topic for a paper," replied Ellie, raising an eyebrow. "Would it have been possible? Maybe. How far along would speciation and evolution have progressed before there was no food?"

Ellie paused for a moment. "These are wonderful questions, class, and I would love to carry on... but you have a final exam to prepare for. If you have questions about the course material, now is the time to ask."

Ellie walked down the long hall on the second floor of the building to her lab. The door was propped open and the lights on. Her lab assistant, Theto, was sitting at a cleaning station, focused on one of the new specimens from Endurance.

"How's it going?" Ellie asked.

With an almost forced reply, and without looking up, Theto replied, "It's going...." He flicked a speck of dirt away with the pneumatic needle instrument and continued working, like a sculptor who had just been rudely interrupted. "I finished cleaning the last vertebrae. They're on the table... there." He pointed over his shoulder with the instrument.

"Let's have a look," replied Ellie, smiling at his dedication, and usual stoicism. She put on gloves and started carefully positioning the bones as she imagined they would have been when they helped support the massive creature. Many months had passed since ADESA had discovered the first fossil fragments. Many new specimens had been uncovered, sent to her lab, cleaned and assembled. The bones were in the best condition of all pterosaurs ever discovered.

Theto laid down his instrument and walked over to the opposite side of the specimen. After a moment of watching her arrange the vertebrae he asked, "Given the size of these, what do you estimate the wingspan to be?"

"Oh... nine, maybe ten meters."

"Hmm. That big?"

"She's a big pterosaur. *Maybe* one of the largest discovered," replied Ellie.

One corner of his mouth turned up slightly as he nodded.

Ellie knew, behind her Theto's normal straight-line keel, he'd just got excited.

"These bones are in pristine condition. I guess being in a giant freezer for millions of years helped."

"It definitely helped," replied Ellie as she rotated the vertebrae around, studying their shapes. She then looked up at him and smiled. "You're doing excellent work. Still, we probably have a year's worth of cleaning."

"Well... slaving away here and my dissertation is all I have," Theto sighed. His eyes then widened just slightly. "But professor... a research assistant trip to Antarctica would be..."

"I'll think about it."

Ellie was thrilled with their first discovery. The trips to Endurance, working with Nick and the team there, showing them how to extract and handle the fragile bones, was exciting. Yet she was also frustrated. She wanted to find something new, something never seen before. While the pterosaur bones they had unearthed were interesting, she knew they were not earth-shattering. Even though only a few had ever been discovered, pterosaurs were known creatures. But she knew if there was one last place on Earth to make a big discovery, Antarctica was that place. And, although not the big score she was after, this was a promising start.

———

Levelling off at a smooth cruising altitude en route to one of his projects in Indonesia, Jonathan settled in for the long flight. He had just closed on a portfolio of zinc, copper, and silver mines in western South America—a major deal he had been working on for over a year. Sitting in his favorite chair in his private plane, he touched a control on the table, slid his finger from top to bottom and watched the windows fade into the fuselage dome as the dark opaque interior slowly became transparent. He gazed out, looking across the clouds and blue sky, content, if only for a while. Like all deals, the thrill of the chase was now behind him. It was time to pass things over to his subordinates and find the next prey.

He rocked back in his chair and picked up his tablet to review the latest progress update from Endurance. After the first section of the report, his mouth turned up slightly. It was exactly the news he needed to see. He had been pressing Nick for some time now. Maybe he had pushed a little too hard. There were delays, but he knew why. The environment there was the hardest conditions his team had ever experienced. Sergey's machines were wearing out quicker than expected and required more maintenance. The crew had to be rotated more often. But nothing ever went according to plan in the mining business. That was why he hired project managers who had perseverance coursing through their veins. And Nick Standish was the best he had.

Aside from their pterosaur discovery, concentrations of elements from boring samples were high. Some of the highest readings he had ever seen. The samples ran deep and long. Nick was still working on mapping the discovery, but this was enough for now. Together with the fossilized creature that Ellie was piecing together, Endurance was beginning to show promise on both fronts. His plan was working.

The last section of the report was titled *T11 Anomaly Analysis*. There was no data. Just a summary of the effort. The crew had attempted, several times, to extract boring samples from a section of the dig site. Every attempt failed. The drill

45

bits could not pierce whatever was buried there. More scanner readings yielded nothing useful. His engineers had never hit something they couldn't bore into at any of his sites. And they had hit some hard crystal structures buried in the earth, but nothing modern drill bits couldn't pierce right through. He was intrigued. However, his experience was telling him it was likely a waste of time. Never had any strange discovery at any of his mines turned out to be of any real value. They were always outliers, one-offs—solitary discoveries, not part of a bigger something.

He knew Nick had unilaterally decided to excavate the site to figure out what the anomaly was. He could be a renegade at times, like a bloodhound that had caught a scent. Not the side of Nick that Jonathan particularly liked, but it was something he had to tolerate. Ellie was interested because fossilized remains of some ancient creature were discovered close by. Not that there was any connection, but she wasn't ready to rule out the possibility.

Jonathan shifted his gaze to the clouds skirting by and the blue sky fading into the hazy horizon in the distance. He didn't completely share their interest. Yet, with the upbeat results, he had enough good news to go along with a little side project. And he was now curious. What could be so hard? *Maybe something new... worth millions per ounce.* He chuckled as he laid down the tablet and picked up his drink.

Sitting in his urban bachelor apartment, Diablo—as he called himself online—pulled his black hair back in a ponytail and leaned forward, studying the image on his screen. It showed a round metallic structure resting on thick legs secured to what appeared to be concrete footings. It was parked in Antarctica, a long distance from anything else man made. If he didn't know better, he would think it was an alien craft. He spread his fingers on the control pad to enlarge the image, then he panned between the structures. He squinted. *Looks like underground passageways.*

Some time ago, he and his team of alien hunters had discovered Z-Scan Technologies and their ADESA system. Curious about what ADESA might find buried under the Earth's crust, they began researching the company and tracking their projects around the world.

Satellite images of Endurance were on one of Diablo's screens, along with some new data Khasimir had surfaced. On the other, he and his team continued an online message thread—text messages were low tech but hard to legally pin on someone—all studying the same data, on their own screens, in their corners of the world.

Akashi: *This was definitely machine generated—ANOMALY in floor section at T11G4B24—that's cryptic.*
Razputin: *Anomaly could be a code word. They could have found a piece of some craft and they don't know how to describe it.*
Diablo: *T11 must be their own coordinate system. Khas, this message was sent to Nick Standish?*
Khasimir: *Correct. He's the first one I've tapped into. I set our filters loose to scan all his message archives and this is the first one that surfaced.*
Diablo: *Any luck getting into the others?*
Khasimir: *Working on it. Just trying to stay under the radar.*

It took me a while to find this hole. They're using some high-end security software. The sweep patterns are irregular, but my timing algorithms are getting close to matching them. Once I get that down, I'll be able to dig where I want.

Razputin: *Come on, Khas. It's been months. Are you losing your touch?*

Khasimir: *Ha, ha.*

Razputin: *Just yanking your chain, dude.*

Akashi: *D could go to Antarctica and do some old school spying.*

Diablo: *It's bone-cold there. But hey, if this "anomaly" even slightly smells like alien I'm going.*

SIX

Station Athena, Mars

Gabriele and Enrico made their way along the subterranean corridors that laced through the engineering, medical, social, and recreation sections of Station Athena. It was a five-minute walk to the other side. Gabriele was running close to her meeting time with the Commander. Two minutes on crowd chatter caught their attention—Athena's social central was busy. Fresh light streamed in through the glass dome that covered that section of the station. Drones maneuvered across the exterior of the dome, blowing off the thick layer of red dust and cleaning the surface.

Gabriele looked around the hall that adjoined the food galley. It was full. Travel gear lined the walls. The main wall displayed a video stream of the Earth-to-Mars Transporter, docked at the Mars Space Station four hundred kilometers above them, waiting to be boarded. Overlaid on the video was a countdown to departure, the current time—in Universal

Time—and a calculation of the estimated days to reach Earth —based on the changing distance between the two planets. She stopped for a moment to admire the new cruise ship. "What do you think?" she said to Enrico. "Those new class EMTs look nice, don't they? I heard they come with an Italian chef."

Enrico looked at Gabriele for a second, wanting to believe her. "Yeah, right."

She felt her tablet vibrate. "I've got to go. What bay are we in again?"

"Three," he replied, smiling. "We will be ready in an hour."

Gabriele continued down the main artery to the west side of the station. With a few seconds to spare, she slowed down as she approached the Commander's office before knocking lightly on the door frame.

Robert Van Der Berg looked up. "Gabi, come in. Give me just a moment to finish this."

Gabriele laid her computer on the table and walked around it to the transparent wall. Manned robots were excavating trenches for the corridors to the new wing.

"Even after being here for as many rotations as I've been, that view doesn't get old," said the commander, rising from his chair after touching *Send* on his screen. "Mesmerizing, isn't it?"

"Yes, it is," replied Gabriele, looking out over the construction work at the endless rocky terrain and the pinkish-red atmosphere.

"The east expansion is taking shape there. It'll be complete when you return as commander," said Van Der Berg confidently, joining her at the window. "When I started with IMTEC thirty years ago, Athena was our only base. We had maybe ten scientists here full time. Hard to believe, but you'll be in charge of nearly two hundred and thirty. You'll also be overseeing construction of Orion. That's going to really step up our exploration efforts to the east." The commander paused and peered out into the distance. "Gabi, you'll be one of a special few leading our expansion out here. It's demanding work, but there's no other job like it. It's intoxicating." His voice trailed off.

Gabriele looked up at the commander, at the angles in his cheeks, his focused eyes, and lean stature. She knew the old man had sacrificed family and many things in life to be in this elite group leading the charge into space. She stressed about her life—in her forties and not getting any younger—with no family of her own. But like Van Der Berg said, she too was intoxicated by the job.

"I know you're heading to Chronos for a couple of days. I wanted to tell you before I depart tomorrow, I'm thrilled you accepted the position. Over the past six months since you got back out here, I've seen you manage some stressful situations. You're a natural. You're perfect for this job. I'll rest better with you as one of my commanders out here."

"Thanks, Robert. And I'll have peace of mind knowing you'll be running IMTEC, keeping all the partners happy. Which does not sound like a fair trade."

Van Der Berg chuckled. "I agree. I would rather be here. But HQ didn't really give me a choice. All the countries partnered in this endeavor have spent trillions, and we're not yet over the self-sufficient threshold. They want me there to keep the presidents and prime ministers informed and on board as we press on out here."

"Robert, I know the scanning technology isn't living up to what we were anticipating. We're starting to phase in the next generation of machines. And, to hedge our bets, I've recruited Z-Scan's lead scientist, Dr. Rachel Dibaba. She's accompanying us on the next rotation to work with Enrico and the team."

"You think she can help?"

"I do. She created ADESA. I believe bringing her to Mars, to the source of the data, she will be able to tweak that AI system's algorithms, modify the scanners, adapt the technology to better fit this environment." Gabriele knew there was a lot of pressure from the IMTEC partners to improve their resource yields—to achieve self-sustainment.

"Sounds promising. Let's hope she can manage out here. You know as well as I do, not everyone can. With that said, come take a walk with me." Van Der Berg headed out of his office.

"Sir?" Gabriele followed. "My crew is waiting for me to head to Chronos."

"This won't take a moment. Come on, I have something to show you."

They turned right and headed towards the main social area. When they rounded the curve, the applause started. The social area was filled with the entire crew staying at the station and with those departing for Earth.

Van Der Berg looked at her and smiled. "This is for you, Gabi. I thought we would have a little informal promotion celebration before you take off. The official one will happen when you return. By the way, I had Jordan move your departure to Chronos out an hour."

"Oh, my. I don't know what to say. Thank you. Thanks everyone."

Van Der Berg looked around. "Well, I think we surprised her."

The crew cheered more.

"I just wanted to say a couple things before we have a little dry bubbly," he continued. "First, I wanted to thank Gabriele for her dedication to our mission. As we all know, this can be a trying place at times, and is not without its risks and surprises. Gabriele has shown us all her masterful skills at leading with a clear head and genuine concern for her crew. That's why I am thrilled to announce she will be taking on the responsibility of Commander of Mars."

Everyone applauded again.

"It's a position she will share with two others in rotations. Her appointment is effective immediately since I'm departing. With that said, I have a couple things for you." He looked around the area. "Jordan?"

"Here I am, Sir." She snaked through the group and handed him a bag.

"Okay, first, you're going to need a proper name plate for the office." He pulled out a long, triangle-shaped block of metal with *Commander Rousseau* laser-burned across one face. Below her name it read, *Planet Mars*. "We had the machine

53

shop fabricate this. The official one will be waiting for you on your next rotation."

Gabriele looked at it for a moment, then held it up and looked over at the shop crew. "Thanks, guys! I think I prefer this hand-crafted model."

"And, to remind everyone you're in charge." He removed his commander badge and attached it to her jumpsuit. "Yes, that will do it. You're official now, Commander Rousseau." He shook her hand, then looked around at the group. "I am now a section leader for the next two days. For any commander issues, don't come see me."

The group laughed at their old commander.

"Okay, let's have some of that Mars-approved bubbly stuff."

An hour later, Gabriele walked through the bay door.

The pilot was pacing around slowly, waiting for her.

They shook hands and walked towards the aircraft. "How does the weather look out there, Captain?"

"Sunny and clear skies all the way, Commander."

Gabriele grinned and then walked up the stairs to the craft and through the main hatch. She looked around as she entered. Jordan and one of the engineers were talking.

Enrico was on his computer. He looked up. "Glad you could finally join us, Commander."

They fist bumped as she sat down and secured her restrainer.

Twenty minutes later, they were navigating west towards Station Chronos.

Gabriele peered out the window and surveyed the rocky surface as it passed by. The endless desolateness was strangely intriguing. Like all the other scientists on these flights around Mars, she often caught herself wondering. But it was nearly impossible to imagine life there when looking at the terrain. Not a single tree or blade of grass anywhere on the planet.

"Hey, Gabi, what are you thinking about?" asked Enrico, nudging her.

She pulled her focus back inside the craft. "Oh, just thinking. Even as long as I've been coming here, sometimes I still can't help but wonder if this place was once something very different."

"Well, we keep searching for signs, and if we get the drones online at Leto we can start searching further north."

Gabriele turned and looked at Enrico. "Speaking of scanning. How's that last grid at Chronos coming?"

"Just waiting on the report from ADESA."

"Can't wait to see it," she said as she reclined her chair and slowly closed her eyes. She felt content; satisfied. The position of Commander of Mars was a big step up. With Van Der Berg departing, she'd have six months as Commander to work into the position before she returned to Earth.

Two thousand kilometers west of Station Athena, Gabriele's eyes snapped open as she lifted out of her seat under the restrainer and then slammed back down. She squeezed her arm rests. The craft dove, then banked left, then hard right. The interior emergency system flashed. Twenty seconds later, the pilot recovered to their flight pattern.

"Hey, crew!" shouted the pilot, glancing back through his rear-view mirror. "Sorry about that. Everyone okay?"

Gabriele breathed in and exhaled a couple of times as she turned and peered around at everyone. "Yeah, we're all okay," she replied. "What was that?"

"I don't know, Commander," the pilot replied, shaking his head. "The controls just stopped responding for a moment, then it all came back. Never had that happen before."

SEVEN

Station Athena, Mars

Six months later

Heading along a footpath back to Station Athena and now pressing through the windstorm that had picked up, Gabriele stopped and looked up. She felt the pressure waves in the atmosphere from the thrusters slowing down the surface-to-space transporter in the distance descending onto the landing pad. She loved being outside and watching the ships land and take off. She smiled and felt exhilarated being there, feeling the force from the landing and the rawness of the windstorm. She needed this final walkabout before the long trek across space on her return to Earth.

"Gabriele," came a soft assistant's voice inside her helmet. "The shuttle will be departing in two hours."

Alright, time to get packed up, she told herself.

The surface-to-space shuttle was designed for one thing, to move crew and cargo between Mars surface and Mars Space Station. Mar Space Station was also the docking terminal and transfer facility for staging between the shuttle and EMTs— Earth-to-Mars Transporters.

Gabriele boarded the shuttle and found her seat among all the crew returning to Earth. Once the countdown started, she rotated back ninety degrees to the liftoff position, then closed her eyes and relaxed for the short ride into space. The count-down meter ticked down 6, 5, 4... The shuttle shook hard as the primary engines roared to life, overtaking the hum of conversation and pushing the craft upwards.

Ten minutes later, Gabriele opened her eyes to the absence of all engine noise. She rotated her chair back upright and peered out the side portal. Ahead, the terminal was coming into view. The docked EMT class spacecraft was hard to miss. Techni-cians working on its exterior looked like small insects hovering around. Minutes later, she felt the sudden jolt as the dock extender latched onto the shuttle.

Onboard the transporter back to Earth, sailing across space on the long monotonous trek back home, all the passengers worked hard at passing the time. And there was a lot of time to pass. Lots.

Gabriele awoke within a minute of the time she always woke up. She heard someone walk by her door. *Probably heading to the gym*, she thought. *Get up, stick to the routine.* Minutes later she exited her quarters into a dark hallway. The ship's lighting was still in night mode.

The inbound trips returning to Earth differed greatly from the outbound ones to Mars. During outbounds, each day was filled with planning the work to be done on Mars. Then, on Mars, every day had a packed schedule with little down-time baked in. There were no weekends or holidays or time off. No one ever complained about boredom while on Mars. The ride back was an altogether different game.

Gabriele waved her ID in front of the scanner. The gym door opened and she headed in the direction of her first station. *I'm in the right place,* she noted as she wrinkled her nose. The subtle, humid aroma of human exertion hit the back of her throat.

"Morning, Commander," came a familiar Italian accent.

"Enrico," she replied, surprised. "You finally got in the early bird session. Who'd you replace?" She looked around the room to see who was missing.

"I was top on the waiting list. I don't know who, but someone was a no-show yesterday." Enrico set the dumbbell he had been lifting back on the rack. "You snooze, you lose, right?"

"That's the rule," she replied, then turned and headed to a free running pod.

After stepping on the tread-pad, the bell-shaped environment dome lowered over her to the floor. "Gabriele, what enviro setting would you like?" asked the virtual assistant.

"Let's do a 10k race along the Northern California coast, light breeze, sun, a few clouds, and medium competition. I want to feel the ocean and the participants."

"Please wait one moment while I generate the scene."

Gabriele started off at a slow pace. The round interior of the dome surrounding her brightened. A warm breeze picked up and flowed through her hair and running shirt. To her right, the ocean waves rolled in against the coastline as virtual runners passed her. She lengthened out her stride.

As she worked to maintain her pace she thought about Enrico. Seeing him there, handling the weights, and straining, aroused memories of occasional interludes together, when he could massage away the stresses of time in space, or help wile away the boredom of long trips back to Earth. She drifted into what else he could do with his strong hands and then caught herself as she fell further behind the pack. She shook off the memories and caught up.

Over time, their relationship had changed. He was a close friend now, someone she could trust to give her honest feedback without sugar coating it—something she needed now that she was Commander.

In her private quarters, slightly reclined in her chair, feet up, Gabriele flipped through pictures on her tablet. She landed on one of her and Michael together from the last time she was back on Earth. They were on the terrace of a marina restaurant in California, overlooking the ocean. *That was a great trip,* she thought. She kept scrolling; her brother and his family, the view of the water from Michael's back porch, her and Michael scuba diving during another trip. It helped her space depression, but not that much this time.

She looked herself over in the mirror on the side panel, pushed her hair up and back. A moment later, she grabbed her bathroom bag and headed to the washroom. After returning, she checked the mirror one more time and practiced her smile for the video.

She pulled up the messaging app and touched *Record*.

"Hey, Michael. I was just flipping through some pictures from our trip down the California coast. I loved that trip. It was perfect. And it gave me some fun memories to help through the time out here. I just wonder how you managed to look great in every single one and I looked like such a goofball." She winked and smiled. "Anyway, just thinking about you. I'm sure on your end you're thinking, oh god, all these messages, she's suffering space depression again." She raised her brow and sighed, "I think I am..."

Gabriele set her breakfast plate down next to Enrico. "Morning," she said to the group as she glanced around the table.

"Morning," replied Jordan. "We were just talking about the next rotation. Looks like the scientist from Z-Scan was confirmed. I saw her name on the team roster. Dr. Rachel Dibaba? Is that correct?"

"That's her."

"I read her bio," said Jordan. "She sounds brilliant." She then glanced at Enrico. "You've met her a few times. What's she like?"

"Brilliant, as you pointed out," replied Enrico. "Outgoing, pleasant, fun to be around." He then cleared the smile from his face. "But... I understand she doesn't think too highly of mechanical engineers."

Jordan raised an eyebrow. "You kind of lit up talking about her, Enrico. I saw your eyes get happy. Do you have a thing for Dr. Dibaba?"

Enrico laughed. "No, no. We've just met a few times, to test out the latest gear from Z-Scan."

Gabriele tried to stay out of the middle.

"Oh. I see," said Jordan. "You meet Dr. Dibaba a couple times. She's a hot computer scientist—a rarity for sure. You then talk our Commander here into bringing her onboard for a little off-planet alone time trip to Mars."

Enrico chuckled. "Your imagination, Jordan... kind of scary sometimes."

Gabriele smiled at Jordan as she sipped her coffee. "Enough on Dr. Dibaba. You said you had something to discuss with us. I saw a report you flagged for me to review. One from our last rotation. Was that it?"

"That's it," replied Jordan. "So, last time out, towards the end, we were wrapping up some reports. In one, three drones had malfunctioned at the same time. It's been a while. Do you guys remember?"

Gabriele nodded. "Sure. A crew started at the site... what? Maybe a couple months ago?"

"Correct," replied Jordan, pointing at Gabriele with her fork. "I am sure you also remember our last excursion to Chronos? When it seemed the pilot lost control?"

"Like yesterday," replied Enrico.

"Me too. So, I decided to go back through the equipment logs for that craft on that day. You know, to see if there was anything out of the ordinary."

"Did you find something?" asked Enrico.

"No, nothing. But I started to think about where it had happened. We were about two-thousand clicks west of Athena."

"That sounds correct," noted Gabriele.

"Remember where those drones malfunctioned?"

"Same coordinates?" asked Enrico.

Jordan glanced at both of them. "The marker where the turbulence started... it's not far."

"How far?" asked Gabriele.

"Half a kilometer."

Enrico raised an eyebrow. "Has the site work reported anything unusual?"

"Not that I've seen," replied Gabriele. "Just some traces of silicon and iron, if I recall. Whatever they've found hasn't pushed the site into a higher queue. At least not yet."

"I dug into the deep scanner reports," said Jordan. "They still report an unknown. There's something there. Gabi, we should bump it up so it will get more attention and resources."

"Jordan, you know it's pointless. You know how the sorting procedures work. Without some significant probability of something useful being there, we can't allocate the equipment and machines. The costs are too great. And it was a half a kilometer away. Sounds like nothing more than a coincidence."

Jordan leaned forward. "We still have no explanation for what happened to us during that flight or to those drones. IMTEC hasn't found anything. I tore those drones apart. Aside from the typical maintenance issues, I found nothing. You don't want to pull rank just to see? Aren't you curious, Commander?"

Gabriele sat her cup down. "This isn't the first strange coincidence we've encountered on Mars. *You* know that. You have nearly as many years there as I have." She knew the costs. On Mars all projects were complex and expensive. Mobilizing the excavation machines, robots, life-support pods, and power systems was complicated enough. Then there were the schedule adjustments, reallocating engineers, and the approval process. No changes were simple matters. Hard analysis and rigorous planning drove IMTEC. She also weighed the fact that she had just made commander. She didn't need any rogue, fruitless ventures sitting on her list of achievements. She knew Jordan was right. Still, knowing IMTEC's relentlessness with such matters, no explanation for either incident was very unusual.

"Okay," she replied. "Put both events in one report with significant detail. Anything useful that was found within a half kilometer radius. All your work. Everything. Make it shine with facts. I'll need the justification."

"Yes!" replied Jordan.

EIGHT

Endurance Site, Antarctica

Inside the excavated chamber of ice, Nick, his crew, and robots reached the pinnacle of the anomaly object, buried nearly a meter under the surface. He knelt down in the center of the hollowed-out room and brushed away the last layer of soil. After finding the tip of the object, he continued scraping away the frozen dirt until he had exposed a quarter meter of its surface.

He studied it for a while.

"What do you think, Nick?" asked Francisco, squatted down opposite him.

"Hand me that scanner there behind you."

Nick took the device with his gloved hands, turned it on, and faced it towards the black rock. The screen on the scanner reported:

> _scanning... analyxfjkweo5420zing.... material signature 32jkesp~- recognized_

"What?" He turned the device off and back on.

"What's wrong?" asked Sergey in his helmet's mic.

"I don't know. The reading was all garbled. Just rebooting it."

Sergey's eyebrow raised.

Nick faced the scanner towards the object again. It reported:

> _scanning... analyzing... material signature not recognized_

The surface temperature displayed in the right column. He made a mental note, then faced the scanner at the soil away from the object.

> _scanning... analyzing... material signature recognized_

He looked at the temperature reading for a while, then pointed the scanner back at the object for a second reading. Then a second time at the soil. He looked up at his crew. "Looks like we found our heat source."

"Think it's just a giant rock?" asked Francisco.

Nick took a while to respond, then looked around at the crew through his clear helmet. "It doesn't look like much more than that. Let's keep going."

By the time they were ready to call it quits for the day, the crew had removed two more meters of soil. The object had now taken shape. Its rough pinnacle sloped down from its peak like the top of a raw chunk of black marble. Flowing down from the top, the roughness smoothed out as it met the perfectly flat polished sides. It was like the sculptor had finished the faces of the object to give it form but left the top raw to show its origin.

Nick was a geological engineer. He knew there were natural hexagons in nature. Beehive honeycomb, and many crystal systems of minerals grew in hexagonal shapes. He had studied them in school. He had seen many with his own eyes. He knew of nothing like this in nature—of this size. It was enormous. "I'll schedule the deep scanners to run a sweep of the chamber when we're done," he announced to his team, "to try to see how much more is buried. But from what we've dug up, if I were to guess what this is, I would say it's an ancient meteorite. I suppose it could also be an overgrown crystal structure. I've just never seen one this big and with this dark color."

"Maybe everything here grew super-sized... you know, before the ice wiped it all out," joked Francisco.

"Maybe," replied Nick. "Before we call it quits for the day, let's take a sample now that we've uncovered this thing... whatever it is."

"I brought the hardest drill bits we have," said Sergey.

"Now that we can touch it, let's take a small chunk with us," replied Nick.

With a hammer and a chisel, Nick strode back to the rock and looked for a crevice. After finding his spot, he positioned the chisel and held it firmly. He then raised the hammer and hit the head square on. The hammer vibrated in his hand; the chisel deflected off the object. "Damn, I don't think I hit it hard enough."

Sergey chuckled.

"I hear you, Sergey," said Nick into his helmet's mic. He placed the chisel in another position, then raised the hammer and pounded the head again, giving it more thrust. Again, nothing broke loose. "Damn, boys, we have one hard fucking rock here," he said, dropping the chisel. He backed up, thought for a moment before turning to Sergey with a laugh.

Sergey was smiling.

"All right, I know what you're thinking. Machine over muscle. I just had to try it."

"I was wondering when you'd come around," said Sergey. "Step back and let me show you how to do this properly." A few minutes later, after mounting the hardest bit he had, Sergey returned to the face of the object next to Nick. "Ready?"

"Give it a go," replied Nick.

Sergey powered up the pulsing drill, spread his feet apart to brace himself, and then pushed the spinning bit against the object. The drill bit just danced around the surface, finding no traction. He braced himself again and then slowly pressed the drill against the object, holding it firm. The bit just danced to the right again. He stopped the drill, took a step backwards and looked at Nick who was grinning. "You think you can hold it steady?"

"Maybe," he replied, not so sure he could, knowing Sergey was pretty strong.

"Here," said Sergey, handing him the drill. "Let's see if all that weight training has done any good."

Nick took the drill. He then stepped up to the object, braced himself, tightened his biceps to hold the drill tight in position, then slowly sped up the bit. It instantly tracked to the right, not piercing the surface in the slightest. He lowered the drill by his side and backed up. He thought for a moment, then turned and surveyed the crew. "Anyone else care to prove their manhood here?" They all laughed. "I've never ran across anything this hard. Let's call it quits for today."

He glanced around at the crew. "I could use a beer. Anyone else?" He got a couple of grunts, which he took for yes.

Before long, the crew were making their way back down the main line.

Nick and Sergey hung back for a moment. Nick held the scanner out and pointed it at the object. "Watch the temperature," he said. "Watch it as I move the crosshair around the surface."

"It's not changing," said Sergey.

Nick then pointed the scanner at the earth a distance from the object.

"I see."

"Sergey. This thing is maintaining a consistent temperature well above its surroundings. I don't know of any element or crystal structure that does this."

"Hey," said Sergey as he placed his hand on Nick's shoulder. "Humans and scientists have never been here. We are the first ones, man. We probably know less about what's under our feet than what we know about all of space. I am sure we will encounter things no one has seen before."

The men studied the object.

Nick glanced at Sergey. "Yeah. You're right."

"Like you said, it's probably just a meteorite. What else could it be?" asked Sergey, glancing back at the object, eyebrow raised.

Sitting on his terrace, Jonathan looked up after rereading the progress report from Nick. He gazed out at the calm Mediterranean. A few grey clouds moved west to east. Years ago, he would have been more curious. After decades of digging deep mines all over Earth, and running into unknown objects—meteorites, crystals, or mixes of elements—that looked interesting but never amounted to anything of real value, his curiosity waned.

His tablet chimed. A message appeared.

Endurance team call

He picked up his glass and strolled back inside his villa into his office. Activating the screen on his desk, he joined the call he had scheduled for that afternoon. Nick and Ellie were already online.

"Hello, team," he said while studying their backgrounds. "Ellie, judging from what's behind you, you're either camping or doing some field work somewhere."

"A bit of both, really," she replied. "We're at a cave site west of Johannesburg. I'm here with a crew of grad students working with some new scanners, compliments of Z-Scan." She smiled.

"Find any anomalies?" asked Nick.

She laughed. "Nothing like what you've surfaced."

Jonathan grinned. "So, Nick, looks like you and your crew have found the source of this heat?"

"We definitely found it. Exactly what we found, I'm not sure."

"I was just reviewing your report again," said Ellie. "The data shows it's maintaining a really consistent temp across all its surfaces. Boy, it's enormous too. Think it's maybe a large crystal structure?"

Nick nodded slowly. "Possibly. Giant crystals have been found before. Near one of Jonathan's projects in Mexico, massive selenite crystals were discovered a long time ago. But our scanners can't identify the material. So, I'm thinking it's a meteorite. Or maybe some elemental structure we've never encountered."

"Can you image the entire object?" asked Jonathan.

This time Nick shook his head. "Not yet. The bottom is very deep, and the resolution of the scanners degrade too much at that depth to see any real detail. We first need to excavate two, maybe three more meters. Then I think our scanners will see the bottom. The thermal readings are what's really puzzling."

"Do you think it's some type of reaction?" asked Jonathan.

"I just don't know, guys. I think we need an expert looking at this data."

"I had thought about this earlier," said Ellie. "I know a top astrophysicist who would gladly look at the data. If this is a meteor, Arnaud will know. Jonathan, what do you think?"

Jonathan thought for a moment as he looked at Ellie and Nick. He didn't like the direction this conversation was going. Sending boring samples off to labs for material analysis was one thing, but getting more scientists directly involved was something he really didn't want to do. He could see this consuming more and more of the team's time, as well as machines for more excavation, more monitoring, more analysis. It also meant more exposure, ergo more potential for spies from competitors to get wind of their findings. Or, worse, alert the media.

"It is bizarre, I agree," he replied. "Such a large rock-type structure being warmer than the frozen earth around it. I don't believe we have ever run across anything like this at any of our other sites. Have we, Nick?"

"No. Never."

Thinking quickly, Jonathan said, "Come to think of it, we wouldn't really know if we had. The earth's temperature in our mines rises the deeper we go. Listen, team, I'm intrigued as well. But that said, this little discovery is turning out to be physically big. Excavating this thing, putting safety systems in place, and everything else needed to carry out this project properly is consuming too much time and resources. Nick, I see the utilization reports. And this isn't anything we are actually looking for. My experience is telling me we should park this for a while and continue expanding our tunnels, mapping out resource veins and deposits and hunting for remains of prehistoric life. We can come back to it another day, after we have a bit more success under our belt."

"If that's what you want," replied Nick unenthusiastically.

Surprised, Ellie replied, "Jonathan, this isn't just another rock or crystal. This is a very unusual discovery. You both just agreed. It's generating heat somehow. We can't just leave it. What if it's some new useful material structure never discovered before?"

Jonathan looked at Ellie for a second. He now realized she was a scientist interested in discovering not just the life that once covered Antarctica, but other interesting things as well. He also heard the disappointment in Nick's response. Maybe he should let it go a little further. He knew he could stop it at any point. It might mean Ellie getting frustrated, but he could deal with that if he had to.

"All right," replied Jonathan reluctantly. "Let's see what your colleague thinks this is. Send him the data."

Ellie smiled. "Nick, his name is Dr. Arnaud Davesne. He lives in Paris. I'll connect you two."

"Great! I'll hook him up with the data feeds."

Jonathan looked back at his screen. "I need to go, you two. Let me know what this Dr. Davesne discovers. As always, let's keep the things we learn quiet. Make sure Dr. Davesne understands as well."

Sitting on the sofa in his executive office, the CEO of Cobalt Energy Global, the biggest competitor of JDC Resources Group, read a one liner message on his tablet:

Concentrations are high in samples. No large deposits yet. Some anomaly detected under the surface. Excavation underway.

He paused and thought for a while about *his* failed attempts in Antarctica. But he knew the issues of supply and demand in the world. He knew Jonathan was right in forging forward. Someone just needed to find and map the folds and large veins and then show the world what was there. *Keep digging, De Clare,* he thought to himself. *I am sure you will eventually find our payday. You always do.*

He then deleted the message.

NINE

Endurance Site, Antarctica

Days after their arrival at Endurance, after hours of upgrading systems and integrating new scanning gear, Rachel strolled into the control room and plopped down at her favorite workstation. She picked it because it sat in the middle of the room, facing the clear, curved glass wall that gazed outwards. Snow-covered ice stretched out in all directions, meeting a mountain range in the distance. Screens on the side walls monitored every part of the operation, both above and below the glacier. It looked like a command deck of a starship that was exploring a frozen planet.

Rachel pulled her headphones up over her ears, turned on some background music, then opened up her messages. One from the International Mars Terraforming and Exploration Coalition was at the top, followed by one from Commander Gabriele Rousseau, and then another from Z-Scan with the subject, *Rescan Report*. She opened the one from IMTEC first. It was formal, as always. The first part was a straight up reminder to complete certain documents online by a specific date. The next part was her training schedule leading up to the departure date. Rachel then opened the message from Gabriele.

Hello Rachel,

I want to welcome you to my team and to let you know I am very excited to have you onboard for our next rotation out to Mars. You should have received your training schedule from IMTEC by now. It's a detailed, rigorous plan designed to get you in physical and mental shape for the time away from Earth. Like myself and others who go through the program routinely, you'll find it both challenging and rewarding at the same time. It is the key to having a successful, productive time on Mars. Your assigned IMTEC advisor will help you navigate the process however, I want you to know I am here for you as well if you have questions or concerns...

After finishing Gabriele's message and reading through the training schedule, Rachel leaned back in her chair and gazed out of the glass wall at desolate Antarctica. *It's really happening,* she thought. Her stomach churned, her chest tightened slightly. As the time of her departure to Mars grew nearer, a million thoughts surfaced in her mind. It all became more real.

Rachel moved on from the IMTEC material and continued through her messages to the one from Z-Scan. She opened the auto-generated report and skimmed through the familiar records of ADESA anomalies, looking at what had changed since the last report. Near the bottom, she stopped and thought for a moment.

"Hey Rachel," came Nick's voice. "I found you," he continued as he strolled into the room.

Startled, she turned.

Nick rolled a chair over and looked at her screen. "What are you working on? You look deep into something."

She pulled her earphones down around her neck and pushed her hair behind her ears. "I was just reading this report from ADESA... an anomaly she's flagged on Mars. Just one in the backlog."

"Didn't you once tell me you get a lot of those on Mars?"

"I did. And we're working on improving the results there. But this is something else." She pointed to the screen. "This is an internal report. One that gives us more data to help with tracking down issues with recognizing materials."

Nick rocked back in his chair and put his hands behind his head as Rachel continued.

"As ADESA builds signatures of new discoveries in her memory, she periodically retraces previous discoveries—things she didn't recognize in the past."

"Other unknowns?" asked Nick.

"Yes, but also things where her certainty wasn't that high. To see if she can now figure out what the anomalies were and to improve her confidence in past decisions."

"Makes sense."

"This report shows me re-scans where something has changed. Sometimes the changes are positive and sometimes not. It all helps in improving her algorithms." Rachel pointed at the screen again, this time to one line. "See that line?"

"Yeah." Nick squinted and read it. "What's *END09081*?"

"She just cross referenced an anomaly on Mars to that discovery."

Nick unlocked his fingers from behind his head and rocked forward. "That's here. That's Endurance, right?"

"Yes. That's the index for *your* anomaly discovery, *here*."

"What does that mean? There's another one of these objects on Mars?"

"No, no," replied Rachel, after a moment. "She's just saying a couple of the characteristics look similar. But her confidence level is so low, the information is useless for anything other than debugging. I just thought you would find it interesting."

Nick noticed her brow was slightly furrowed. "Yeah. Wild," he replied, intrigued. "You think there's something to it."

"It's nothing more than a coincidence," replied Rachel, staring at the screen; sticking with the statistical conclusion.

The southern hemisphere faced the Sun at that time of year. Sunlight bathed the Endurance compound for nearly twenty four hours a day for several weeks. Then, over six months, it slowly tapered back down to several weeks of complete darkness. One evening—according to the time, not the bright glow outside—some of the crew were making dinner. Others were playing cards. Nick helped with the food while Rachel and Sergey took part in the poker game. Rachel was a numbers wiz who knew the odds, while Sergey was a quiet master at reading the opponent.

"Okay, last round. Time to eat," announced Nick.

Sergey, Rachel, and Francisco were still in. The pot was real money. Sergey noted that Rachel had leaned forward a bit more, that her playing pattern had deviated slightly. He upped the stakes enough to make them think he was holding a good hand, but not enough to spark suspicion. Rachel and Francisco folded. Sergey laid down his cards.

"Shit, I'm getting another beer," said Francisco, standing up, pushing his chair back.

"Not again," said Rachel. "You had nothing, again. Just a pair."

Sergey raised an eyebrow. "Stick with your usual playing pattern. Don't think too long."

Nick laughed. "Kalashnikov is reading you, Rachel. He's a master at subtle body language."

"What am I doing?"

"Little things you are not even aware of. We'll play another round or two later. I'll show you."

Later that evening, Nick and Rachel were in her quarters, laying in her bed. Nick was on his side, looking at her and her computer while thinking. She was reading logs from the day's activities.

"Hey, so when you are traveling to Mars, how will we communicate? Will I be able to reach you? You know, like how we talk here on Earth?"

Rachel looked up from her tablet. "What do you mean?"

Nick wanted to talk. Or perhaps he just wanted some attention, he wasn't quite sure. He rolled over on top of Rachel, grabbed her computer, set it down on the side, and rubbed his beard against her.

"Oh gosh, what are you doing," she said with slight exasperation.

Reality was setting in. She would be gone for a long time; on another planet; millions of kilometers away. "I know I won't be able to wake up next to you and play with you when you are gone to Mars, but will I be able to call you there? Video chat? I'm curious what IMTEC will allow."

"Real-time chatting will not work. The signal delay is too long. But we can send messages. Like we do when one of us isn't reachable or is busy."

"A year is a long time."

"You'll be busy with Endurance. The time will fly by."

"Yeah, I guess."

"I am sure Jonathan will bring on other females," said Rachel, not showing any concern, playing a game.

81

Nick kissed her. A little longer this time. He wrapped his arms around her to bring them as close together as possible. Then he rolled them both over, putting her on top. "So far, they've done well. You know, picking you for the team. Maybe my luck will continue." He played along.

Rachel grabbed his right nipple and gave it a slight twist.

Nick smiled, then grabbed *her* nipples.

Next day, inside the subway station, Nick and Rachel suited up.

"You know," Nick began, helping her seal her boots and gloves, "wearing this suit and spending time in these cold conditions will be nice practice for Mars."

"It's like a space suit, isn't it?"

"It is a space suit except it's not equipped with the gear to keep it pressurized. It's the only thing we could find that could handle these temperatures. I looked up data on Mars and the temps are about the same. Cool?"

"Super cool!" said Rachel, smiling.

They grabbed helmets and walked down the corridor through the thermally sealed door into the elevator room. Nick pressed the button. Rachel watched the floor meter above the doors. 480, 500, 520...580. The doors opened. A dirt covered rover exited on its way to the warehouse for maintenance.

"Remember, it's a bit of a ride down," said Nick, looking at Rachel with a suggestive raise of his eyebrow.

"You got something in mind?" Rachel gave him a light shove towards the elevator.

He grinned.

The ride to the bottom was just short of a freefall in subzero air.

Nick got close to Rachel. "You know... we're the first human couple down here."

"You said that the last time I was here."

He then kissed her softly.

"You're a great kisser, Nick." Rachel said with a smile. "But this beard..."

"I'm diggin' it," he replied with a grin.

"What's that noise?" asked Rachel quickly, looking down. "It's getting louder."

Nick smiled. "It's okay. It's just the ice skimmer running up the outside of the shaft."

Feeling the air temperature drop rapidly from frigid to unbearable, Rachel started to feel anxious. She put her helmet on, secured the seal, and activated the environmental controls. The warmed air through the breather helped. Nick checked her helmet to make sure she had fitted the seal, then he put his on.

Slowly, the metal cage screeched to a halt. The floor meter showed *B*.

"Ready?" said Nick, looking at her through his face shield.

Rachel stepped out of the lift and studied the room taking it all in again. "It's like we just descended into the world's most secret war bunker."

Nick chuckled. "Not much could get to us here."

To her right, a large debris transporter entered the service lift headed up top to dump a load of ice and rock. Another transporter exited a charging room. Two smaller dirt-covered debris-haulers were rolling in from the main line—their beds full of rubble.

"Come on, I'll have a small transporter follow us and carry a few tools." Nick walked into the front charging room, glanced across the control panel on the wall, and selected a fully charged machine. A moment later, the top light on a transporter activated as it detached from its charger and rolled towards the entrance, following Nick's path. Inside the tool room, he selected a few instruments and a couple of tripod lights before placing them on the transporter. Then he took Rachel's gloved hand and tugged. "All set, let's go!"

Opposite the lifts, the tall roller door to the main line tunnel flew up.

"Every time I come down here it's like the first time," said Rachel, excited. Her eyes wandered around the rough walls. "The blue ice. I never can remember how brilliant it is." A series of lights along the ceiling of the tunnel activated in succession, illuminating their path ahead. "It's like a fantasy world." She rubbed her gloved hands along the glass-like walls.

Ahead, a transport rover approached carrying a load of ice. It slowed slightly as if to say, *I see you, don't worry,* then it weaved to one side and sped up again.

"Which tunnel are we going to?" asked Rachel, watching their progress on the Endurance site map on her tablet.

Nick heard her loud and clear. "T11," he whispered.

"Sorry. Did I scream it? I forget about the mics inside the helmets. I see T11 on the site map. It looks kind of curvy. More than the other tunnels."

"You'll know why when we get there," Nick replied.

Fifteen minutes later, at the entrance to T11, he stopped. "Okay, now you'll see why it's curvy."

A few minutes down the path, Rachel suddenly understood. "We're descending."

"That's right. We're following the terrain and it's going down, possibly descending into a valley. The end of the tunnel is nearly twenty-eight hundred meters under the surface. If we do discover we're in a valley, maybe we will find a cave. Isn't that the best place to find fossils?"

"Maybe. I don't really know. I mean, I've been to plenty of sites with Ellie and they were all caves."

In a short distance, they rounded the corner at the end of the tunnel and stood at the top of the ramped floor to the chamber. Atlas—the boring machine—sensed their presence and paused from its work, excavating the room around the object. Atlas scanned the walls of ice and relayed the data to ADESA. ADESA analyzed the information and responded with the next instructions for Atlas. The machine worked non-stop, excavating away the ice, exposing more floor surface area. As Atlas removed ice, the size of the small room became a sizable chamber. Reinforcer beams lined the walls and ceiling.

"Atlas is a monster, isn't it?" said Rachel as she walked down the ramp. "I forgot how big of a machine he is."

"Yeah, it is the machine that makes this project work. Once he's finished clearing away the surface area around the entire object, we'll continue with the excavation."

Rachel walked up to the black rock jutting up out of the Earth in the center of the chamber. "It's much larger than I imagined from watching the video streams."

Standing by her side, Nick took off his glove and put his hand on the face of the object. "What you are seeing is just the pinnacle of this thing. There's so much more still buried. Touch it. It's warm."

Rachel removed her glove and placed her palm on the object's face. She then turned and looked at Nick. "Do you think it's decaying internally?"

"There has to be some type of reaction going on inside it," replied Nick. "But we haven't been able to pierce its surface. So, at this stage, we're just guessing. Ellie has brought in a physicist to do some research into it. We're feeding him all the data. Maybe he can figure out what it is."

The whole scene started to take shape in Rachel's mind. She was in an ice-walled chamber, nearly three kilometers under a glacier, staring at a massive black rock-like object that was giving off heat. She put her glove back on and walked around the chamber. "This is just bizarre," she said uneasily.

Nick checked out Atlas, but more he listened to Rachel's voice for markers—signals of high levels of anxiety leading to panic. Yes, she had been through the psychological training that was required of everyone at Endurance, but seeing this unusual object introduced a new source of tension. *She sounds okay,* he noted. He looked over at her. "Hey. Like Sergey once told me." He feigned his best Russian accent. "We are exploring unknown region of Earth. This land's been buried under ice for millions of years. We're bound to find unusual things down here."

Resting on a parked excavator, Rachel took a picture of Nick standing in front of Atlas. She smiled. "You look like you're in a space suit with your transformer pal behind you."

Nick walked over, sat beside her, and put his hand on her thigh. "You know we could make history down here."

"How's that?" She didn't look up.

"You know."

"You're amusing, Nick Standish. Tempting... but no! It's too cold down here. And this place is creepy."

He grinned, "What's creepy about a huge, hexagonal shaped rock standing perfectly straight, emitting heat, and under three kilometers of ice and frozen earth?"

"Exactly," she replied as she pushed him. She was half his size. He didn't move much.

He laughed. He knew the playing would help ease her mind.

"Don't forget what happened to that rover," she said as she turned and walked around the chamber, her arms folded tight. "This just feels weird, Nick. Anything else happen since that issue?"

"Nothing really notable," he replied with a shrug. "I did have a thermal scanner wig out on me once. When we uncovered the top of this thing, I was scanning the surface... recording its temperature, and the reading came back all jumbled. I rebooted it and then it worked fine. It's probably just a big meteorite. Or maybe an overgrown crystal structure, somehow electro-statically charged. I've seen some big ones. Some four or five meters in diameter, maybe ten meters long."

"But this rock, or whatever it is, is much bigger than that," Rachel pointed out.

"Yeah, that's right. That's why I wanted to show you. This thing is like fifteen to twenty meters across. Maybe bigger. Bigger meteorites have hit Earth in the past. I've done some research."

Rachel looked at Nick. "But don't they disintegrate when they hit? And do meteorites, or those crystals like you mentioned... do they give off heat? Like this?"

Nick hesitated. "No. I don't know of any that give off heat for this long."

TEN

Sunlight brightened Ellie's lab, illuminating the dust covered bones and artifacts on the shelves from her field projects at sites around the world—clues to ancient creatures that once roamed the Earth.

Ellie propped her feet up on the side of her desk and kicked back in her chair as she reread Arnaud's brief note before their call.

Found something fascinating. Object's temp oscillates and is predictable. You need to see this...

She accessed his profile at Sorbonne, in Paris. He was older now, more professorial looking than the last time she saw him. They had met at Witwatersrand. The university had recruited him for a multi-year engagement to teach and to help grow the school's space research program. After his sojourn in South Africa he returned to Paris to head up the physics department at Sorbonne. Ellie skimmed his professional history. Arnaud was now a world-renowned astrophysicist, a leading expert in the chemical makeup of things in nature and physical phenomena in space, an advisory scientist to IMTEC and other leading space agencies. *I definitely recommended the right scientist*, she thought.

She hadn't spoken to him in some time. They had exchanged messages but no face-to-face time. After Ellie had introduced Nick and Arnaud, Nick had taken over and connected them into sensor data streams from Endurance and managed the day-to-day interactions with Arnaud's team.

It was time for their call. She found Arnaud in her list of colleagues and touched his picture. *He likes to talk,* she reminded herself.

A moment later, he appeared on the wall-screen in front of her desk.

"Hey Arnaud. How are you?" she said, smiling.

"Not bad for an old guy like me," he replied calmly. Arnaud's longish, unkempt hair was greying, aging an otherwise youthful face that saw little sunlight. Behind the small glasses were deep, attentive eyes that rarely blinked. "You are looking lovely as ever. How are things at Wits?"

"Great. Just working on a couple projects here in Africa, and, as you now know, a big one in Antarctica. By the way, I just read your note again. I'm intrigued."

Arnaud laughed. "I am as well. I have a lot to show you."

"I'm ready to be blown away."

"I think I can do that and more," he replied as he stood up.

Ellie watched. He backed up and moved his camera to face a wall of screens.

"Everything clear on your end?"

"Perfect."

Arnaud pointed to the monitor on his left. "What you are seeing there is the time-series temperature data read off the surface of that object. Looks like nothing useful, right? Well, when you back out," he touched a control at the bottom of the screen, "and look at the data across a longer span of time, it looks like this... do you see?"

"I do. Looks like it's oscillating."

"It is." There was a slight tremble in Arnaud's voice. "It's a wave, Ellie. The surface temperature is cycling up and down like a sine wave, a long rhythmic movement, something akin to a resting state. Rhythms in nature are consistent as well when in a resting state but they vary ever so slightly over time. Whereas this object's temperature rhythm doesn't vary at all when it's in this low-level condition. We modeled this pattern and can forecast it with extreme accuracy. It's very consistent, very predictable." Arnaud paused for a moment, then said, "It's like a machine."

Ellie's eyes widened.

"There's something else." The data advanced forward a few minutes. "See the temperature rising? It's quick, not linear. It reaches a peak then hoovers there for a while before decreasing and then syncing back into that sine wave pattern. This is not exactly a scientific way of framing this behavior, but it's almost like this thing is sleeping comfortably in a non-dream state, and then it hits a REM cycle and everything goes haywire. Then after a while it settles back into this low-level sleep state. We have had no success modeling those erratic episodes."

"Are there more of those perturbations in the pattern?" asked Ellie, now leaning closer to her screen.

"There are many of them."

"Are the intervals between them predictable?"

"No, not at all. They appear to be random, but as you know the stimulus could be there and we're just not seeing it."

"Absolutely fascinating," replied Ellie. "What do you think it is?"

Arnaud played with the whiskers on his chin. "Great question." He thought for a moment. "All I know, with any degree of certainty, is I don't believe the heat is from a reaction. Reactions die out over time or, I guess I should say, we've discovered none that don't. To answer your question, we need to do more research. Our next step is to focus on these disruptions, but we need more data. A lot more data. Starting with the full history of video feeds and the ongoing live stream."

"I'll talk to Nick after our call."

Arnaud looked at his notes for a moment, then looked back at Ellie. "I also need data streams from some special plasma-based equipment I have here."

"Easy enough. Nick can pick it up at the Endurance facility in Melbourne. You just need to ship the gear there."

"I think we should also scan its surface for micro shifts in reflected light. I have sensors for that as well."

Ellie smiled. "Arnaud, just send me your Christmas list and I will get it to Nick."

Arnaud grabbed a stool and sat down in front of the camera. He then reached up with both hands and rubbed the back of his neck slowly. "Ellie, I have analyzed many meteorites—ones that hit Earth, ones that had been found on Mars, the Moon, and many that had been landed on to study. None maintained a surface temperature well above their surroundings. I know of no natural material or anything that has been discovered in space that exhibits this behavior. This is a first. Given where this object is sitting adds to the mystery. Bottom line? We're going to need a lot more time. You and the team there stumbled onto something that is a real enigma. Something very different indeed."

"It is intriguing," replied Ellie, thinking about the random, chaotic temperature swings. "What do you think, Arnaud? Is it some oddity of nature? Or something from somewhere else?" She then smiled slightly, "Is it a paper for a science journal, or... material for some alien hunting media?"

Diablo and his team of alien hunters had many projects on their radar, but Endurance had quickly moved up to center of the screen. None of the other cases were as intriguing, or as adventurous. Antarctica was a giant mystery to those who were curious, and Diablo and his team knew something was hiding there.

Their folder on Endurance grew. They learned about the exploration team, their backgrounds, and their lives outside of Endurance. After some time and patience, Khasimir had gotten into Witwatersrand systems. He found Ellie's messages. Then he found Arnaud. Then Diablo found Arnaud's tech assistant, János—the key he had been looking for—a poor graduate student from eastern Europe. After exchanging information online and offering a hefty consulting fee, Diablo had finally convinced János to agree to a meeting.

Diablo arrived at Gare du Nord in central Paris late afternoon. He pulled on his heavy overcoat, gloves, and scarf before exiting the train and making his way through one of the busiest stations in Europe. The Sorbonne Université campus was on the other side of the Seine, a nice forty-minute walk south. Four blocks from the campus, he entered the cafe where János had agreed to meet.

It took time for Diablo to get János to lower his guard and to understand the nature of the work. But winning over someone was a skill Diablo had worked on and discovered he had some talent for. Computer hacking served its purpose in his work, but sometimes the old ways, simply finding an insider and paying them well for information yielded the best results.

"I'm a scientist," said Diablo as he rubbed the beard filling in along his jaw. "I studied physics like you. My entire team are scientists, and experts in their fields. You see, outside of our day jobs we hunt for signs of alien life."

"But why in this way?"

"Sometimes big corporations and governments hide things... things that might get in their way. But we all live on this planet together. Shouldn't you and I know if something alien has been dug up somewhere? Shouldn't such information be shared with everyone?"

"I guess," replied János with some reluctance.

"I am only interested in discoveries that look or smell like something from somewhere else. That's it." He then laughed light-heartedly. "We just want to make sure some alien discovery doesn't sit in a closet collecting dust somewhere."

Two hours after meeting and several cups of coffee later, János understood. All he had to do was direct the data and video feeds from Endurance to Diablo. That was it. It was a very simple, harmless act. Diablo reassured him they were only using the data to see if there was an alien connection, nothing more. No one would get hurt. János would remain anonymous, just like all of Diablo's other sources he had paid over the years. It took some convincing, but János finally came around.

Diablo pulled out his mini tablet, accessed one of several transfer accounts he used, and sent the first payment. It was a lot of money for such a simple task.

"The payments will come every month until we don't need the data any longer," Diablo clarified.

János frowned. "How do I know you're not with some government?"

Diablo looked at János curiously, then replied in a deliberately friendly tone. "Well, I would think a government would just go take the data from the Endurance Project if they really wanted it." He didn't want to piss off his new recruit in their first meeting.

They left the cafe. János turned right, and Diablo turned left.

———————

Days later, sitting at a table in his flat, Diablo read a report—surfaced by Khasimir's hacking—titled, *Endurance Project - Initial Analysis*. In his nearly ten years of alien hunting, he had never run across anything like this. Something like a meteorite that maintained an *internal energy source*, as Davesne had put it. But more perplexing was the fact that, later in his report, he referred to it as *machine-like*. It was time to put all other projects on hold and focus on Endurance. Diablo turned to his other screen and pulled up his team's running communication thread.

Diablo: *Just finished reading Dr. Davesne's report. This is a game changer. We need to stop everything else and focus on this. We're going to need a way to corroborate his findings. Something more than just 'his' data. I have an idea.*
Akashi: *Hey, D, I just jumped on.*
Diablo: *Have you read the report?*
Akashi: *Sure did. Mind blowing stuff. What's your idea?*
Diablo: *All big corporations spy on each other. Just like governments. I am 100% sure JDC's biggest competitor has a spy on that project.*
Akashi: *Brilliant. I like it. I'll start on the research. We'll*

*need Khas doing his network cracking magic once we're confi-
dent which competitor to target.*

Diablo: *You know what this means? If we can find a second
source? Holy shit! This is what we've been hunting. This is it
A, I can feel it.*

ELEVEN

The JDC aircraft landed at Rand Executive Airport in Johannesburg and taxied to a parking space in front of the passenger lounge. It was eleven degrees outside, cool and crisp. Jonathan exited the jet for some air and briskly walked the length of the tarmac, working through his list of calls for the day—calls to board members to hear how meetings went, calls to project managers of mines and resource fields on every continent, calls to lawyers representing JDC in environmental litigation, investors, and follow-up calls.

Ellie arrived at the gate for the private terminal, cleared security, and made her way into the passenger facilities. She looked out onto the covered parking lot of private aircraft and saw Jonathan walking around his jet with a phone device in his ear, talking. As she made her way across the tarmac he waved and held up five fingers.

The plane assistant recognized Ellie, greeted her, and took her bags. Ellie boarded the jet and made herself comfortable at the executive table, in the seat that faced the front of the plane. *Jonathan can sit facing the back,* she decided.

After a while, the assistant came into the cabin. "Dr. Mayfield, Jonathan will be a few more minutes. Can I bring you something? Sparkling water? Cappuccino?"

"Water would be nice. Thank you."

Ellie watched Jonathan through the side window. He stretched and then locked his fingers behind his head as he looked up at the sky. *How did he manage to keep such nice hair with so much stress?* She smiled slightly. He looked like a rock star who had aged to a more distinguished regal look and now favored relaxed business attire.

A few minutes later, Jonathan concluded his call and boarded the plane. He ducked slightly as he entered the door.

"Ah, Ellie," he smiled, "such a pleasure to see you again! It has been too long." He held out his arms.

"Hi, Jonathan," Ellie replied, standing and greeting him with a light embrace. "Great to see you again as well."

The cabin assistant softly interrupted. "Jonathan, lunch has been delivered, and the pilot suggested we take off soon."

"Let him know we're ready."

The aircraft maneuvered out of the parking lot and onto the runway to their starting position. After a brief pause, it quietly sped along and then lifted into the air. Once they reached a cruising altitude, it leveled off to a smooth glide.

Jonathan leaned forward in his chair and took a drink from his glass. "This plane has an interesting little feature I've been dying to show off. Are you ready?"

Ellie raised an eyebrow. "Do I have a choice?"

"I'll take it slow," he replied as he touched a control on the table between them and slid his finger from top to bottom.

Ellie's eyes widened as the dark interior walls of the craft slowly morphed from opaque to transparent allowing the bright sunlight to stream in, rendering the top half of the fuselage as a clear glass dome.

"Amazing, isn't it?" he said calmly.

"Breathtaking. But I don't think I would like this if we were flying through a storm."

"*That* takes a little getting used to," said Jonathan, raising his eyebrows. "Would you like me to darken it again?"

"No, you can leave it. I am getting used to it," she replied, while clinching her arm rests and watching the field of white beneath them fly by.

As lunch was served, their conversation moved towards Endurance.

Ellie was just finishing her dessert when Jonathan said, "I've arranged a dinner for this evening with a delegate from Norway. She is the new head of their Ministry of Justice, which oversees the Polar Affairs Department."

She finished her plate and sat back. "I take it you're preparing me to accompany you?"

Jonathan smiled. "Something like that. They've started asking some questions about Endurance."

"What types of questions?"

"Details on what we're doing. Environmental questions. We've created quite a mountain of excavated ice and rock at our site. I am sure we now show up as bright as day on their routine satellite scans."

"I don't think I would be of much help with those types of questions."

"I'll handle the questions. I would like you to tell her about your field work in Africa and the relationship with Antarctica; the pterosaur discovery, and what else you believe we might find."

Ellie thought for a few moments while sipping her espresso. "Are any other countries requesting information?"

"Some have. But Norway is more important to keep happy at this point."

"I see."

"As long as Norway is comfortable with our work then all the other members should be as well."

Ellie had left the politics to Jonathan. As Endurance progressed and after their first big discovery, she felt herself being pulled in more. She had listened to Jonathan and, as always, weighed what he said with a dash of skepticism. *He is a savvy businessman. Everything he does and says is a means to an end*, she thought, as she looked out of the glass-tube they were flying in.

Inside the grand auditorium, the Minister of Foreign Affairs from the host country—in this case, the Netherlands—welcomed everyone to the annual Antarctic Treaty Meeting. The hum of audience chatter quieted down. The Minister then started his opening talk.

Jonathan half listened while thinking about the dinner with the delegate the night before. The woman was very inquisitive and well versed in the Endurance project. Her questions were direct and revolved around one point; *were there any mining efforts underway at the site?* Jonathan knew going into the meeting she was in a green party, and her questions affirmed this. It was obvious she didn't appreciate her country having an agreement with his company. Nevertheless, he had kept his tone respectful and assured her they were not mining and that he was acutely aware such actions would reflect negatively on Norway. He described their explorations under the glacier and how their work was benefitting science. Ellie showed the delegate images of the pterosaur and explained the significance of that discovery to the world of paleontology.

After thinking back through their conversation again, and again, looking for holes or something he said that he should not have, Jonathan tuned back into the Minister on the stage. The man was now reviewing the history of the Antarctic Treaty Committee System, and the spirit of peacefulness it had fostered among countries. Antarctica was humanity's top example of how countries could settle disputes peacefully. The Treaty itself had been proof of cooperation and an inspiration for other multi-national projects.

After a while, the Minister's voice took on a more somber tone. His facts became less aspirational and more reflective of the slightly graver world situation. He emphasized the significant increase in the human population since the Treaty was first signed in 1961, the consequences of an advanced society and its demands for natural resources, the mounting pressure to divide up Antarctica, and the pressure from member states for their land claims to be recognized.

"He just hit the point of this whole meeting," whispered Jonathan to Ellie. "More humans need more stuff, which means more resources are needed."

The Minister was a skilled politician and knew how to make his points without putting specific countries on trial. However, the audience of business leaders, interest parties, and politicians from every country clearly understood the history lessons of greed and expansion he alluded to. He ended with reminding his audience of the Arctic and the confrontations there in the last decades between the United States, Russia, and China and how that escalating conflict had come within a hair's breadth of all-out war. A war that would have surely devastated the entire world. He concluded with a mandate for all members to strive for resolution through diplomacy.

Jonathan sat, reflecting for a moment. He knew—without being singled out—that his efforts to open up Antarctica were being alluded to. At times, he had even felt the Minister's eyes directly on him. He understood the Minister's talk with crystal clarity, but the facts did not place the blame on him. Global *demand* for natural resources was driving the escalating tensions around Antarctica.

Underneath Jonathan's charm and sophistication, he was very much a realist. With several decades of experience under his belt, in his line of work, he had seen a lot of human nature—

the good and the bad. He knew the lengths people and countries would go to get what they wanted. But he didn't play on the demand side of the equation. He was simply meeting a need and would do what he could to come out on top.

He nudged Ellie lightly with his shoulder. "Well, that was a bit of a cold shower, wasn't it? Let's go find some coffee and maybe something to eat. I didn't have any breakfast."

After the opening of the Committee Meeting, a series of presentations were scheduled throughout the day. Jonathan planned to sit through a few. Not because he really cared about the content but because he wanted to be seen to be caring about the content.

Politicians being voted out, new ones being voted in, and other interested groups coming and going meant every year brought a new swath of fresh attendees. Most knew very little, if anything, about Ellie's material; how plate tectonics—the movement of the continents—had unfolded over time. How Antarctica came to be and the role it played in the evolution of life on Earth.

Late morning, Ellie breezed through her presentation in the main auditorium, reaching her main point after forty minutes. "Fossil discoveries play a primary role in helping us understand our Earth," she said, standing on the stage. She pointed towards the center of the image of Earth on the theater screen behind her. "Notice all the markers in eastern Africa. Many discoveries that have helped fill in our understanding of our planet and our history have been discovered in that little region of Africa." Ellie clicked the control in her hand. Africa, Antarctica, and the other continents all drifted and rotated back towards each other on the screen, connecting, forming one large landmass—Gondwana.

She took a few steps across the stage, pointed to eastern Africa, and then drew a short line with her finger to northern Antarctica, circling an area of land. "Based on the evolutionary history of the continents, and the hotbed of discoveries in eastern Africa that I have shown here, my colleagues and I believe there are many more important discoveries to be found in this region of Antarctica. *This* is where our Endurance Project is hard at work."

Ellie strode back to the podium and motioned to the virtual room assistant. The theater screen turned black. "And now I have a short video showing footage of our project and how it's progressing." The auditorium lights dimmed. A timpani-filled soundtrack radiated through the room. The title, *Endurance - Discovering the Lost World of Antarctica*, fizzled in on the black screen. After a moment, the title faded away to a short film of the development of the project.

The video ended with the cover of a scientific journal showing the Endurance team with Ellie and Jonathan in the center holding bones of their pterosaur. The title read, *Paleontologist and Team make Big Find in Antarctica*.

The video was Jonathan's idea. He wanted to leave the audience with an image of the purpose of the project. Behind all the technology, money, and years of work, was a real scientific purpose; something that would benefit the world.

Jonathan stood in the back of the room, applauding along with the audience. He reminded himself, *keep it professional*, as he watched Ellie on the stage. Endurance was too important. He was proud of this project—excited.

Ellie pushed through the revolving door and exited the hotel. She took a band from her wrist and pulled her hair back in a tight ponytail before crossing the street and setting off running. She headed north along the wide path that abutted the waterway encircling the old city. While she ran, she thought about Endurance and the team. She loved the project. It was the most ambitious, exciting thing she believed she would ever do. She loved the team; Nick, Sergey, Rachel, and, of course, Jonathan. They all had the same explorer drive she had. But, given that the speeches at the conference got bleaker every year, she now wondered more about Earth's shrinking reserves, how things would unfold in Antarctica, and what that could mean for Endurance. After their pterosaur discovery, and the preserved state of its bones, she really believed this was her chance to find something. Something that would change her world of paleontology. She wanted to better understand the risks to Endurance and, more importantly, to her work. With the Treaty Committee meetings and presentation behind them, it was time for their annual talk.

Evening arrived. Ellie met Jonathan in the lobby of their hotel and the two walked into the old town of Utrecht to a canal restaurant. Their table was outside, under large old trees overlooking a waterway. An ambient fusion band filled the air with music, providing cover for the private conversations of business executives and local politicians, all working on deals and investment ideas.

They started with a bottle of wine Jonathan had suggested. The owner of the restaurant personally delivered it and filled their glasses.

Jonathan lifted his glass and looked at Ellie. "Cheers, Ellie. To Endurance. Your presentation was perfect, as always."

"Thanks, Jonathan." She smiled back as they clinked glasses. "To you, Nick, Sergey, Rachel, and the whole team."

"Yes, to the team indeed."

The two continued talking for a while, catching up on the topics missed in their Endurance calls. A third of the way through dinner, the owner showed up and poured more wine.

Ellie took a sip from her glass and set it down. "Jonathan, the Minister's opening speech this morning was quite somber. Like a cold shower, right?"

He smiled.

"Every year they get more dismal. It seems the pressure is really building. At first, I was somewhat skeptical about the Treaty's demise. But now, I wonder how much longer it will survive."

Jonathan sighed. "We've exhausted older mines. You see them all over South Africa. All the mines there were depleted and abandoned decades ago. New deposits are getting harder to find. The Arctic and Greenland, considered the last rare element reserves, are being rapidly depleted. Now, after spending significant time in Antarctica, we can both attest to the continent having no indigenous people that would create a humanitarian issue. It has no government to topple; no land-based wildlife that would pose animal rights issues."

"Don't forget about the penguin colonies," said Ellie, casting a serious look at him.

Jonathan smiled. "Okay, a small animal rights issue. Penguins aside, as you've now seen with your own eyes, with the technology we possess, not even a two- or three-kilometer layer of ice can get in the way. The only thing standing in the way of outright resource-stripping there is a weakening treaty. To many countries, companies, and profiteers, it's prime for exploiting."

"How do *you* see things unfolding with the Treaty and then playing out there?" asked Ellie. "I often wonder, would there be conflict or not? The Minister didn't really go there, but he sure alluded to it."

Jonathan thought for a moment. "Well, if history is any guide, land claims and disputes over claims are rarely resolved peacefully. I think confrontation will boil up to the surface and... it could get nasty for a while."

"I know this will not happen tomorrow," said Ellie, "but let's say countries do lock horns over land claims. Everything around Antarctica would be in disarray for years. Maybe Endurance would no longer need to be a scientific led project. Assume you've now mapped out significant gold and mineral deposits. What happens to Endurance? And I guess, to be more on point, what would happen to my work? I just feel like we are on the verge of discovering something for the history books."

"Ellie, naturally I am interested in digging for gold in Antarctica. Hell, I believe there's a decent chance the Witwatersrand gold beds run close to our site. Whenever I see certain terrains, I immediately wonder; what could be under the ground? Could there be lithium or cobalt or palladium? I love the mystery. And now with the robotic mining machines I own, ADESA, and Endurance, we can truly discover Antarctica. While the prehistoric world has always been fascinating to me, I've learned more about the role Antarctica played since you started consulting with us. It wasn't always just a block of ice at the bottom of Earth, right?"

Ellie smiled. "No, it wasn't."

"I want us to make history. Who knows, maybe we will find another ancient human-like race."

"I don't think we will find that," said Ellie. "But you never know." She then frowned at Jonathan, not really answering her question. "Jonathan, what's the plan when you find some large vein of something valuable? What's the plan if and when the treaty goes away? What's the plan for my work?"

Jonathan heard the concern in her tone as he took a drink from his glass of wine and set it back down. He had to be straight up with her. "Ellie, I do believe the treaty will collapse, and I believe we will discover significant deposits of metals and valuable resources. When that day comes, will I walk away from your work? Today, I would say no, but I can't make such promises about the future. Business is complicated. I have investors I am accountable to. The world changes."

Ellie understood. Jonathan's message was clear. The future was uncertain, and he didn't care to tie himself to commitments he didn't need to. "Jonathan, I've never asked you this, but what if we never find anything worth mining for? Or you do find something, but mining remains forbidden? How long before you shut it down?"

"You know I have investors I am accountable to," Jonathan replied. "But that said, Endurance is what we call a frontier project. We've spent more on other ventures that never panned out. At least here we will have some scientific discoveries to hang on our walls, right?" He smiled, raised his glass, and took a drink.

Jonathan's world was complex. Ellie liked the excitement. The adventure of uncovering prehistoric life in Antarctica was beyond words. At first, she believed he couldn't justify Endurance's presence in Antarctica without her. Without him, she could never truly explore Antarctica. But, as every year unfolded, she began to see the person Jonathan really was —and the power he wielded—more clearly. She began to catch glimpses of the motivations behind his suave character and his intelligence. Ambition. Power. If she ever got in his way, he would easily progress on without her. Ellie pondered their conversation. She never fully trusted him. After this year's conference, she wondered even more. Was she just a piece in a game to help him towards an end? Or were his interests in science sincere?

It was late when they called it an evening and walked back to their hotel.

At the entrance, Ellie turned and looked at Jonathan for a moment. Then she said, "Breakfast at eight?"

Jonathan smiled. "Perfect."

They said goodnight and retired to their individual worlds, in their individual rooms.

TWELVE

IMTEC US-West Campus, Seattle Washington

Gabriele returned to her office from physical therapy, sat down at her desk and reached for her cup, reminding herself to put her fingers through the ring. She felt the unexpected weight of her arm. She felt the added weight from the cup. Since stepping foot back on Earth, she had already dropped more than a few glasses.

She touched her computer to check her messages. *Mars Site Excavation & Activity Report* was at the top. She opened it and looked for anything interesting.

"Knock, knock!"

Gabriele looked up from her screen and saw Van Der Berg at her door. "Robert. Morning. I would stand but..."

"Earth gravity is a bitch, isn't it?"

"Yeah. Seems every round trip is a bit tougher."

"That's age working on you. Wait until you're an old bastard like me. It'll take you twice as long to recover. So, last time I saw you I promoted you to Commander and then you took off on a mission to Chronos, if I recall."

Gabriele leaned back in her chair. "That sound right. And you hopped the next transporter back here."

Van Der Berg smiled. "I guess I did. Well, welcome back."

"Thanks. You must have caught an earlier flight up this morning."

"I did," replied Van Der Berg with a nod. "I have back-to-back meetings here and wanted an early start. Listen, Gabi. I was just reviewing the last activity report on the flight over. Have you had a chance to look at it?"

"Not yet. I was just opening it when you walked in."

"A line item in the report flagged a block in a quadrant out near Chronos. The crew there has found something." He reread the data on the tablet in his hand. "Looks like the material signature is registering as unknown, hence the flag. I am sure our scientists are doing their research, but I was curious to see if you have any first-hand intel on that site? I know it will come up in the briefing later this morning."

"I'll look into it and let you know what I find."

Van Der Berg stepped back towards the door. "I don't think we've run across a material we couldn't identify in quite a while."

Gabriele nodded. "I agree. I'll look into it. By the way, I'll be off-grid for a while after today."

Van Der Berg looked a little surprised. "Oh? Plans?"

"Yes. With Michael."

"Ah," he said with a smile. "You need to talk him into going to Mars with you, to help expand our life sciences programs."

"Yeah, right," she laughed. "That will never happen. He would prefer a firing squad."

Van Der Berg laughed and then waved goodbye as he turned around. "We'll catch up more later."

Gabriele forced herself to sit up straight. She then opened the activity report and scanned it. Midway down the page she saw the flag—*subsurface mass, material signature unknown.* She recognized the range of the coordinates and knew of only one active project in that quadrant. She navigated on her screen to the active sites repository and opened the most recent analysis report. The summary points were clear: unknown mass detected, nearly three meters deep, slight temperature variations, no detectable radiation, boring samples unsuccessful. She then pulled up a video stream from the site. The timestamp in the footer indicated it was ten days old. Some excavation equipment was there, but no pod yet for the crew. *This was just the wildcatting phase*, she thought, using an old oil prospecting term she used to refer to the phase-one operation —the basic excavation work needed to expose whatever was there.

Endurance Site, Antarctica

Layer by layer, the machines stripped away the earth to expose more of the anomaly. For ten million years, the ice sheet had pressed down on the frozen soil—compressing it, freezing it, preserving it in time. Breaking it up was tough, even for Sergey's best machines.

Jonathan held firm on his agreement with Nick to only have the team work part-time on the anomaly. It was not to be their focus. Nick and Sergey had allocated a small pool of machines to work on the site. Their plan was to first tunnel around the complete circumference of the object to expose all its faces. Layer by layer, they would remove earth, lowering the ramped floor running up to the object, and then lowering the floor of the tunnel around the object.

Nearly three months had passed since kicking off their plan. The small cadre of machines had worked nonstop. They had cleared a tunnel around the six-sided object and exposed its top five and a half meters. Each of the two longer sides measured just over eighteen meters and were perfectly parallel with each other. The two short faces on each end were just under ten meters each. The object was far larger than any crystal struc- ture Nick could find in the global geological databases.

It was late. Some of the crew watched a soccer game in the galley. Nick sat in the control room, rocked back in a chair with his feet up, talking to Rachel on his tablet. On one wall, a video feed displayed the mysterious object's chamber.

Sergey strolled in with a cup of black coffee—his signature drink—and took a chair a respectful distance from Nick and watched his machines at work. They had lowered the ramped floor another layer, another meter. It was like watching water being slowly drained out of a flooded chamber, revealing an ancient monolith standing in the center.

Nick whispered, "I'll call you tomorrow," then touched *End*.

"How is Rachel?" asked Sergey, his eyes still on the wall-screen.

"She's great. Her training for Mars starts soon."

"You like her a lot, don't you?" Sergey came over and picked up the controls next to Nick and returned to his chair, studying the video feed on the wall while slowly rotating through the tunnel cameras.

Nick uncrossed his arms and stretched them behind his head. "I do. I really like her. I miss her, Sergey. Seeing her every couple months just isn't enough. At any rate, I'm meeting her in a few weeks."

"What have you planned?"

"She talked me into going surfing in South Africa."

"Isn't that home for her?"

"It is."

"Sounds like she's taking you to meet Mom."

Nick laughed. "Maybe."

After making his rounds, switching through the cameras in all tunnels, Sergey returned to the object's chamber. There, he slowly rotated counterclockwise around the room, moving from one angle to the next. When he reached the display showing the right face of the monolith, he stopped. He gazed at the screen for a moment, then stood up and walked towards it, studying it. "Have you seen this?"

"Seen what?"

"Something is there," mumbled Sergey. "Some kind of marking."

"What camera is that?"

"It's the right face."

The two men watched the excavator in the chamber nudge forward, removing the next layer of soil from the face of the object. A transporter pulled up behind the excavator. The excavator raised its debris bucket and rotated it backwards, dumping its load into the transporter bucket. It then continued forward, digging and exposing a few more centimeters of the object's face.

Sergey backed into his chair, laid down the control pad, and picked up his coffee. The excavator edged forward again. As it did, soil fell out of the engraved marking.

"Something is carved into the face," said Nick.

They watched the excavator. It took its time. The marking gradually rose out of the earth floor like a long arc. Nick pulled his chair closer to the screen.

Half an hour later, after the excavator had moved another meter forward, the marking had gradually arced across the face.

Nick zoomed the camera in closer, squinting at the screen. "It looks like a perfect arc of a circle from here."

"Yes... it's clean and symmetric," mumbled Sergey, scratching his graying beard.

"We need to focus on this side," said Nick. "We need to see what that is. Can that excavator do another sweep?"

"Sure," replied Sergey. "But after that, we'll need to lower the rest of the floor and the entry ramp."

"Cool. Let's do it. Let's also send in two more excavators to work on the floor."

Sergey rolled his chair up to a computer, put on the reading glasses that were hanging around his neck, and logged in.

Another sweep by the excavator did not reveal much more. It was late. They decided to give the machines a few hours to work before checking again.

Nick woke early, his mind unable to settle after what he'd seen on the chamber cameras. He pushed through his weight workout—just like he did every morning—and did a five-k on the running machine before he showered and made his way to the galley. Sergey and a new geological engineer—on rotation at Endurance—were already there, discussing progress on a new tunnel.

"You are an hour earlier than usual," said Sergey, greeting Nick. "Didn't sleep well?"

"Yeah. Couldn't stop thinking about that object. You gents?"

"You know, at my age, nothing keeps me awake," replied Sergey.

"Are you settling in?" Nick asked the geologist.

"I am. Still learning the machines and systems, but I'm getting there."

"Why don't you join Sergey and me this morning? You can get together with Francisco and the other guys about the new tunnel plans later. We're going to T11. I'm interested in another geo-engineer's take on it, what we discovered there."

Later that morning, the three men met in the subway station. They suited up, rode the lift to the bedrock level, and made their way down the main line to T11.

"What's the biggest crystal you've seen?" Nick asked the engineer as they entered the mouth of T11.

"I guess maybe a meter in length. I've seen images of the ones in Chihuahua that are maybe six to ten meters."

"We've stumbled across something a little bigger," said Nick as they rounded the corner at the end of the tunnel and then stopped at the top of the ramped floor.

The geologist turned his head from side to side as the chamber lights brightened, taking in the size of the room and the black object projecting up from the earth in the center. "Good... god! What is that?" his voice quivered.

"It's a little side project we've been working on," replied Nick excitedly. "Let's check out the marking." He turned and walked down the right side of the ramp, making way for a transporter full of debris on its way out. Sergey and the geologist followed. After rounding the right side of the object, Nick stopped midway along the path and turned to face the marking. After the excavation work, it was now stretching the full width of the giant object's face.

"Is this your side project? You're into stone carving?" asked the engineer.

Nick and Sergey looked at him.

"Not exactly," replied Nick. "We discovered this engraving last night. The excavators cleared away the top half yesterday, and then Sergey reprogrammed their clearing pattern so they would continue working this side overnight." He took off his glove, knelt on a knee, and cautiously ran his fingers along the engraved edge. "It's smooth as glass. Not a single scratch or chip."

Sergey removed a scanner from his belt, positioned himself at the center of the object's face, then activated the device. Its lasers swept the engraving end to end and relayed the measurement data to the site computers.

Nick stood up and said, "Touch it," to the engineer.

The man looked back at Nick. Then he removed his glove and placed his palm on the surface. After a moment, he moved his hand to another spot. "What is this," he mumbled into his helmet's communicator.

"That slight heat you feel... it's oscillating slowly up and down." replied Nick.

"I don't know of any crystal type structure that maintains a temperature like this, above its surroundings. Much less one that's oscillating."

"Crazy, isn't it?"

The geologist put his glove back on and backed up. "Yes. I don't know what to think. And this engraved marking, it looks like some type of symbol."

"I know what you're thinking," said Nick. "What could have made this?"

"No human," replied Sergey. "It's been here far too long." He knelt down with a trowel and dug away the soil at the bottom of the arc. After removing as much of the frozen earth as he could, he glanced over at Nick who was now squatting next to him. "The marking continues around. Maybe it's a complete circle?"

"Whatever this is, we have to continue excavating," said Nick. "We need to see it, the whole marking. Let's get these machines working, and let's bring in another excavator."

Sergey stood and looked at Nick for a moment. "You're obsessing over this thing, Nick. What's the rush?"

"It will only be for a week, max," replied Nick. "Jonathan won't like it either, but we have to figure out what this is."

THIRTEEN

Jonathan exited the tall glass doors of JDC headquarters onto the cobblestone street. He flipped up the back of his collar and put his black gloves on as he walked along the lake to the train station. It was a cool day, overcast, like it usually was this time of year. The water on the lake was choppy and no sign of Mount Rigi, just heavy fog in the distance.

Forty-five minutes after Jonathan found his seat in first class, the train arrived at the Zurich Bahnhoff. He exited the station and headed south towards the lake of Zurich.

Two minutes before the hour, he entered the hotel.

The maitre d' immediately greeted Jonathan. "Guten Tag, Herr De Clare."

"Guten Tag," replied Jonathan with a respectable German accent. He followed along to his usual table. Aleksander owned the hotel, practically lived there when in Europe, and seemed to conduct all his business there, at the same table.

"Ah, my friend." Aleksander stood and shook Jonathan's hand.

"Good to see you, Aleksander," replied Jonathan, then looked at the waiter. "Ein cappuccino hätte ich gern."

They took a few minutes to catch up on general business, new acquisitions, personal adventures, as well as recent purchases of yachts and jets. The waiter returned with Jonathan's coffee. It was now time for him to show Aleksander why he'd asked to meet him.

Jonathan pulled out from his bag a tablet and placed it on the table between them. "I have something to show you," he said in a serious tone.

"Did something surface with this anomaly object at the Endurance site?"

"Yes," replied Jonathan, cracking a slight smile. "Your spies keeping you informed?"

Aleksander laughed. "Just a guess."

Jonathan smiled and touched an icon on the screen. A full image of the object in its chamber appeared. The image slowly morphed as the scene moved from one camera angle to the next. The last image showed the half-arc marking engraved in the object's face.

Aleksander gazed down at the screen through his glasses. "Oh. I see," he said, while watching the images change from one to the next. He saw workers in their thermal suits standing next to the object. Now understanding its size, he looked up at Jonathan, no longer smiling, and confused.

"This is the anomaly we found that is giving off heat." Jonathan circled the marking with his finger. "The crew just uncovered that engraving. There might be more to it." He paused for a moment. "Up until now, we thought it was just some type of ancient meteorite. Something decaying internally that would create the heat."

"And this marking changed your thinking, if I am understanding correctly?" said Aleksander.

"You could say that," replied Jonathan firmly.

Aleksander noted Jonathan's change in tone.

"Aleksander, that thing has been buried there for millions and millions of years... since long before any of our ancient ancestors roamed Earth."

Gazing at the tablet, Aleksander pondered the images, the size of the object, and the marking. "So, what made this marking? That's the question, right?"

"Yes, but there's more," replied Jonathan. "Our professor wanted to have a colleague of hers help us with the analysis. His name is Dr. Arnaud Davesne. He's a well-known astrophysicist. In short, he's discovered the surface temperature moves in a very consistent, predictable rhythm."

"What does that mean?"

"It means that the heat is likely not coming from some type of nuclear decaying process. It means we don't have a clue what this thing is or where it's from."

Aleksander took off his glasses and looked at Jonathan. "I understand now why you wanted to meet. This could become a problem."

"Yes, a real big fucking problem," sighed Jonathan. "First the heat signature and now this engraving. I don't care what it is or where it's from. This is not what we are looking for. It's of no value to us. You know I've run into unusual discoveries in other mines. I know where this goes. Inquisitive scientists or maybe archaeologists catch wind of it. They then come knocking on my door with government restrictions in hand stating what we can and can't do in the area while they do their research. This could quickly become a big nightmare."

"What do you plan to do?"

"Nothing," replied Jonathan. "Maybe bury it and then keep the project moving forward."

"But you have a curious scientist on your team."

Jonathan leaned back in his chair and drank his coffee for a moment as he thought about Ellie. He smiled. Maybe it was her adventurous side. Maybe it was the fact that she was a researcher, searching for something deeper. Yes, he admitted to himself; he had been attracted to her since the first time they met. Often, when together, he wondered where their relationship could go. Yet, she was an unknown variable in this situation.

"Yes. What to do with the professor?" He already knew where she stood. She would not just bury the discovery and walk away. She had already engaged another scientist. Maybe Davesne had shared his insights with other colleagues. *Who else knew?* he wondered.

124

"Sounds like you need to put some controls in place, Jonathan. Check for leaks. Make sure the media doesn't catch on and make sure your team doesn't stray too far."

Jonathan shifted his focus from Ellie and Dr. Davesne back to Aleksander and Endurance. "Yes. I'm already working on it. Nothing's getting out. Nothing."

The competitor received a message from his informant:

We're finding ores. Here's some concentration readings from recent borings. Also discovered something bizarre. Can't explain. Here's an image...

Decent concentrations, he thought. He opened the picture; studied it for a while; then sat down at his desk. He zoomed in on the object, knowing the image was from deep under the Antarctic glacier. Workers in thermal suits were small compared to the object in the center. He stared and thought for a long while. *Damn De Clare. What did you find? What is that thing?*

Matt Brown, a scruffy junior analyst in a building of hundreds of analysts for NIOPS—the National Investigative Office of Private Science—spent his time on the United States government clock, chasing leads. S3—the computing technology at the center of NIOPS—surfaced those leads for him to investigate. Twenty-four hours a day, seven days a week, it probed all data sources it could find, searching for suspicious activity. It searched records of scientific endeavors and projects that dabbled in areas of science that had some meaningful chance of becoming a public concern, or anything that could be considered a genuine threat to the world. Projects like the biotechnology advancements in the past that had put enormously destructive weapons in the hands of underground radical groups. Those kinds of developments needed to be tracked, visited, and terminated if the need arose. NIOPS worked closely with sister organizations in other governments to monitor subjects in a coordinated way. With the vast majority of such scientific work being carried out inside private corporations, NIOPS and its counterparts around the world were a public necessity.

Matt Brown returned from lunch, finished checking out his favorite sites, and began reviewing updates on the S3 dashboard. There was a new case in his inbox. S3 case folders were not overviews, executive summaries, or written out content. They were collections of unique types of information; pictures, video clips, articles, white papers, media content S3 thought were connected in some way.

Matt looked at the first of three pieces of information. It was a document from a shared repository at a university in Paris, France, written by a Professor Davesne. The subject line in the document read: *Endurance Project - Initial Analysis*. The summary was brief.

Surface thermal readings exhibit a consistent oscillating behavior akin to a long sine wave. Behavior is predictable within an acceptable margin of error.

Interesting, Matt thought. He closed the document and opened the next one. It was a list of the sources for the data points in the folder. He closed that document and then opened the last. It was a snapshot taken from the Endurance media site. The picture showed the main station, perched on its thick metal legs. It looked like a UFO parked on a frozen planet. Matt pondered the image for a while. *Cool fucking building,* he thought. *What exactly are you guys up to?*

FOURTEEN

It was twenty-one degrees outside. The sky was bright and clear with no rain in sight. Beau, Ellie's white labrador, laid in the seat beside her while the rover navigated out of the city. Ellie loved Johannesburg—the multiracial culture, the modern cosmopolitan life. But leaving the city of thirty million humans and escaping to farmland and rolling hills and raw nature reminded her of where she grew up. It cleared her head, gave her time to think. She watched the landscape pass by as her rover's autopilot drove on. She remembered when the terrain on that stretch of country road had been nothing but brown grass with a few trees sprinkled around. Now, it was covered by long stretches of healthy tree farms growing engineered varieties, ones that can thrive on less water. Millions of years earlier, it would have been lush all around with towering trees, and vegetation of all varieties, with bizarre-looking animals trotting around. *And in just a short distance from this I will be in the Cradle*, she thought. *Looking for remnants of the very first humans. In a spot on the planet where we somehow, someway got a start.*

Sixty-four kilometers northwest of Johannesburg, the rover turned off the main road onto a gravel path, then drove on for a short distance across a brown, scrubby plain before parking next to a group of tents. Ellie climbed out of the machine and stretched. The air was fresh and dry, the sun soft on her face. She loved being in the field. She grabbed her backpack and strolled towards the tents. Beau hopped out of the rover and followed.

Standing outside, watching a mini drone enter the mouth of the cave, Rachel turned when she heard the bark and saw Ellie. "Hey," she said with a smile. "You made it!" They embraced.

"I'm happy you could come by for a while," said Ellie.

"The timing worked out. I have a break from training and wanted to come and see my mother. Plus, Nick is meeting me here. I'm taking him exploring around South Africa." Rachel grinned. "I brought you a present. One just flew into the cave. Come in the tent, I'll show you the latest greatest from Z-Scan."

"Hi, Professor," said Theto, Ellie's assistant.

"How's it going out here?"

"We're testing out some scanner upgrades Rachel brought us."

Rachel picked up a micro profile drone from their worktable. "I brought these test models with me. They're hot out of development. You told me you needed a high energy scanner on a tiny drone to get in tight spots."

Ellie picked up one and set it in her palm. "Amazing."

"The energy pulses these guys send into the earth actually push them upwards. We had to work out algorithms to compensate for that motion."

"There is a small chamber in this cave we can't access. This will surely get us in there. I can't wait to try it." Ellie's eyes smiled as she inspected the little guy.

"They're not bad," said Theto.

"Not bad?" asked Rachel.

"We are getting a much deeper scan with a step up in resolution," replied Theto with a hint of a smile.

"Are you finding anything in the chambers?" asked Ellie. "Every square inch of these caves has been picked over by many before us. If there is anything remaining to be discovered here, it's buried in the floors of the caves."

"Earlier we found a couple teeth and those bone fragments there." Theto pointed to the table. "They were about a quarter-meter under the surface."

"That's promising," said Ellie. "We should explore that area further. Let's also start searching the registries to see if we can find a skeletal match."

Late afternoon at dusk, daylight faded, attention spans waned, and fossil hunting slowly turned to pouring glasses of South African Syrah. Conversations around the table slowly turned from the caves and their recent discoveries to topics more interesting to young wine-softened minds.

Ellie started on her second glass of wine.

"Professor, are you working on any new discoveries in Antarctica?" asked a doctoral student.

"We haven't found anything new since discovering the pterosaur, but I believe that was just the beginning. Working in Antarctica and tunneling under the ice sheet is painfully slow."

Theto, standing by the side listening in, spoke up. "What's it like in the tunnels? Crawling through the caves here and into the different chambers is one thing. Thousands of meters down an ice shaft then traversing tunnels maybe kilometers long just sounds stressful."

Ellie shrugged. "You try not to think about it when you're down there and you trust the work of the engineers. They install tunnel reinforcers every few meters. Sensors everywhere monitor for the slightest shifts in the ice. Anyway, we spend little time in the tunnels. A fleet of robots coordinated by Dr. Dibaba's AI technology do all the work. We only go into the tunnels when something interesting surfaces."

"What's the strangest thing you've found so far?" asked another member of the crew.

Rachel looked at Ellie. The one thing Jonathan was very sensitive about was information flowing out of Endurance. He was adamant about releasing information in a controlled manner, and only after it had been vetted by his organization.

"The blue ice, I would say," replied Rachel casually.

Ellie smiled. "Rachel was there last, working on the scanners. Tell us about the tunnels."

Rachel thought for a moment. "They are bigger than you might think. I guess maybe eight or ten people could walk side by side down them. The ice walls and ceiling are this brilliant cerulean blue. Sensor lights are installed along all the tunnels. They are all well lit. It's freezing. That's probably the most unnerving thing. You can't breathe the air for too long or it will hurt you. We wear thick suits and air locked helmets with environmental controls. They're actually space suits."

"Rachel was getting in some practice before her journey to Mars," said Ellie, igniting another long conversation that required more wine.

Ellie was up early the next morning, having coffee and checking messages from the university.

"Morning," Rachel called, strolling into the tent and slumping into a chair.

"Sleep well?"

Rachel rolled her head slowly from side to side. "Eh. I love camping out here under the stars. It's amazing. But the sounds at night sometimes... you know, it can be like a bug symphony."

Ellie got up. "I made coffee. Would you like a cup?"

"Yes, please."

"So, when is your scheduled leave date for Mars?"

"October eighteenth."

"Exciting, isn't it?"

"Yes, and I'm a bit nervous. Who would have thought this girl from South Africa would be going to Mars?"

Ellie heard the excitement in her voice and saw it in her high cheeks and smile. "A genius girl from South Africa, with a penchant for tough Australian men."

"Nick? He's just a big teddy bear. Looks tough but gentle on the inside. I do like him... and the chemistry is good."

Ellie laughed as she sat down. "Chemistry is important."

"So, I've been wanting to talk with you about Endurance. On our last call, Jonathan was different. He didn't want to explore this discovery any further."

Holding her cup with both hands, Ellie took a sip from her coffee before replying. "I believe it's spooked him. Spooked is probably not the right word, but you see what I am saying. He doesn't want to invest any more time and money in it."

"I don't know why, Ellie, but I had a bad feeling when walking around in that chamber. And with what happened to the rover that discovered that thing... we still don't have an answer to what caused it to malfunction."

Ellie saw Rachel's face change. "You're concerned for Nick."

"Yes, I am. And for the whole team there."

"Hey. That's common in this type of work," replied Ellie. "Exploring caves and unusual places always surfaces strange things that work on our psyche. We all have anxiety in those places as well."

Rachel nodded slightly, agreeing.

"Nick and Sergey are highly experienced engineers. *And* they have the best tech monitoring the integrity of those tunnels."

"There's something else," said Rachel, after taking a sip from her coffee. "It's about ADESA. And Mars."

"Sounds interesting."

Rachel explained to Ellie the anomaly that ADESA had flagged on Mars.

"I see."

"These cross references happen. When they are low on the confidence scale we ignore them. This one's no different."

Ellie noticed the question mark in her tone. "But you don't believe that fully. You think there might be something to it?"

Rachel took a slow breath. "I don't know, Ellie. Just with all the weird things surrounding this... thing, this... object. It's just one more data point, I guess."

Ellie understood clearly what Rachel had explained. ADESA's confidence level on this cross-reference was so low it was almost irrelevant. Yet, even so, it was hard to ignore.

The sun slowly rose and warmed the tents and the air. Rachel and Ellie continued catching up over the morning while the crew began working. Then noon arrived. It was time for Rachel to go and meet Nick. Outside the main tent, Ellie and Rachel hugged and said goodbye. Ellie waved as she watched her friend drive off across the trail to the main road. She knew it would be awhile before they saw each other again.

FIFTEEN

Arnaud sat on a stool in his lab in front of a wall of displays. One showed a live feed of the object's chamber. Another screen displayed a rendering of the object slowly rotating. Numbered markings on the surface of each side indicated where sensors and scanners read data. Another screen monitored the results of those scanner readings.

"Professor, the size of that object is just bizarre," said his assistant, János, studying the image on the screen. "It's like a ten-story structure buried there. And that engraving is a very strange thing."

Arnaud had to admit, the more they dug, the more unexplainable this anomaly became. He looked at his graduate student. "Yes, I agree. We've analyzed many unusual things in my labs. Some more bizarre than others. So, you removed all environmental influences?"

"I modeled every effect, Professor. All the machines coming and going, the humans, everything. We've removed all ambient effects. The data is clean. We've isolated the object."

"Okay, let's see the first sample."

János pressed *Play*. The most interesting metrics were overlaid at the bottom in a two-row, three-column grid. When the video started, the human-distance metric started decreasing by roughly forty centimeters every second. Twenty seconds into the video, the actual and predicted temperature values started increasing in lockstep—a few digits, then no movement, then a few digits. The surface numbers in the right column first held at zero, then decreased in a continuous pattern. Then they stopped. Forty seconds later, Nick and Sergey walked into the chamber in their thermal suits and helmets and progressed down the ramped floor. A rover carrying tools and gear followed behind them.

"Stop there." Arnaud looked at the screen on the right and studied the quadrant titled *Model Error Metrics*. "Okay, let's see the next sample."

János advanced the video to the next time marker. Four crew members entered the chamber, worked a while, then exited. The next sample just showed Sergey with two robots. Arnaud kept pressing them through the different scenes.

Two hours later, János stretched his arms above his head and yawned. "Well, Professor. Should we continue?"

Arnaud didn't flinch. His eyes were glassy and wide open. He looked at the sample counter. It displayed 43. He looked at the error metrics again. *Mean Model Error - 00.01. Model Success Rate - 99.99.* He didn't need to see any more. The evidence was there, right in front of their faces. They now understood the source of the erratic temperature swings: humans.

"It senses humans," announced Arnaud. "It sees them coming through meters of ice. And it differentiates between humans and machines."

That evening, Arnaud sat in his office and thought through his analysis. He'd tested their models on hundreds of samples. His colleagues had corroborated every detail. Yes, the underlying temperature and surface changes were predictable with near perfect accuracy. The evidence was sound.

Ellie and the Endurance team would arrive at his lab in the morning. "They are not going to believe what I am about to show them," he mumbled to himself, gazing out the windows at the rainy night. "It's a machine. A functioning machine that senses humans."

SIXTEEN

Endurance Site, Antarctica

Under the clear dome of the observation deck on top of the Endurance main station, Nick studied the dark, clear sky. A continuous sheet of bright stars covered the night in all directions. *No man-made light around here,* he thought. He gazed out, found Mars, and watched it for a while. The planet shone brightly that time of year. He thought about Rachel. He had never really thought much about what might be out there in space. Earth had provided enough interest in the past, but that had changed. That was before he knew his girlfriend was heading off planet for a year. That was before they discovered something that was looking more alien than Earth-like.

Off in the distance, Nick spotted the cargo transporter. Ellie and Jonathan were on board. Nick was not looking forward to this visit. Since the team had uncovered the marking, Jonathan had become significantly more engaged. It had begun to feel like Endurance was the only project he had. The meeting with

Arnaud was the real turning point. Nick remembered seeing Jonathan's face after Davesne showed them the analysis. He changed. He became more controlling. Even though JDC Resources Group ran over a hundred and fifty projects around the world, Endurance was now where Jonathan focused his attention. He told Nick it was time to see the object with his own eyes.

The aircraft slowed to a hover and then started rotating as it descended onto its landing pad. Nick went downstairs, suited up, and made his way through the thermal lock into the entry staging room. As he lowered the platform to the surface level, he saw the air transporter's bay door open. Ellie and Jonathan stepped out and started towards him. He could tell from Jonathan's stride he wasn't there to revel in their discovery.

After a dinner together with the team, exhaustion from their trip set in and brought an early end to the day for Jonathan and Ellie.

Nick was up early. The environmental settings still portrayed night throughout the main station. He wanted to get his routine in and check all systems before Jonathan was up pacing around.

Sitting in the control center, he reviewed all dashboards on the monitoring screens and read through all logs and ADESA alerts. There were no issues for him to worry about. He then kicked back and checked his messages. There was a video message from Rachel. He smiled and pressed *Play*.

"Hey Nick. Sorry, I know it has been a few days. This training is intense. I haven't had too many free moments..."

"She looks happy," said Ellie, entering the room.

Nick glanced up. "Yeah, she really does." He let the message finish.

"You miss her, don't you?"

"I do."

"I heard you're a decent surfer."

Nick grinned. "I thought I was too until Rachel and I went out."

Ellie smiled.

Jonathan walked in a few minutes later.

"Morning, Jonathan," said Ellie.

"Good morning."

"Are you two hungry?" asked Nick, noting Jonathan who seemed ready to get the day under way. "We should eat something before we go down in the tunnels."

"Okay," replied Jonathan, somewhat reluctantly. "Let's eat and then go see this machine-object thing, shall we? We can start planning our next steps later."

Nick didn't know exactly what Jonathan meant by *next steps*—he believed he was running the operation well.

It had been nearly a year since Jonathan's last visit. A lot had happened since then. He was ready to walk and talk, and Nick was prepared with the site details.

After breakfast with the crew, Jonathan, Nick, Ellie, and Sergey donned arctic suits and helmets and slowly made their way down the main line. Nick covered the details of each tunnel for Jonathan; the location of boring samples that had been retrieved, the mineral deposits that had been mapped, the team, equipment, and progress on new tunnels.

At the mouth of T11, Nick and Sergey removed the erected barrier. Jonathan had demanded they stop all work down there until he visited and had time to assess the object. Nick peeled back the cover on his sleeve, accessed the embedded tablet computer, and activated the tunnel lights.

It took ten minutes to traverse the declining curvy tunnel to the end. They turned left at the last corner and stopped at the head of the chamber. Overhead and perimeter lights turned on sequentially, illuminating the carved walls and monolithic structure in the center. Their conversation ceased.

Jonathan peered around the chamber, taking in every detail. He then paused and studied the monolith for a moment. "I did not realize just how enormous this thing is."

Nick heard the awe in Jonathan's voice, then headed down the ramped floor and along the path under the scaffolding. The others followed.

"Nick, what's the width of the long sides again? Eighteen? Nineteen meters?" asked Jonathan, counting his steps along the posterior side.

"About eighteen meters," replied Nick. "Each of the four shorter sides are a little under ten."

Jonathan rubbed his gloved hand along the face and said with surprise, "It's smooth as glass."

Nick turned the last corner and walked along the path abutting the sixth side—the face of the monolith. The marking, a groove the width and depth of a human hand, etched with precision into its face, made a perfect circle. Three engraved shapes like long pointed daggers, equally deep as the circle, stretched across the crest pointing east, west, and south. The tips of the east and west cross marks nearly reached the edges of the object's face.

Ellie walked up to it, took her glove off, and laid her hand on its surface. After a moment, she moved her hand to another spot. "It's definitely warm," she announced excitedly. "Even after eons of time." She then moved her hand along the right outer band of the marking. "Not the slightest flaw."

"And it's aware of us," mumbled Jonathan. "It knows we are here."

Standing at the opposite end of the object's face from Jonathan, Nick heard the awe in his voice. He knew this thing had just become as real for Jonathan as it had for him and the crew.

Ellie put her glove back on and looked at the full arc and its cross markings. "Nature..." she sighed into her mic, "did not make this. This object is not from Earth. It can't be. Nothing here could have engraved this so long ago."

"I don't think we could do this even today," admitted Nick, turning his head slightly from side to side. "We can't scratch the surface of this, much less carve anything in it. Can we, Sergey?"

"Maybe it's from Earth," Sergey called from his position nearby. "But whatever carved this was not."

Jonathan, Ellie, and Nick looked over at Sergey.

He chuckled. "It was just an idea. But, yes, it's the hardest thing I have seen. We've tried chipping and drilling. The drill just dances around the surface, not making the slightest scratch. This thing just laughs at us when we try."

"How deep are we here?" asked Jonathan.

"A little over twenty-six hundred meters," replied Nick.

Jonathan looked up at the top of the chamber. "And how far are we laterally from the main station?"

"Right at twelve-hundred meters."

Nick and Sergey knew what Jonathan was thinking.

"How much more is buried?"

"We don't know the exact depth, but, from drilling and deep scanner readings, we estimate sixty meters," replied Nick.

Ellie stopped walking and looked at Jonathan. "What are you thinking?"

He took a moment to finish his idea, then looked at her. "How to extract this from our site and take it to some research facility."

Ellie could not sleep. She got up and meandered down the stairs to the main floor of the station and found Jonathan, alone in the control room, staring at a display, watching a video feed of the object's chamber. "I see you couldn't sleep either," she said quietly, entering the room.

Jonathan aroused from his thoughts. "Care to help me figure out our game plan here?"

Ellie rolled a chair over in front of the screen, sat down, and listened.

"I am trying to think down the paths this discovery could take us," said Jonathan. "It's an exercise I go through with all my projects at big forks in the road. Call it risk analysis. If I didn't do this, I would have been in financial ruin a long time ago."

"I'll help if I can."

"The problem is, I can't find the paths. What the hell is this thing, Ellie?" he sighed. "I'm sorry. But there's no explanation for what this object is. Not long ago it intrigued us. It was a fun mystery. After Nick dug up a little, we thought it was some ancient meteorite. That was possibility number one. Then an overgrown crystal structure was possibility number two. Neither of those options would have disrupted our progress. But it's not one of those." He looked over at her. "It's possibility number three. This monolithic thing is not something we can figure out. It's something not from Earth. Or so it seems. What Davesne showed us was mind boggling. Disturbing is more like it. This thing... this *machine*... is aware. It's intelligent. It senses human presence. And it seems interested in us since it has no reaction to anything else."

"It is unbelievable, isn't it?" said Ellie softly. "In this most remote spot on Earth, so far removed from all life, we stumbled across this other-worldly thing. It almost feels like a dream. I guess it's slowly changing my perspective on things. I haven't wasted much time thinking about aliens. *Are there others out there?* type questions. My entire life has been digging up our past. But now I really wonder. It is a significant scientific discovery."

"Oh, I agree," replied Jonathan, leaning forward. "It's a profound discovery. Unimaginable. Let's say it's not from Earth. This thing looks like it's a product of something intelligent. It's some kind of advanced alien machine. Our project would then take on a whole new level of interest." He paused for a moment to gather his thoughts. "Endurance sits in something like a neutral zone. If the world starts believing this obelisk thing is alien, every government will want access to it. That's where the path becomes very unpredictable. Not to mention very uncontrollable. Our project would become a giant government lab. We would not be allowed within a thousand kilometers of this place."

Jonathan pushed his fingers through his hair and interlocked them behind his head. He closed his eyes and breathed slowly. After a moment, he opened his eyes again. "Ellie, I believe it has become clear that we've found something not from Earth. *Where?* Who the hell knows? *Why?* We will probably never know. But I know for a fact the world has never seen anything like this. This will be a first. This will change the world. Once this gets out, we will lose control of Endurance. Everything we have invested here will be lost. Do you understand what I am saying?"

She saw where he was going. This thing represented little to no value to him. He saw it as a big obstruction in the way of his pursuits. "So, you want to move it," she replied, sensing his frustration.

"Maybe," he said with a nod. "Just exploring all possibilities. We need time to work on a plan. Maybe we can split that chamber and tunnel off from Endurance. Move in another direction. I don't know right now. But we have to shut this down. Seal it off. Lock it up until we can figure things out. This can't get out. We must make sure all the information flowing to your team of scientists is locked down tightly. The research needs to stop until we can figure out what we're going to do."

Ellie heard the stress in his voice, saw the muscles tensing in his neck. She took a moment to choose her words before she spoke. "Jonathan, we can't just bury such a profound scientific discovery until some day when we are prepared to deal with it. If we do conclude it's alien, then the single biggest question humans have looked up to the heavens and pondered gets a partial answer. The advanced technology this thing could hold is unimaginable."

"No doubt," replied Jonathan. "But you and I know that governments will not see it the same way. If what Davesne is saying is true, then defense organizations will first perceive it as a potential threat until someone can prove it's not. This place will be crawling with government agencies. Look at this thing, Ellie." Jonathan stood up and walked to the wall. "This doesn't look friendly. Quite the opposite. What does that symbol mean? These cross markings look like swords. It almost looks like a warning."

Ellie studied the object. She agreed. It looked more like a weapon than anything else. She turned back to Jonathan. "Arnaud knows about this, his colleagues, who corroborated his work, know. Nick, Sergey, other engineers, and scientists who have been here on rotations know. This discovery isn't a secret."

Jonathan sat back down and took a breath. "Ellie, we need to hit pause for a while on this. Let's keep moving forward and focus on the actual reasons we are here."

Ellie looked back at him and didn't respond. She didn't have any better options at the moment.

SEVENTEEN

Diablo and his crew had run across some odd things before while scouring the planet for signs of aliens, but never anything like this. They each had read Dr. Davesne's most recent report titled; *Endurance Project - Machine like Intelligence*. This ancient obelisk was aware. Never had the alien-hunters seen anything like the object on their screens. Arnaud's assistant had come through on his end and Diablo had continued the payments like clockwork.

Razputin: We have more than enough information. The world needs to see this!
Akashi: What do you think we would get for this, D?
Diablo: A shit load. But the minute this story goes live, our source would cut the wire. We've got to corroborate this, guys.
Akashi: But if we wait too long, we risk someone else leaking it.
Khasimir: I agree with Akashi.
Diablo: This is too big. Too unbelievable. No media will pay

up for this without something from a second credible source. And I'm just curious what this Dr. Davesne and his team will discover next. What if it comes to life? I don't want to miss seeing it.

Razputin: *I agree with D. Look at what we all just read. It's a sentient machine. Maybe we give it a few more weeks.*

Diablo: *Khas, any luck with that competitor, Cobalt Energy?*

Khasimir: *I've gotten into their network. Definitely not as sophisticated as JDC. I just need time to get into the CEO's communications. That's who I should be targeting, right?*

Diablo: *Absolutely. Any messages from a spy would go directly to the top. Guys, I am sure governments would love to get their hands on all our data. Let's keep our sources and data locked down tight.*

S3—NIOPS's data mining system—scoured the global network of computing storage systems, searching for information and patterns it had learned to recognize. Patterns that often led to serious threats.

Sometime after Diablo and his crew read the latest report from Davesne's team, S3 had crawled its way around the world's information networks to a massive data center sitting on almost free land in the middle of nowhere. It was running on cheap computers and providing computing power for those on tight budgets. Buried inside the storage systems, S3 found an archived version of Diablo's Endurance folder. It made a full copy of the folder, created a reminder for itself to revisit this location occasionally, and then moved on. It then updated

Matt Brown's Endurance case folder with newly discovered data.

Matt Brown was sitting at his desk at NIOPS headquarters working on other cases when he received a new alert from S3. The Endurance project was by far the most interesting one he was working on. He dropped what he was doing and opened up the Endurance case. New data files were highlighted. He went straight for the image file and opened it. A three-dimensional image appeared on his screen of an object suspended in space, rotating slowly. Matt saw the marking on its face. "That's fucking cool looking," he said, a little too loudly. The exclamation attracted the attention of a colleague, who wondered over and squinted at the screen.

"What is that?"

"I'm not sure," replied Matt. "I'm working on something that surfaced in Antarctica. S3 found this and thinks it's related. It looks like a physicist has been monitoring sensor readings from something discovered there, some big project called Endurance. Looks like a group of scientists are exploring the Earth's surface under the ice, looking for fossils."

"Are there more pictures? Any video footage?"

"Just a couple stills."

"Any resemblance?"

"A little," replied Matt. "Here I'll show you." He pulled up the other images S3 had found.

The colleague leaned forward, studying the pictures and the 3D image on Matt's screen. "They do look similar. Is there any info on what that physicist found?"

"There's this. It looks like a newer version of a report I saw earlier." Matt opened the data file. "But you know all this shit can be faked just to throw us on a wild chase."

"Some people have too much time on their hands," his colleague agreed. "What does the report say?"

"It talks about the surface temperature readings of something he is analyzing," replied Matt. "The readings oscillate up and down like a sine wave. It appears what he is analyzing is this thing, but I need to dig deeper to really figure it out. I am guessing S3 found the word Endurance embedded in the report and thought it might be related."

"Why don't I ever get anything interesting like this?" sighed his colleague.

"'Cause you're not cool like me."

"Yeah, right. Anyway, what are you going to do next?"

"I'm writing up my analysis. My guess is it'll get escalated once my report circulates."

NIOPS, and its counterparts in other countries, were interested in private endeavors into any areas of science that had a potential to become a serious danger to the world. It was sometimes viewed as a feeder organization to other more specialized offices within the United States intelligence agencies. One specific area of science that received a lot of attention was AI. Within intelligence agencies in all world governments, there were groups whose sole mission was to monitor private sector advancements in artificial intelligence. Since the advent of evolutionary software, rogue AI systems were a genuine threat all world governments took seriously.

When NIOPS surfaced the Endurance Project, the data was shared with sister organizations in other governments. However, the sharing didn't stop there. Sister organizations had sharing agreements with other countries. As new data surfaced, it too was shared. Countries who were not in the sharing club simply stole the data.

Not long after Matt Brown had submitted his report, a computer system owned by a higher-up office stopped by the NIOPS data archive and checked out the Endurance folder. Inside the folder, a report from Dr. Davesne used the words *aware, machine,* and *intelligence.* Those words, together with the scientific language of the report, registered a high probability the report was real. The higher-up office's system took less than one second to classify the Endurance Project as AI with a realness factor of ninety-two percent. Once the AI classification had been applied, the office took control of all further research. Matt Brown's lead list at NIOPS no longer contained any reference to Endurance. The Endurance folder and its investigation were now the responsibility of a specialized office, where it received a lot more attention.

The new owner's access level to global information sources was close to the highest in their government. Their core data gathering and analysis system was one of the most advanced in the intelligence community. Their funding and resources were unlimited—a requirement to get out in front of questionable AI systems before they did any real damage.

Agent Steven Goodman, a career intelligence man, loved his work hunting down AI systems that could become a danger to the world. He landed in the agency directly after his university studies, methodically rose to the level of senior analyst and had no interests in progressing to management. Analysis and field work were his passion. As part of the investigative team assigned to the Endurance project, he took charge of the effort with his usual *all-in* level of effort.

After days of digging through the project folder, studying the data, and organizing the various pieces of information into a coherent picture in his mind, he was ready to begin a draft report. He stared at the images of the object on his screen while spinning a pen around his thumb, not knowing where to start. The subject was unlike anything his office had ever come across. He leaned back in his chair and pushed his glasses up the bridge of his nose. *This doesn't look man made*, he thought. *What is this?*

EIGHTEEN

Gabriele walked up the right side of the forty-four foot cruiser towards the bow as Michael cast them off at idle speed, slowly easing out of the narrow slip and turning a hard right up the channel out of the marina. After securing the buoys, she stepped down into the cockpit, her sun hat secured snuggly under her chin.

"Ready to take the helm?" asked Michael.

"I am."

"Just keep her on the right side of the channel and head straight out into the bay."

Gabriele took her hat off and pushed her hair back in the breeze. She closed her eyes and faced the warm sun for a moment. She loved sailing. It was old school—using wind as your propulsion and navigating by sight. It was something basic and simple; something at the other end of the spectrum in her life, something to balance the tensions from space travel.

Out in the bay, the wind blew a steady twelve knots.

"Ready to raise the main?" asked Michael.

Gabriel flicked the switch labeled *M* on the controls panel. The head of the mainsail powered up the track in the mast, lifting the sail body out of the boom. The wind filled the sail, powering the cruiser through the open water. Her heart rate picked up. Feeling the pressure on the wheel as the craft sped along, she grinned, spread her feet further apart, and tightened her grip.

Michael pulled the bill of his hat further down and smiled. "See the little island straight ahead? That's our heading. The helm is yours, Commander."

They arrived at the island marina in the early evening and parked in an overnight slip.

After dinner and a stroll around the village, they sauntered back to the boat. Michael refilled their drinks below deck. Gabriele reclined in the cockpit under the dark sky and studied the swaths of stars, identifying landmarks like experienced navigators would once have done on those waters.

Michael walked up the steps from below, sat beside her, and gazed up at the night sky.

"I know I ask you this every time we're together again..."

Gabriele chuckled. "Have we found any signs?"

"I know you would tell me if you had, but I still like asking."

"There *is* something. A new discovery site a team is working on. I haven't been there."

"What did they find?"

Gabriele walked Michael through the events; ADESA flagging the area near Station Chronos two years earlier, the drone malfunctions, the unexplained loss of control during their flight over the area.

When she finished, Michael let out a breath. "Wow. So, the crew there now are excavating the site?"

"They've just started."

"No idea what it is?"

Gabriele shook her head. "So far, all analysis has come back dry. It's looking like something new."

"Think it's some kind of alien artifact?"

Gabriele laughed. "No. At least not yet. I've seen all the images and video of the site. It looks like a black rock, some kind of dense mineral structure."

Michael picked up his glass with a thoughtful look on his face. "In a symposium I sat in on recently. This quirky astrophysicist from Berkeley gave a talk on other life in the universe, and why we haven't encountered aliens given the vastness of space and the number of planets."

"Sounds à propos," replied Gabriele while stirring her drink.

"Essentially, he argued that we would be fools to assume there's no other life in the universe. We should go about our ventures in space assuming the opposite."

"I agree."

"But he got on this really big picture idea of how the designers of the universe wanted us to compete with each other, so they limited our resources and even made them hard to get to."

Gabriele laughed. "They are definitely hard to find on Mars."

Michael grinned. "After an hour or so on many tangents the old guy finally got to his big point. That advanced life forms with a decent understanding of nature would abandon uncontrolled growth and consumption. They would then attempt to control other life that does not hold itself to the same restrictions."

"So, in his world of limited resources the strong will control the weak in order to protect their way of life."

"Something like that," replied Michael.

"We do that to each other already. I can only imagine that would play out in other civilizations as well, if they exist out there."

"That was one of his key points. The things that drive our behavior, things like limited resources and competition, are woven into the fabric of the universe. They'll drive behavior everywhere, not just here on Earth. It was at this point the lecturer got a little dark."

"What do you mean?" asked Gabriele.

"It was a little thought experiment. Do you know the story of Easter Island?"

"Vaguely. One of the Polynesian islands, right? I don't remember it being a happy story."

"Exactly. According to some researchers, the natives of Easter progressed rapidly after landing on the island a long time ago. But after cutting down all the trees, their resource for making canoes for fishing was gone. Their quality of life went in reverse. Given their remote location in the South Pacific, of course they also destroyed any hopes of making it to any neighboring island."

"Tragic ending, like I thought," replied Gabriele.

Michael took a drink and set his glass down. "It was, but it's just a little what-if experiment. Okay, so now imagine you and I and our tribe are on an island not too far away, watching the natives of Easter and their behavioral patterns. They've depleted resources on their island and are now reproducing rapidly and inhabiting an island closer to us. We're more advanced though. We learned the role trees play in blocking wind from crops, preventing soil erosion, the time it takes for them to regrow and, more importantly, that too many of us is unsustainable. And we're now becoming anxious about these Easter Island chaps. They don't seem to be learning quickly enough to avoid disaster and we know there's a limited supply of islands around."

"I see where this is going," said Gabriele. "We view these other islands as our reserve supply of resources. This other clan, if not contained, could get into our supply, creating a risk to our well-managed way of life."

"Yes, exactly. So, now we're in the present. Assume another race out there got a million years' head start in life. A million years ago, it's questionable whether Homo sapiens had fire. But since then, we're now venturing to Mars. Soon it will be even further. And our pace of advancement is speeding up. A million years from now, how much more advanced will we be?

"A lot."

"Now assume that race embraced these Laws of Nature. We would expect them to try and control others, like you said. The question is, how would these guys go about it? More importantly, how would they view us as we expand out into space and get closer to their little corner of this universe?"

"What did the lecturer think?"

"He thought they would do whatever it took to control civilizations who couldn't control themselves."

"Did he think humans fall into that category? Some out-of-control life form?"

Michael looked at Gabriele and raised an eyebrow, "He did."

She stared up at the stars for a while, contemplating the vastness of space and the tiny little speck of that she'd traveled through. "It's an interesting thought. I get his points. However, we were nervous on our little island because we had no perspective on how big the world is and how much resources there are to go around. Would we have bothered with the Easter natives had our perspective been bigger?"

"He believed we would."

"Why? Why bother?"

"It's about losing control," replied Michael. "At what point in their uncontrolled growth and expansion would we lose our ability to control them? Say they expand out to one more island to the west, then one to the east. Now our troops must cover a much bigger area to control them. Say their behavior continues unabated. Beyond a certain point we lose our ability to control entirely."

"What do you think? Are we uncontrolled consumers of resources? Is someone out there watching us?" She glanced over at him and smiled. "Is that why you're scared to go to Mars with me?"

"Maybe," he replied, smiling. "Let's just say I lack the mojo."

Gabriele laughed as she leaned back and took a drink from her glass. "Wow. I think you gave me all the alcohol. What are you trying to do to me before I leave?"

Michael placed his hand on her thigh. "Want to find out?"

Gabriele grabbed his chin and smiled. "But I thought you didn't have any mojo?"

The adventurous day, dinner, drinks, and a star-filled sky had but one ending in sight. Michael pulled Gabriele closer and kissed her. She kissed him back, a little stronger than he had expected. He smiled. It didn't take long for the exploring to move below deck.

Every day of the two weeks flowed like the first, ending with an intimate time together. They were not ready for it to end, but time was relentless. The days had passed by. Gabriele's next mission to Mars was demanding her time.

Michael drove his truck to the airport manually rather than engaging the pilot. He glanced over at Gabriele as the country road wound through the heavily forested hills. "Gabi, this was the best time together. I loved it. Every day. If I could snap my fingers and have us living the past two weeks over, and over, I would do it. I can imagine sharing my life with you. What do you think of the idea of coming back here with me? Starting a family of little astronauts?"

Gabriele paused for a second and took a breath. This time with Michael had caused her feelings for him to solidify more; to grow. She could imagine a life together with him out on the island. His eyes looked a little glassy and dreamy. She smiled at him. "Michael, are you asking me to marry you?"

He tilted his head slowly. "I'm just asking you to consider it."

They sat comfortably in silence for a while, watching the mountains and water pass by.

Gabriele sighed softly, feeling her emotions rise and fall. "Well, I am bound for Mars. Nothing is changing that. We have another year ahead of us. That's a year to figure it out." She looked back at him as the road straightened. "Yes, Michael, I will consider it. I will probably think about it every day until I return."

As they drove along, and the country roads led into bigger city roads, and the unhinged fun of the time together started giving way to rational thought, they both realized there would need to be significant changes for them to have a life together. But they were starting to think about it.

They arrived at the airport, both sad and a little conflicted and not wanting to say goodbye. They kissed. They hugged. Gabriele could see Michael's eyes were wet.

"Hey, I almost forgot." He reached into his pocket. "I made these from the two stones you brought back last time." He took her wrist and fastened a woven bracelet around it. He then put the other one on his wrist. "That should help us think about each other and spending the rest of our lives together."

She looked at him and teared up. "I'll wear it every day." She kissed him again, then turned away slowly and walked towards her flight.

NINETEEN

IMTEC Launch Facility

Inside the Earth-to-Space Transporter, the ground maintenance crew completed their final inspections of all systems, exited the main hatch and sealed it. Every seat was filled with someone who was heading to Mars for a year.

Gabriele looked over at Rachel. "This is about the time all the old-timers like me nod off until we hit space."

"You're not old, and I know you're joking," replied Rachel, looking at her nervously.

Gabriele laughed. "Unfortunately, for your first ride to space you got stuck in this vertical transporter. We're carrying a lot of cargo to Mars lately. Gear for Orion, the new base. It's old school, but you need big heavy thrusters to lift heavy payloads out of the atmosphere. It's a real adrenaline rush, and a bit bumpy, like you probably learned in your training, but it's also the fastest way to space. We'll be out of the atmosphere quicker than you can ride a big wave into shore."

"I don't know about that," replied Rachel, half smiling, feeling her stomach tense up. She watched the countdown: *9, 8, 7,* before the primary engines roared to life, rattling the cabin like an earthquake. She closed her eyes and sucked air in through her nose and then pushed it slowly out of her mouth. *3, 2, 1, 0.* The thrusters ignited, the force punching her back into her chair. The shuttle shook hard as it ripped through the Earth's thick atmosphere. Two minutes later, the noise subsided and the shaking smoothed out. *The pressure feels like three Nicks piled on top of me,* she thought.

Rachel opened her eyes and looked to the right. They were exiting the upper atmosphere and now speeding up towards the space station. One minute later, all noise stopped. The pressure was gone. Her arms could float free.

"Quite a ride, huh?" said Gabriele, rotating her seat forward 90 degrees.

Rachel grimaced. "That was much rougher than training."

"It's kind of hard to simulate that many Gs." Gabriele pointed out of the portal. "That's an Earth-to-Mars transporter, our home for the next thirty-six days."

Rachel turned and gazed out. "It's massive."

A docking breezeway in front of the EMT extended outwards. The shuttle decelerated to a crawl and then crept forward, slowly rotating into position, like docking a passenger ferry along a pier. The breezeway connector latched onto the side of the shuttle and pulled tight, forming an air lock over the main door as the G simulator slowly ramped up.

Inside her assigned room, Rachel finished unpacking her things and then, without hesitating, she laid down on her bunk, exhausted. Her eyelids grew heavy. Thoughts in her head washed around in a haze. Her breathing slowed.

Two hours later, after what felt like only a moment, Rachel heard someone at her door. She slowly opened her eyes, looked around, and then sat up. "Just a moment." She stood slowly, took two steps, and then opened the door to her room. "Gabi." she rubbed her face. "Sorry, Commander."

Gabriele smiled. "How are you doing? I am sure the excitement of it all is starting to settle in."

"Yeah." Rachel yawned. "I guess I dozed off for a while."

Gabriele glanced around Rachel's quarters. "Nice. Looks like you got a deluxe cabin."

Rachel knew she could stretch her arms out and nearly touch two opposing walls. "Are you sure?"

"We don't want you camping out in here too much. Come on. Let's go up to the bridge and watch the crew take us out. This'll keep you up so you can get in sync with the sleep cycle of the ship."

Rachel followed Gabriele down a series of passageways leading from the rear of the ship to the front. Up a staircase and then down one more pathway, the two women walked through the open entry onto the deck.

"It's smaller than I expected," said Rachel.

Gabriele laughed lightly. "Not quite the starship deck you expected?"

"No. Not at all."

"The EMTs are really just cargo ships that spend most of their time in space on autopilot. The crew here are needed mainly for docking, departing, and monitoring the ship's systems. They also stay in constant contact with Earth, Mars Station, this station, and Station Athena. Come on, I have something else to show you."

On the other side of the deck, Gabriele stopped at a large portal window. Rachel looked out at the giant blue Earth beyond the glass in front of her. All the training, then the ride to space, and now seeing her home planet sparked something inside her. "Oh, wow," she sighed, focusing her gaze on South Africa. She then looked further down to Antarctica capping the bottom of Earth. She wondered if Nick was there and what he was doing. Thoughts from her last visit to the site surfaced. Images of them in the chamber walking around that giant black object crept in, sparking a tinge of anxiety.

"Are you okay?" asked Gabriele with a smile.

Rachel turned towards her. "Oh. Yes. It's just a bit overwhelming."

"It takes us all by surprise the first time we see her from out here. Amazing, isn't it? It makes me well up inside every time I come up here and see her."

After a while, they walked back to the observation level on the other side. "We're nearing our launch time," said Gabriele. She pointed to one of the overhead screens. "The display there will now cycle through different views of the exterior of the ship while we shove off. Then, as we move out away from the station, we'll begin rotating slowly. When we're about a kilometer out, we'll start accelerating forward on our path to Mars."

"Should we sit down?" asked Rachel, still excited.

Gabriele laughed. "Sorry. No adrenaline-driving blast-off like in the movies. Speeding this cargo box up and slowing it down is an excruciatingly slow and boring process. But once we reach our top speed, sometime tomorrow, I'll bring you back on deck."

"Cool," replied Rachel, watching the screens as the ship pushed away from the Space Station.

Two weeks had passed since departing from the space station. Gabriele sat at her usual table in the galley and worked on her breakfast while reviewing the most recent site scanning report on her tablet. The early morning crowd was drifting in.

"Morning, Gabi," said Rachel, sitting down across the table.

"Hey, thanks for coming."

"What's up?" asked Rachel.

Gabriele noticed the energy in Rachel's tone and smiled, pleased that her recruit was adapting quickly. She rotated her tablet around. "This is a scanning report, one of many reports I receive routinely. This one is of a quadrant near Station Chronos. Some time ago, ADESA flagged an area there. Since then, we've been excavating where the anomaly reading occurred. The short story is we found something and are working on figuring out what it is. It could be some new elemental structure." Gabriele pointed to a line item in the report. "This new detail just surfaced."

Rachel sipped her tea and read over the data. Her smile faded. Her eyes drooped slightly.

Gabriele noticed the change in Rachel. "Given ADESA's sub-optimal track record of false-positives on Mars, what do you think of this?"

Rachel leaned back in her chair. "Wow. ADESA's confidence has grown substantially. The probability of this cross-match is now significant." After a moment she looked back at Gabriele. "I don't know. Another one of those on Mars is just too... unbelievable."

"Another one of what?"

"Something discovered at another project ADESA supports," sighed Rachel. "But, Gabi, I... I don't know. There must be something wrong with ADESA. A bug in an analysis subsystem somewhere."

Gabriele saw Rachel was wrestling with this conflict. "So, you think it's not an error?"

"No. It has to be an error."

"But ADESA has come to the same conclusion from two distinct sets of scanning data," said Gabriele. "And one was very recent."

"They discovered something very unusual there," said Rachel. "And I just don't believe it's possible for another one to be on Mars."

"Have you been to the site?"

Rachel hesitated. "I have. A few times. It's a big project. They're tunneling under the glacier in Antarctica. Exploring. Hunting for fossils and natural resources."

"Fascinating."

"It is." Rachel's eyes lit up. "It's very ambitious. ADESA runs the scanning there in much the same way as on Mars. A small fleet of rovers scan the tunnels they are digging and then send their data to ADESA."

"Sounds familiar. What have they discovered?"

"When I was last there, the crew had not excavated much of it. They've since uncovered more. I don't know how to describe it. It's a big black rock-like object, like a giant meteorite."

"Doesn't sound bad. We run into all kinds of unusual things like that on Mars."

Rachel slid her tablet over. She pulled up a recent video sent to her from Nick, rotated it around, then looked at Gabriele. "You haven't run into anything like this." She pressed *Play*.

Gabriele watched the video scene slowly move around the giant monolithic object, and then she looked up at Rachel. "You're right. What is that?"

"No one knows," replied Rachel. "A team of scientists are studying it. All they have are theories. Some have suggested it's some type of alien artifact."

Gabriele sighed and took a drink. "Where in Antarctica is this?"

"In the interior where the glacier is deep."

"How deep? Do you know?"

"I think something like three kilometers."

"So, whatever this is has been there for a very long time."

Rachel nodded. "Oh yes. Millions of years."

"Whatever this is, it's ancient. I now see why you think it's an error, or just a coincidence."

"What are you planning to do on Mars?" asked Rachel.

"We will continue to excavate the site, while you dig into ADESA and make sure she isn't suffering from any cognitive issues."

Rachel smiled. "I'm on it, Commander."

After Rachel left, Gabriele's smile faded. The possibility of two of these objects intrigued her. She rotated her tablet around and played the most recent drone footage of the Chronos site. The wildcatting team had done their job. They had dug a crater that gently sloped down from all sides to a center point. *The soil must be soft*, she thought. In the center of the crater, the tip of a black object rose up a half-meter from the surface.

TWENTY

On the deck of his hundred-and-forty-meter yacht, making its way across the Mediterranean en route to Rhodes, Jonathan heard the chime of a new message on his tablet. He set his glass of wine down and touched the screen of the computer. A message from Aleksander was at the top.

Following is from a friend of a friend, an investor in one of your competitors. Looks like we have a spy…

Jonathan stared at the message. It contained concentration readings from their most recent borings. An image of the object was at the end. He grinned slightly. *I just love this business*, he told himself. *We all spy on each other, we steal each other's best engineers, we squeeze each other when we can.* If it wasn't for the treaty and the fact that Antarctica was a frozen block of ice year-round, he would care more. He knew other mining outfits were nipping at the edges of the continent. There had been fits and starts there for decades. But none were building a sustainable approach. He chuckled. *There's only one other group who has the balls and the capital to even think about doing what I'm doing.* He knew it was Cobalt Global. Most likely through one of the engineers who rotated in and out of the Endurance site. He could buy Cobalt with the stroke of a pen, but that would take some of the fun out of the game. He smiled. They were about the only group left who gave him any actual competition.

Jonathan looked at the message again. He didn't care about the data in the message, but he did care about the image getting out.

He breathed slowly to calm himself as he looked out at the blue water flowing by. He had known he couldn't keep this sealed off. *Impossible,* he thought. He was a fool to ever think he could. Gazing at the stern of the craft, he knew then he had focused on the wrong end of the problem. He should have been building his plans assuming the news *would* get out, not trying to keep it under wraps. He now wondered how long it would be before the discovery found its way to the open media. How much time he had to build a new game plan before governments and everyone else started knocking on his door?

Diablo waited for his contact in a small cafe in Budapest, just across the street from the Keleti train station. He had done business with this informant for many years. He was a respectable reporter of the science arm of the largest media conglomerate on the planet. Diablo had trusted him in past dealings, but he didn't trust anyone enough to share this information online. It had to be face-to-face, and the fee had to hit his account before he would turn over the full folder. He sipped his coffee and waited. Two minutes after the time they had agreed to meet, the cafe's door opened and his contact strolled in, shook hands with Diablo, and sat down.

"I'll have a coffee," the Brit said calmly to the waitress. Then he looked back at Diablo. "So, mate. Let's have a look at what else you've uncovered. I just traveled across Europe to get here. Given what you delivered last time, I'm more than a bit curious."

Diablo looked at his contact and slowly said, "You have never seen anything like this. I hope you have the authority to pay a very big fee."

"If your information is as good as you claim, I can pay."

Diablo pulled his pad computer out of his bag, placed it on the table between them and pressed *Play*. He had worked hard on the presentation, showing only enough data to seal a deal, and no more. He was very careful not to give away too much, but he still needed his contact to understand the data was real, from the source, and that there would be more to come if he paid up.

As the video finished playing, Diablo pulled the tablet back towards him and sat quietly. He knew it would take time for it to sink in.

After a lengthy silence, the contact finally spoke. "This will be doubted by everyone."

"It's hard to swallow," Diablo replied. "Doubt will be the first reaction. But it is as real as you and I sitting here. You saw the data and images from the second source. It's all there. This story has the potential to change the world, my friend. Aside from miracle workers in the ancient past, nothing so mystical has since surfaced."

"How much?"

Diablo had come to the meeting with a number in mind, but after gauging the expression on his contact's face after seeing the material, he doubled that number. The contact wanted to see the presentation one more time. Diablo obliged.

"Do we have a deal?"

The contact paused for a long minute. Then replied, "Same account as last time?"

"Same account."

Minutes later, after he saw the money appear in his account, Diablo slid the computer across the table. "It's all there. Everything."

Diablo waited until his contact had left the café before entering a simple message to his crew into his personal device. It contained just the fee. He smiled and pressed *Send*.

Media stories of the discovery in Antarctica captured the world's attention. The mysteriousness of the object buried there enthralled the public. Fueled by the media, the belief that it was alien caught fire around the world. The idea of other intelligent life existing millions of years before humans was pushed by the scientific observers. Religious groups worked to reconcile this concept with their foundations. Others believed the whole thing to be a complete fabrication.

As the world began to understand the object wasn't just an ancient stone monument but some type of machine that was aware, defense departments and ministries of defense took notice. The lack of knowledge and understanding of the object moved it into the realm of a potentially un-contained threat. Some governments contracted with JDC to scan remote sections of their countries. Who could say more of these objects were not scattered around on every continent?

As interest grew, the will to do something grew with it.

Larger governments wanted to take the lead but were quickly reminded of the Antarctic Treaty. At the same time, no country owned territory in Antarctica. Countries claimed areas, but the Treaty suspended all claims while it was in force. Simply put, an unquantifiable potential threat sitting in a neutral territory with no clear policy in place to give direction provided all the ingredients for confusion, disagreements, distrust, and growing tensions.

TWENTY-ONE

Agent Steven Goodman and his boss walked with purpose into their boss's office. The Director of Intelligence for the United States sat behind her desk, awaiting their arrival.

"Come in, gentlemen," said the Director. "Help me understand this discovery in Antarctica." She met Goodman's handshake with a firmer grip and no smile. "I read your report on the Endurance Project. Not bad. I can't wait to hear more."

Mr. Goodman looked up at her through his thick glasses thinking, *not bad?*

Two walls of windows overlooked green forests in the countryside on the outskirts of Washington, DC.

"The Office of the President is asking to be briefed on what they are seeing in the media," started the Director, not wasting a minute. "The President himself is asking why he knows nothing of this alien discovery."

Because we have to do real homework, unlike the fucking media, thought Goodman while holding a smile.

"So, you gentlemen are our top AI sleuths, is that correct?"

"We strive to be, Ma'am," replied Goodman's boss.

"From reading your report, it seems you've caught a big something in your net?"

"Something definitely interesting," replied Goodman. He kind of liked this director. Tough, but not so damn dry like the old bastard she had replaced.

"Aside from what's in your report, what else do you have for me? Any details on the team who discovered this?"

Goodman jumped right in. "Ma'am, may I?" he asked, pointing to the computer controls.

"Yes, please."

Goodman logged into his group's project repository and showed her biographies on everyone involved with the Endurance Project, both directly and indirectly. He described their roles, their relationships with each other, educational backgrounds, and other personal details. He showed her files on each of the scientists, their backgrounds, and their contributions to the analysis of the subject. Rachel's bio he held until last.

"A few days ago, Dr. Dibaba sent a message to Mr. Nicholas Standish. He's the site manager of the Endurance Project. In her message to Mr. Standish, she talked about ADESA, the AI system I described in my report, and how it had identified something in a remote location on Mars."

"Fascinating, but what's the connection?"

Goodman paused for a moment then replied, "She said the sensor data from that discovery on Mars matched the readings from the subject in Antarctica."

The Director's head nod was slight, but Goodman knew that even this tiny movement reflected her interest. "Now that's new information."

"Ms. Director, I am headed to Melbourne to try and bump into Mr. De Clare," said Goodman. "He's a hard man to get a meeting with. I believe a chance meeting might be more efficient. It's time we engage and talk about his little project."

The silver JDC jet landed at a private airport on the outskirts of Melbourne, Australia, and taxied to the company's hangar. Ducking at the door, Jonathan exited the craft, carrying only a small tablet, and walked towards the facility transporter, awaiting his arrival. He eyed the men exiting the hangar office. It was essentially just three glass walls connected to the back of the hangar with a door. He recognized the facility manager in cargo shorts and a t-shirt and the maintenance guy in a jumpsuit, but not the suit with them. He stuck out like an accountant in a strong man competition. Jonathan stopped at the transporter, seeing the men's pace and obvious intent on speaking with him.

"Mr. De Clare, this man...," huffed the facility manager.

"Mr. De Clare," the suit interrupted. "My name is Steven Goodman. I am with U.S. Intelligence." He extended his right hand.

Jonathan had already pegged him as either a banker or a government guy. Most likely a govie since he somehow knew his itinerary and hadn't bothered setting up a meeting. Obviously, Mr. Goodman was determined to meet sooner rather than later. He shook the man's hand. "Mr. Goodman, you're a long way from home. Care to take a ride?" Jonathan climbed into the transporter. Mr. Goodman walked around and entered the other side.

"Where are we going?" asked Mr. Goodman.

Jonathan pointed ahead at the aerial transporter down the tarmac starting up. "I have an appointment with the captain of a ship I just bought. Have you ever been on-board a nuke-powered icebreaker?"

"Not in this lifetime."

Jonathan cracked a smile. "Today's your lucky day, Mr. Goodman."

Inside the aircraft, the men took their seats and secured their restrainers. The machine's engines ramped up, lifting it vertically for a distance before it tilted its nose and accelerated towards the open ocean.

"So, Mr. Goodman, you have gone through quite an effort to track me down," said Jonathan into his headset mic. "Which one of my operations interests you?"

"Your project in Antarctica."

"Ah, yes, Endurance. One of our new exploratory ventures." Jonathan gazed out the window for a moment, wondering how much information this Mr. Goodman had. "The ice breaker we're about to tour was bought from Russia's fleet for that very project." He then turned back to Mr. Goodman. "The opening of the Antarctic is starting, and our project is helping to make it happen."

"Mr. De Clare, I am with a special intelligence group. Our outfit is responsible for surfacing and monitoring advanced artificial intelligence systems. Specifically, systems that might develop the potential to become a threat to the public. Maybe even the world."

"Sounds like tax dollars well spent."

Agent Goodman smiled. "We've learned from a few incidents in the past. AI systems that got out of control. We're talking about systems that would have caused global catastrophes had no one stepped in. Do you follow me?"

"I do."

"You catch glimpses of some of these incidents in the media. The serious ones you've never heard of. We have learned the only way to protect ourselves is to get in front of these things. Mr. De Clare, you've uncovered something significant in a globally protected neutral territory. Every government on the planet is now tracking your project. It's moved up close to center on everyone's radar screen, and it got there rather quickly. I am sure you've seen your discovery all over the media."

Jonathan knew this meeting was coming. It was just a matter of time. "Yes, I have. It's hard to miss. Endurance is now famous."

"Your project has become a public interest. Not just to us, but the world."

Jonathan gazed back out the window. He saw his new purchase approaching off in the distance. It was easy to spot the massive ship, painted red like all the Russian icebreakers.

"We need information, Mr. De Clare. We need to understand Dr. Davesne's research."

The craft tilted slightly into a long arc to circle the ship and approach it from behind. "Let's tour my new ship, Mr. Goodman. Then we can work out the details."

"We want access to the site, Mr. De Clare. We need to assess this discovery for ourselves." Agent Goodman peered out the window and saw the giant red ship powering through the seas. A bloody mouth and teeth of a great white were painted across the bow. "*She* looks like an icebreaker."

Jonathan nodded in agreement. He looked back at the man and met him eye to eye. "This is going to become a political nightmare, Mr. Goodman. Other governments are going to want the same access."

"We believe you and your team have stumbled onto some kind of alien device. If Dr. Davesne's research is correct, and given his credentials we believe it is, this thing is exhibiting intelligence. We're concerned with the threat potential it could contain."

Jonathan chuckled. "It's buried in the most remote spot on the planet, under a mountain of ice. And it's been there for no less than ten-million years. What threat could it possibly pose?"

Agent Goodman cracked a slight smile for a moment, then it disappeared before he replied, "Mr. De Clare, from what we've learned, it's best to make sure we don't find out."

Jonathan's friendly smile vanished.

TWENTY-TWO

Station Athena, Mars

Gabriele listened to the lead engineer for the Orion project, sitting opposite her in her office, with more than a small amount of frustration. Orion was the single most expensive off-planet project ever conceived and would become the new primary station on Mars. The project schedule was slipping again. On her watch, no less.

"Commander," said the engineer, "assembling the cells of the dome is the issue. It's painstakingly slow. Simply put, the planners at IMTEC were too optimistic." He chuckled. "You know, a rotation on Mars should be a job requirement for those guys. I think that would straighten 'em out."

Despite another setback since she had arrived back on Mars, Gabriele liked this engineer because he didn't sugar-coat anything. She knew the dome over the new station was the most critical component. That was not an area to push. But she wanted to make up some time somewhere before sending off her report.

"Knock, knock."

Gabriele looked over at the entrance to her office and then realized the time.

"Rachel, come in. We're just finishing up." She looked back at the engineer. "Let's regroup later before I send off my report to Van Der Berg tomorrow. I would like to find some time somewhere. Just not with the dome."

"Whenever you're ready, Commander," he replied as he headed out.

Rachel sat down in the chair the engineer had just vacated.

Gabriele tried to park her frustrations with Orion off the side for a while. She rubbed her forehead and cleared her thoughts as she looked at Rachel. She noted the concern on her face. "Everything okay? Sounded like you had something urgent to discuss."

"It's about ADESA and that object discovery in Antarctica."

Gabriele had wondered if that was it. She had caught glimpses of the project now appearing in the media updates from Earth. But all the speculation surrounding it painted it more like sci-fi than something real. "I've seen a couple mentions of it in the news recently. I didn't know what to think."

"It's real," replied Rachel. "Just not quite how the media is portraying it. They are blowing it up more than reality."

"As always."

Rachel took her time. "You know I've been engaged with my team at Z-Scan. We're working through the backlog of anomalies, refactoring code, adapting algorithms to the environment here."

"Enrico tells me it's going well. He said he is seeing some real, tangible improvements."

"It's working. I'm seeing ADESA's performance metrics improve. More than expected actually."

"That's great news, Rachel. Send me a write up when you can. I want to update Van Der Berg. Just know, he's not going to let you go easily after this rotation."

Rachel smiled. "Oh. I don't know if I could keep this up. You know, being away from family and friends. Being here has sure helped me realize how amazing Earth is."

Gabriele grinned. She knew the feeling.

"Gabi... ADESA revisited the anomaly data from the site near Chronos."

"What did you discover?"

"There's no change in her analysis. Actually, her confidence has gone up."

"I see. ADESA thinks it bears similarities to that object in Antarctica?"

"Correct. I've seen all the footage and images from the Chronos site. I've compared scanner data to the same data read off the object in Antarctica. They both exhibit similar heat characteristics, same issues with material signatures, and they even look alike from what's been uncovered."

185

Gabriele smiled. "Incredible, isn't it?"

"I can't wrap my head around this," sighed Rachel.

Gabriele rolled her fingers on her tablet, thinking. After a moment, she looked over at Rachel. "I believe it's time we have IMTEC engage with that group in Antarctica. Let's see what they've figured out. And take you out of the middle of this."

Rachel smiled. "I agree."

"Let's finish this conversation while walking," suggested Gabriele, now energized by this news. "Come on, I'll show you my favorite walkabout path. It's what I do when I need some fresh air, so to say. I'd like to hear more about this project in Antarctica so I can get IMTEC ramped up. Sounds like a little information sharing is in order."

It was early morning and the rising sun behind Van Der Berg warmed the salty air while he sat on his terrace overlooking his pool and the Pacific Ocean and waited for the call. He had met the US Director of Intelligence a couple times, maybe more. He read her terse message again.

Dr. Van Der Berg

An issue has surfaced in the global intelligence community that needs your attention. It concerns this discovery in Antarctica that has surfaced in the media. We have been tracking this project for a while and are now working with the group who made the discovery. I would like to discuss this matter with you as soon as possible...

While reflecting on her message and the stories he had been reading of this discovery, an image of the Director faded in and out on his screen as a soft tone alerted him to her call. He took a deep breath and touched the screen. The Director appeared. He did a quick study of the video background. She was sitting in a large, black, padded seat. *Flying somewhere,* he thought, as he eyed the interior of the government jet.

"Morning, Dr. Van Der Berg. Thanks for taking the time out to talk for a moment. I know you're busy."

"Well, Director, your message laid a nice hook. I'm now intrigued," replied Van Der Berg, in his calm baritone voice. "How can I help?"

"Let's first see if you can." she replied. "When this project came to our attention, something else surfaced along the way that—to be frank with you—was quite bizarre. Before we get to that, I need to confirm a point. One of the scientists who had worked on that exploration project in Antarctica, a Dr. Rachel Dibaba, I believe is now in your organization?"

"Yes, that's correct," he replied. "She's a real AI expert we brought on board to help with projects on Mars."

"So, is Dr. Dibaba on Mars now?"

"She is. She'll be there for a while. What's your interest, Director? If you need to reach her for something, I can arrange communications."

The Director raised her chin slightly, confirming the first fact her call was based on. She then leaned closer to her screen. "No. I don't need to talk with her. It just helps confirm whether or not I am wasting your time."

"I see."

"Dr. Van Der Berg, part of my organization watches the world for advanced AI systems. Rogue AI that could get out of hand, you know, pose a threat to us all. Because of the nature of this discovery, where it is, and what we've uncovered, it is quickly taking top priority here, if you know what I mean."

"It is a fascinating discovery," interjected Van Der Berg.

"We're classifying it as AI with a moderate threat level until we learn more."

"That makes sense."

"I never had imagined Mars would be of any interest to me and my organization," said the Director. "And honestly, this could all still be for nothing. However, given the mysteriousness of this object, we have to run all information to their ends." She sighed softly. "Which brings me to my point. We've come to learn that your scanning technology might have discovered another of these objects on Mars."

She must be referring to the Chronos site, he thought. Recalling the reports from Gabriele, he replied, "Our surface scanning did identify something out near one of our stations and flagged it as an anomaly. At some point, it reported it as being similar to that discovery in Antarctica. Twice, actually. Meaning we had the area re-scanned after the first report. Behind the scanning technology used on Mars and at that project in Antarctica is a common AI system. It helps us identify minerals, metals, and other resources deep under a surface. Maybe that's what you are referring to?"

"Possibly. We're aware of this AI technology from a German engineering firm called Z-Scan. I believe it's called ADESA."

"Yes, that's right," he replied.

"Dr. Van Der Berg, let me see if I understand correctly. This ADESA system, which discovered the object in Antarctica, is the same system that flagged that discovery near one of your stations on Mars. And it suggested it might be the same thing that was uncovered in Antarctica?"

"That's right."

"What did you find there?"

"Not much at this point. I believe a crew has just begun excavating the site. But let's not get ahead of ourselves. The only data we have connecting these two discoveries is through this ADESA system. That technology is still a work-in-progress on Mars. That's actually why we recruited Dr. Dibaba. She's there to work on the scanning technology to improve it, so we get less of these unknowns and more of the known discoveries."

"You're telling me this anomaly on Mars hasn't been marked as high priority?"

"Correct. We currently have a two year backlog of these to work on. Depending on where they are and what else we've uncovered in the area, we give them priorities that factor into our planet-wide program. That said, Commander Rousseau, who is there now, raised this project's priority. It's now getting some attention, although not from this link with the discovery in Antarctica."

The Director leaned forward, her face serious. "Dr. Van Der Berg, the lead scientist researching this object in Antarctica refers to it as an intelligent machine. His research seems to prove it is very aware. So, evidently, no one knows what we are dealing with here. If, by chance, you've found another one of these on Mars then I can promise you all world governments would want to know about it."

"Who's the lead scientist that's making these claims?"

The Director muted and glanced up at someone sitting across from her for a moment before returning. "Davesne. Dr. Arnaud Davesne. An astrophysicist. Do you know of him?"

Van Der Berg thought for a moment. "I believe so. If it's the same Davesne, he's been an advisory consultant to IMTEC off and on for years."

"Is he credible?" asked the Director.

"Yes. Very."

"So, Dr. Van Der Berg. What would it take for me to encourage you to move this little anomaly all the way to the top of your list?"

Van Der Berg smiled. "You just have to ask nicely." He saw the sides of her mouth turn up slightly. He thought that was enough to constitute a return smile. "I'll talk with Commander Rousseau and will be in touch as soon as I have something to report."

"Thank you."

"By the way, Director. How did you come across one of our scanning reports?"

She frowned. "Did I say I had one of your reports?"

He chuckled. He knew he would never know for certain. "Alright. This will take some time. Things on Mars move much slower than here."

Not long thereafter, they concluded their call. Van Der Berg reflected on their brief conversation as he watched the waves crash against the shore. *She's seen information that's spooked her,* he thought. *Davesne has figured out something. This thing in Antarctica is real. 'Aware',* she had said. He touched the screen on his tablet and then began to search through the media for the stories and images of Endurance. He found them quickly, along with hundreds of theories making their way around the online world. As he paged through the images —of the black monolithic object, the ice chamber, the engraved marking across one of its faces, the accompanying text that read, *10-Million-Year Old Alien Object Buried under Mile-Deep Glacier!*—it all started growing in his mind. *What if there is another one of those on Mars?* he thought.

Van Der Berg accessed the project's repository at IMTEC and searched for the Chronos site. He quickly found the live video feed and played it. On his tablet screen he saw the site from the first camera's angle. A piece of equipment blocked the view. He switched to the next camera, then the next, and then stopped. The view was clear. In the center of a small crater a rough black rock poked up out of the surface. He zoomed in on it and enhanced the image, then cropped the view and created a still from the video. His curiosity piqued. He placed the image side by side with an image in the media he had captured. He stared at the tip of the object on Mars, then glanced back to the monolith in Antarctica. *Not much to go on,* he thought. *But it sure looks similar.*

His mind charged at the idea. He even felt his pulse tick up. Over the decades of his career in space, nothing even close to this intriguing ever surfaced. *It's time to find out what that is, Commander Rousseau. Time to bring in the full crew.*

TWENTY-THREE

Mars

Gazing out of the side window and studying the terrain below, Enrico rubbed his expanding goatee and moustache as the air transporter circled the site of the anomaly—a little more than three-hundred kilometers southeast of Station Chronos.

Spotting a flat stretch of surface, the pilot set down his aircraft. Its extended legs contracted to soften the landing. The second craft, carrying an enclosed work pod and life support capsule for the crew, landed a short distance away. After the clouds of fine red dust settled down, the rear loading door of the first transporter lowered, and the crew and machines started unloading.

Weeks prior, deep surface scanners were sent to the site to map out the entire area around the anomaly. The data had been relayed to satellites where it was forwarded to engineers and analysts at Station Athena. From there, a site plan and full excavation details had been laid out for the crew to execute. It was going to be a big, deep crater in loose soil. Ground retaining walls would be assembled around the perimeter and lowered into place as they dug the crater.

Enrico walked the site, navigating with his tablet computer, like a metal detector looking for coins. "One marker here," he said into his suit's communicator.

His robot helper picked up a long metal shaft off the back of a small transporter, stood it up vertically, held it firm, and then pressed the sinker button. The hard jolt from the small, concealed blast shook the machine.

Enrico placed the markers at the four corners of a large square, then slowly surveyed the site. Content with the size of the perimeter, he walked into the existing crater dug by the wild-catting team and knelt to study the object jutting up out of the surface. He had seen the images of the object in Antarctica in the media and knew its backstory from Rachel. He placed his gloved hand on the object to see if he could detect a temperature through the thick, pressurized suit. Nothing.

He stood up and stared at the oddity, studying its surface, its color, its location in the middle of nowhere. The frown on his face was not from wonder. To him, the alien object was not friendly looking at all. Something about it made him want to cover the black mass up and walk away, but he had a job to do. Whether this was in fact another one of those alien objects was the big mystery he was there to help figure out. And the first step was to dig it up.

After a moment, he stood and looked around at his crew. "Let's get this going, team. Commander Rousseau said it's a top priority."

Gabriele watched the live video from the Chronos site on the display in her office. She paused it, walked up closer, and studied the engraved marking on the face of the black, monolithic structure in the center of the crater.

After receiving the request from Van Der Berg to focus on the anomaly, Gabriele had put other projects on hold, combined two teams, and put Enrico in charge. With all the machines, robots, and aerial transport on his wish list, he and his team had exposed enough of the object within the first ten days to know what they had discovered.

The video on her screen switched to the next camera encircling the crater. ADESA had been correct all along. Gabriele had just forwarded all the details to Van Der Berg. Analysts and scientists on Earth were now receiving the images she was watching along with streaming data read from an array of sensors setup around the site.

Everyone on Mars had been watching the tensions on Earth grow, but it was different from being there. They were entirely removed from the situation and the endless media speculation. That had just changed. Excited and nervous, Gabriele picked up her computer and headed to her briefing.

Crews were still arriving. Others out at remote sites were tuning in. The mood in the big meeting hall was charged. She looked around the room for a moment. The chatter quieted down.

Gabriele turned to the wall behind her, displaying a map of Mars. With the screen controls, she zoomed in on the area near Chronos. *Unbelievable,* she thought. Her eyes widened slightly at the thought of being the first commander of IMTEC to present what she was about to show her team.

After a long breath, she started. "Over the past few days, in that quadrant," she pointed at the screen, "approximately three hundred kilometers southeast from Chronos, our excavation team uncovered what appears to be the first alien-like object we've discovered here on Mars, and anywhere off Earth, for that matter. I have to qualify our discovery in this way because, from what we are seeing in the news, it looks like an exploration crew in Antarctica has beaten us to claiming the top prize."

Gabriele looked around the filled hall. She heard some laughter and saw fascination on some faces. On others, she saw question and concern.

She turned towards the neighboring screen. "This is the site where, as everyone can see, Enrico and his team are hard at work." The time marker indicated the video was live. In the center of the excavated crater, the mysterious object stood tall and erect. "It seems we've stumbled upon another one of those objects here on Mars."

Pointing to positions on the image, she continued. "The crew has already set up sensors around it. We're accumulating data from everything we can measure and feeding it to HQ, where they will do all the analysis and determine our next steps." She then paused and looked around at the group. "Questions?"

"Is it putting off any radiation?" asked a scientist.

"Other than a little heat, no. At least none that we can measure."

"Has the crew taken any samples?" asked another scientist.

"Not yet," replied Gabriele. "That mass is very hard. The team hasn't been able to bore into it."

The questions continued for a while. Some she could answer. Many she could not. She didn't want to just pull answers out of the air. These were top scientists and engineers. No answer was better than a fabricated one.

Gabriele looked slowly around the hall. She knew the details and the hype in the media streaming to them from Earth would now translate here. "Team," she said with sincerity. "The object in Antarctica has been buried there for many millions of years. The scientists studying it believe it has done nothing but sit there. I agree, it is bizarre that we just uncovered what appears to be another one." She walked up closer to those seated in front and spoke with passion from her heart. "I joined IMTEC because I was drawn to the mystery of space and what's out here; the possibilities, the adventure, the unknowns, the excitement!" She smiled. "All of you are here for the same reasons. Yes, we're here to do our research and help with our expansion out into space. But we are also fascinated with what we might find. Well, we just found something. Something quite mind-boggling, really. Up to this point, we have encountered nothing that we couldn't eventually understand. With so much time in space behind us and no big, unexplainable discoveries to speak of, this first one is a bit of a shocker. Maybe even unnerving to some of us."

She paused for a moment, meeting the eyes of ones in the crowd wherever she could. "But we are all explorers. And scientists. And we just made a genuine discovery. Something for the record books. We'll be able to say we were the team that found this thing. Right?"

She noted the concern on some faces turning to confidence.

Conversations picked up around the room.

"Team, before I close, I submitted everything on Chronos-330 to IMTEC earlier today. What we do next is in their hands. I will keep everyone informed as it progresses. For now, we all have our work cut out for us. Let's stay focused. As always, my door is open."

It was midday, and sections in Station Athena were taking breaks. The social area was crowded and tables were filled. The main wall brightened with scenes of Mars and other planets, streamed to it from the space station and observation points around the planet.

Jordan ate a chip and rotated her tablet around on the table to show Rachel a video clip. They didn't receive all news feeds from Earth, just what IMTEC licensed and relayed on to their off-planet sites. She stopped the video and zoomed in on the face of the object. "That's an alien-looking thing if I ever saw one. Look at that. It almost looks like a family crest. And it looks exactly like the one at Chronos. To think it's been sitting there in Antarctica for... what did they say? Ten million years? When did the first humanoid show up? Any idea?"

"Something like eight million years ago," replied Rachel. "That's when the human line split with the gorillini line. Your basic primates."

Jordan paused for a moment.

Rachel saw the curious look on her face and smiled. "When you grow up in South Africa, you learn a great deal about the origins of humans. I've also absorbed a lot from a paleontologist friend. I've been helping her for years at fossil discovery sites around Africa. So, what's your idea?"

"Maybe it's what spawned humans," replied Jordan.

"Interesting idea," replied Rachel with an agreeable smile. "But around the time that the human line split off, that object would have been buried under ice and sitting where it was found. But I guess it could have been sitting there for much longer, like since Gondwana existed. Which would have been around fifty or sixty-million years ago."

"Sounds like a stretch to me," said Jordan, eating her chips.

"I guess it could have planted the seed, but then it took fifty million years to work its magic," replied Rachel. "Evolution does take its time."

"You're not buying it?"

Rachel paused and thought about her time with Nick at the dig in Antarctica, then said, "honestly, I don't know what to think." All she remembered was how eerie, strange, almost frightening it had been down in that chamber with that object. She knew some of her feelings were from just being in that chamber, from being under the glacier, a long way down tunnels through ice.

"What if it is alien?" asked Jordan. "It can't do anything sitting where it is, under all that ice, frozen solid like a giant popsicle."

"But that's one of the strangest things. It's not frozen. And, as we now know, neither is the one that Enrico just dug up."

Jordan thought for a moment as she fiddled with the chips on her plate. "Maybe it was just discarded there. Or lost. Or misplaced, like the old cargo ships from decades ago. Containers would accidentally fall off those ships into the ocean and were just left there because the ships weren't aware they had lost them."

"That's an idea," Rachel agreed.

"But we're talking like ten million years ago, right?"

"At least," replied Rachel.

"Well, I'm a decent mechanical engineer. I know even our most advanced gear has imperfections and eventually require maintenance. If this thing has machine-like intelligence and hasn't crapped out in that span of time, then it was made by some very advanced engineers. Which means something out here is way, way ahead of us. Like, way ahead."

Rachel set her sandwich down and took a drink. "Losing one of those objects, like falling off a ship, is an interesting idea, and believable. But losing two?"

Jordan's eyes widened. "Almost seems planned, doesn't it?"

"Yes, it does."

TWENTY-FOUR

Endurance Site, Antarctica

The data from its comrade, two hundred and ninety million kilometers away, was a simple update on progress of the Earth life forms on Mars. The machine woke slightly, absorbed the information, and factored it into all other data it had been accumulating. At the end of its comprehensive analysis, the machine changed. The end result indicated it should shift its state to a higher level of observation. After its internal systems adapted to the new order, it dropped into a new, higher, meditative state, listening again to Earth, observing humankind.

TWENTY-FIVE

Diablo: *Khas, can you tell where the message originated?*

Khasimir: *The Z-Scan scientist, Dibaba, sent it to Standish.*

Diablo: *Where did it originate from? Z-Scan?*

Khasimir: *No. Even better, IMTEC.*

Razputin: *IMTEC? They're hiding something.*

Akashi: *In previous messages to Standish, she mentioned training with IMTEC.*

Diablo: *A, that's right. I have a theory. Khas, can you see the hops the message took getting from Dibaba to Standish?*

Khasimir: *Sure. Give me a couple minutes.*

Akashi: *What are you thinking, D?*

Diablo: *It's just a hunch, but what if she's on Mars? Maybe that training was for an off-planet mission.*

Akashi: *Another one of these on Mars would be unbelievable.*

Diablo: *Yes. It would be a ground shaker for sure if it's true.*

Razputin: *Man, if there is another one on Mars, things could get crazy. Could you imagine that?*

Diablo: Yes, I can. But why would an ancient race put one of these on Mars and one on Earth?

Khasimir: D, you might be right. From when Dibaba sent the message to its next hop took minutes. Every subsequent hop was in the sub-second range. It definitely looks like it came from Mars.

Razputin: Amazing. These alien machines could be on every damn planet.

Khasimir: We need more proof. This lone message isn't enough.

Akashi: Maybe she'll send a pic.

Diablo: Let's hope. Khas, let's keep this channel open. No fingerprints. Extremely light touch. I don't want to get sniffed out.

TWENTY-SIX

Jonathan, Ellie, Nick, and Arnaud stood looking out at the snow-covered capitol city of the United States. The view from the conference room inside the federal building was truly spectacular. They studied the solitary obelisk that rose one-hundred and seventy meters from the Earth off in the distance. They all knew the size and resemblance of the stone monument to the alien machine they were about to present was just a coincidence. Nevertheless, it was surreal to see.

Jonathan glanced around the room. Aside from his team, he recognized only Mr. Goodman. This was the first of several presentations they had to give to world governments. Since Antarctica was a neutral territory, Endurance essentially sat in everyone's own backyard and so everyone engaged with the team on their own terms. The United States had called first.

Live video from the object's chamber at the Endurance site streamed onto a screen that had descended from the ceiling. Chatter around the oblong table slowly subsided.

Jonathan looked at the time, then at Nick. Nick got the point, eased his chair back, and stood up at his end of the table. His hair was pulled back tight with a band, and he dressed in a suit and boots. *He cleans up well,* thought Jonathan with a smile.

"I am Nick Standish, a geological engineer and project manager for a scientific endeavor actively exploring Antarctica. A venture we call Endurance. Some time ago, we discovered something of a mystery in the interior of the continent." He turned and looked up at the object in the center of the screen. "This is from our site. The black obelisk shape you see there is the top third of what we discovered. It is buried a meter under the bedrock layer, roughly twenty-six hundred meters under the glacier that blankets the continent."

He turned to the adjacent screen showing a map of Antarctica. "Our site is located at the green marker which you can see falls within Norway's land claim, an area called Queen Maud Land." He pressed the controller in his hand. "Here are a few images of our site. That is the bedrock staging area at the bottom of the service elevators. And this image shows the main line tunnel. All other tunnels T into the main line. Down a secondary tunnel we call T11, we made our first significant fossil discovery—a large pterosaur creature." He smiled at Ellie. "Professor Mayfield here can tell you more about that if you're curious."

Nick gestured back to the live feed of the object and continued. "A little further down T11, our scanners picked up on something else buried deep in the earth." He pointed to the center of the screen. "That object is what our scanners detected. The round chamber it's in is solid ice. We excavated that room to dig this thing up." He turned and looked over his shoulder at the long-standing Washington Monument. "To give you a real sense of how large that object is, we have a perfect reference structure right out those windows. That object on the screen is larger in cross section than that monument there, and roughly three quarters its height."

All in the room looked out of the wall of windows that framed the age-old structure.

"Mr. Standish, what are you saying?" asked a delegate. "The object on the screen is wider than the Washington Monument?"

"Yes, that's exactly what I am saying. Remove the top third of the Monument there and what's left would fit inside the object in that chamber you see on the screen, with room to spare." Delegates turned to each other and whispered. *That seemed to crystalize everyone's attention,* Nick thought. He then turned back to the screen. "Since we found this, we've been attempting to understand it. We've tried to take samples to determine its material structure. It's far harder than anything we know of. We can't chip it. We can't drill into it. Hell, I remember one excavator losing its footing and falling against one of the object's sides. Nothing ever chipped off. Nothing. And those are heavy machines, weighing in at maybe 800 kilos. At first, we thought it to be a meteorite or some type of large crystal. That was until we uncovered that engraved marking on its face there." He handed Ellie the screen control. "Now I'll turn it over to Professor Mayfield."

Ellie stood and winked at Nick as if to say, *nice job cowboy.* "I am Dr. Ellie Mayfield, a professor of paleontology at Witwatersrand and research scientist on this project. I've been studying Antarctica for many years now. We know from our understanding of the continent nothing could have touched that object for at least ten million years. Ten million years ago, the most intelligent creature on Earth, that we know of, was something not dissimilar to a small monkey. So, what could have made those markings? Making a perfect circle is no trivial matter. Etching a groove like that in stone? Far more challenging. Humans would not have been able to do such a thing until very recent times. And even then, as you just heard, this object is far harder than any material we know of. We've analyzed the width and depth of the engraving with very high precision equipment. There's not the slightest deviation around the marking. For lack of a better word, it's perfect."

Whispered discussions arose around the room again. Ellie paused for a moment.

"Professor, is that a symbol of something?" asked a delegate. "Maybe it's similar to drawings in ancient documents? Or carvings we know of? Or a symbol on early archaeological monuments?"

"We've run it through all the symbol registries and have found nothing close. Keep in mind how long this has been buried and where we found it. We know it has been there for at least ten million years. It's also possible it's been there for fifty million years, maybe longer."

The delegate nodded, pleased by the straightforward answer. "Thank you, Professor."

Ellie smiled. "Now, to take this up a few notches. Dr. Davesne will present to you data that shows this object exhibiting intelligent, machine-like behavior. That it's aware. And not just subtly aware either, but acutely cognizant of humans in its presence."

Arnaud stood and walked over to join Ellie. Like a man accustomed to educating bureaucrats on the complexities of nature, he began at the most basic image he could conjure up. In this case, a visualization of a heartbeat.

On one screen, a line moved from right to left, oscillating slowly up and down like a sine wave. He watched the screen for a moment, then looked around the room at his audience. "This is the object's surface temperature reading." He then emphasized, "It's a very slow heartbeat. I call this its resting state. Not much happening in the chamber, as you can see. Nothing to disturb it from its slumber." He heard a few chuckles. "Let's now introduce a little stimulus." He touched two buttons on his tablet to send Sergey a message. On the screen a moment later, a drone flew into the chamber. It circled around the object slowly before landing. "Its heartbeat hasn't changed," Arnaud said. He looked back at the screen. "Let's now bring a human into the chamber. The Endurance project's master engineer, Sergey Kalashnikov, is standing by, fifty meters away. A couple of things to note here before he sets off. The reading on the screen displays the distance from Mr. Kalashnikov to the object. That distance is also the thickness of the ice between him and the object. The other number, to the right of the distance metric, measures change in the light reflected off its surface. There are sensors all around the chamber that read the reflected light. When this number changes, it means its surface material has been altered in some way so that it reflects light differently. Is that clear?"

"Dr. Davesne, what do you mean by altered?" asked a delegate.

"The object's surface is changing somehow in a way that is causing the reflected light to shift. The object itself could be getting harder."

The delegate's eyes widened as he rubbed his chin. A few others glanced at each other with a bit of concern. "Thank you, Doctor."

Noting that everyone seemed to be sufficiently intrigued, Arnaud sent Sergey the next message and looked back at the audience. "Okay. Mr. Kalashnikov is on his way." The distance metric counted down the meters. "Pay attention to its heartbeat as the distance nears thirty meters." A moment later, the smooth up and down cycle of the wave jumped up a few degrees and bounced around erratically. The distance metric continued to fall. 29, 28, 27. "Now observe the light metric as Mr. Kalashnikov approaches from fifteen meters away." Right on queue the measurement began to decrease, -54, -72, -112. Sergey entered the chamber moments later in his thermal suit and helmet. The object's heartbeat remained in the elevated state, moving up and down slightly as Sergey walked the chamber. The light metric dropped to -184 and remained there.

"To conclude this little demonstration, Mr. Kalashnikov will now exit the chamber." Arnaud sent Sergey a final message. Everyone watched the space-suited figure walk up the ramped floor and then disappear down the tunnel. The temperature reading remained elevated for a while and then slowly settled back down to its resting state. Not long thereafter, the light measurement moved and started ticking back up.

"We could repeat this demonstration countless times and the results would be the same," said Arnaud. "As a matter of fact, the results would be exactly the same, without the slightest deviation from what you just witnessed. My team has built models that can predict these reactions with extreme precision. Meaning, the object's reactions are like a machine. They are exact." He looked at the screens and then back to his audience. "*That* is a machine."

With the control in his hand, Arnaud switched one of the screens to a split dual display. The left half displayed the original heartbeat of the object he had started with, while the right half showed another oscillating wave, one that was similar to the heartbeat but slightly higher on the scale. "This is the last bit of data I will cover," he said, gesturing to the graphs. "The graph on the left is where we started. It's the cyclic rhythm of the object's surface temperature up until just a few weeks ago. The wave on the right is the same sensor data from that point in time to today." He turned to face his audience and walked towards the head of the conference table. "Something has changed inside the object. Its resting state has changed. The fact that this wave has shifted up the scale and not down is worth noting."

"Worth noting in what way?" asked a delegate.

Arnaud thought for a moment before replying, "Maybe it's more awake now. Paying more attention."

"Dr. Davesne, you're a well-respected astrophysicist," said a delegate at the table. "I am guessing you've had colleagues corroborate your findings. And I am sure they were all mesmerized by this thing, like all of us are. What do you and the team here suggest this might be?"

Arnaud frowned, weighing his words carefully. "I just demonstrated this object is exhibiting precise, intelligent behavior. Right now, we have no way of determining whether it's machine intelligence or sentient intelligence. It detects humans approaching long before they are even visible to it. It could be detecting us from much further away but just not showing a measurable reaction. There's an energy source inside it. It doesn't show the slightest bit of surface degradation, yet we believe that it has been buried here for many millions of years. Its surface changes somehow. It morphs, yet it is harder than anything we know of. Mr. Standish and his team have also had machines malfunction in its presence. Analysis has determined a potential cause of those malfunctions to be high energy pulses. Yet we don't detect any radiation emanating from it, aside from the traceable heat. Given everything we've discovered to date, we must conclude it's not from Earth. Because its responses are very calculated, I believe it's a machine. An intelligent machine."

"A machine for what purpose, Dr. Davesne?" asked another delegate.

Arnaud took a moment before responding. "Maybe a probe of some sort. Maybe a *weapon*." His last word resonated. It changed the tone in the room. It changed the focus of the rest of the meeting.

Jonathan watched the reactions and studied the room carefully. Even though more meetings were to follow in Europe and with the Asian governments, he knew the path that *one* word would forge. *Weapon.* Given the size of the object, it was just a matter of time before the idea would bubble up to the surface of every defense department on the planet. Like a splinter under the Earth's skin, it would fester. They couldn't do much with it in its current location. Eventually, someone was going to want it bad enough to remove it from his site. And knowing any attempt to monetize an alien object would almost certainly lead to nationalizing it, that was exactly what he wanted.

TWENTY-SEVEN

Endurance Site, Antarctica

"What's that little guy for?" asked Nick while sitting on a stool and watching Sergey work on a drone. No one else was in the warehouse. The machine maintenance section was Sergey's, and he had made that clear to the multi-government research crew now overseeing all experimentation on the object.

"Cute, isn't it?" replied Sergey. "Rachel brought me a few of these on her last visit. He's our new eyes and ears down T11." Sergey plugged the micro drone into a computer, touched a button on the control screen and turned around to Nick. "Aren't you curious about what they are up to?"

Nick raised his eyebrows. "Definitely, since they won't tell me what they're bringing in."

"I suspect they're setting up something. Maybe something experimental. Something to penetrate its surface."

"And we should know what they are up to," said Nick with a grin. "After all, we found it first. Send in your little spy and let's see what these government deviants are up to."

Mounted on the back of a small rover, Sergey's spy drone was transported to the tunnels. At the bottom of the elevator ride, the drone lifted off the back of the rover and quietly flew down the main line, made a left into the mouth of $T11$ then flew to the end into the chamber where it nestled quietly into a perch with a bird's-eye view of the goings-on with the object.

While working on his maintenance backlog, Sergey observed the government team passively, noting their diligent progress over several days as the scientists set up and configured a device they had uncrated. When the progress stopped, he knew the day and time of the experiment had arrived. He quickly made a call to Nick.

Once Nick had arrived, the two men studied the government scientists in the chamber. There were only two in there. From their actions, they were obviously communicating a lot, but the audio between their suit communicators was not picked up by the spy drone.

"What do you think this device will do," asked Nick, glancing at the screen while watching Sergey replace the tracks on a rover.

"Hard to say. I would think it's some type of heavy particle beam. Something that might penetrate that object's surface." Sergey finished connecting the track and glanced up at the screen. The lead scientist was giving a thumbs up towards a camera. Sergey put down his tools and walked over. "Whatever it is, I think they are about to give it a go," he said to Nick, who was now milling about.

Inside the chamber, the scientists gathered behind the shielded control panel at the back of the room. The figure Sergey had pegged as the head scientist looked up at the main camera and gave another thumbs up. After pressing a few controls, he looked back at the object.

"That damn thing is alive," said Nick, seeing its surface move.

In an instant, the engraved marking on the face of the object began to morph and change shape. The cross markings moved inwards, touching in the center of the ring. The crest began to glow. A thick, shimmering light poured out, encasing the monolith. As the light envelope sealed the object inside, the energy in the shield resonated outwards in a dense sonic wave, throwing the scientists and their equipment against the chamber wall.

Sergey grabbed Nick's shoulder. "Go call the lift!" he shouted as he ran to the side wall and pressed the emergency alarm.

***

Diablo sat at his wooden table inside his sparsely furnished flat and watched the activity in the chamber on his display. The video feed from Arnaud's lab remained on 24/7 since Diablo's contact had granted him access.

His team had patiently watched the chamber, studying the scientists and their actions, noting the equipment they had recently installed. The video stream provided eyes in the chamber, but they could not hear the scientist's communications. The scientists appeared to be carrying out experiments. But none had involved a device like the one they had been working on for the past few days. Diablo knew they were about to attempt something big.

He had dedicated one of his many screens to watching the chamber and what was happening to the object. The screen was divided into six smaller screens, each displaying a video feed from a different angle.

Seconds before the scientist engaged the device, the marking came to life. The image of the chamber on his screen vibrated. All camera angles shook as the force that emanated from the object lifted the scientists and flung them backwards against the wall, leaving them sprawled across the floor. Then the shimmering of the shield dimmed. The engraved cross marks slid back to their original position. The energy field was gone.

Inside his lab, Arnaud and his team of scientists—who had recently been recruited into the multi-government group monitoring Endurance—watched their experiment at the Antarctic compound unfold. They saw the machine's marking illuminate and then shroud the object in an energy field. They heard the deep rumble that resonated in the chamber as their two colleagues were lifted off the floor of the chamber and thrown backwards, landing on the frozen ground.

Arnaud was mesmerized. "Oh my god," he said out loud as his heart raced.

Late that night, in the dim light of his study, Arnaud replayed the scene over and over. He watched the metrics from all the sensors in the chamber. In the instant before the object nearly killed his colleagues, the force field flickered and the ambient energy reading in the chamber went off the scale. It was at least an order of magnitude more energy than the cutting device could produce. The picture was crystal clear. The object defended itself against its foes with a force field. What happened next was unclear. Did it attack them? Or was that an unintended consequence of its defense? *Why attack?* he wondered. It clearly had the upper hand with technology. Humans had nothing close to a force field. That was still just science fiction. *Maybe it was just a residual effect,* he thought. *Or... maybe it was a warning.*

After watching the scene a final time, Arnaud let it play on as he reviewed the details in his mind. With help from the Endurance team, the scientists were back on their feet, exiting the chamber as quickly as they could. He watched the object, almost wanting it to do something else. It did nothing. Now exhausted, he leaned back in his chair, studying the metrics and graphs on his screen. He suddenly realized the object's thermal measurement had not returned to its usual resting state, remaining elevated, long after the chamber had been vacated. It moved around, slightly up, then down, then up quickly. The movement wasn't uniform like before. This was the second time its steady-state readings changed. *It must be thinking,* he thought. *Crunching lots of data and thinking.*

Melded into his chair, and staring at the screens on his desk, he knew this was a game changer. A real turning point. It appeared as if the machine had attacked his colleagues. It recognized they were a potential threat and took action. And it now appeared to be in a different state of mind entirely. Maybe this is its *alert* state, he pondered. Regardless of what it meant, Arnaud knew this event was now being viewed by every government that was a part of this coalition research group, as well as several who weren't. *What will they do?* he asked himself. He gazed out his window at the dark of night, thinking. *They all just witnessed an alien machine attack humans with technology the world could only dream of. And it happened on Earth.*

If that was just the shot across the bow, what else can it do?

TWENTY-EIGHT

A few minutes before the start of his briefing, Agent Goodman activated the display in the intelligence agency's private conference room. He pulled up the subject matter for the briefing—three highly classified reports that had just surfaced.

The previous day, Goodman had accompanied the Director of Intelligence to an early morning meeting with the President of the United States and his staff. Inside the presidential briefing room, they had watched the footage of the object defending itself. Top scientists, presidential advisors, and heads of defense and intelligence agencies discussed and at times argued loudly. Scientists wanted to study it, to learn about its forces. Defense wanted the force field technology. They knew if their top weapons contractors could harness that power, it could be a game changer. However, the object had just shown the world, in very clear terms, that it had no interest in being prodded.

Reflecting on the previous day's meeting, Goodman knew the material in his briefing would fuel his country's efforts to get out in front of this alien object.

Right on time, the Director walked in with her assistant and took her seat at the head of the conference table. She calmly folded her hands together and said, "Okay, Agent Goodman. After yesterday's meeting, I am eager to see what else you've dug up."

Goodman touched the pad in his hand and activated the display on the wall. "These are intel reports we intercepted coming out of the AsiaPac and EasternEuro regions."

The Director took her time reading every detail, then replied, "I see. It seems there are many eyes watching. Looks like global interest is growing. I take it you've run these through the deep analysis group?"

"Yes, we have, Ma'am. There's an eighty one percent probability the first two are already exploring covert ways to get to the Antarctic site. Also, just a point to keep in mind, some countries in the AsiaPac Group are the ones that have been pushing hard to divide up Antarctica. They desperately want access to the resources there."

The Director thought for a moment. "And this alien object with unimaginable powers, no doubt. Well, whatever the reasons, they're obviously no longer interested in just being spectators, are they? How about others?"

"We're monitoring everyone," replied Goodman. "No reason to think there aren't others watching as well."

Diablo met his media contact at the same old cafe in Budapest around the same time of day as their last meeting. Taking in his surroundings, he spotted the same old men sitting outside playing chess and smoking cigarettes. He walked in and noted instantly the same heavy-breasted barista displaying her goods quite proudly.

This time his contact was waiting for him. Diablo took a seat across from the Brit and ordered a coffee. The two men spoke for a long time about the last folder, the object, and what had happened since. The global response had far surpassed their imaginations.

The man was excited to see what Diablo had brought him this time. "Hard to believe you've uncovered something that can top your last find," he said with a raised eyebrow as he leaned forward, sliding his cup to the side.

Diablo removed his tablet from his bag and laid it on the table. He placed his hand on it, looked at the Brit and said, "It's more unbelievable. But once again, it's as real as the last." He spun it around and pressed *Play*. Inside the object's chamber, the scene unfolded with crystal clarity. Diablo watched the man's expression when the object came to life and emitted the energy wave that threw the crew backwards against the wall. Minutes later, the scientists slowly came around and the presentation stopped.

The man looked up at Diablo. "Unbelievable. It can defend itself. It really is some type of alien machine, like that Davesne guy claims. This is crazy!"

"That's not all," replied Diablo. "This next piece is going to blow your mind." He played the second presentation. The scene started in dark space, moving towards a small planet. The image grew larger and larger until its red surface gave away its identity. The scene descended to the Mars surface and traversed across the rolling terrain past Station Athena, continuing westward, skirting along the equator for a moment before reaching a crater. The man leaned forward closer to the screen as he watched the scene hover around a black mono-lithic structure standing erect in the center. He saw the marking on its face and recognized the object immediately.

After Diablo and his team had discovered the first message from Rachel to Nick, they focused on getting more proof of what was happening on Mars. A single message was not enough to convince the world of another alien machine. They knew someone, some crew member, would have taken a picture or a video and sent it to someone on Earth. It would be impossible for everyone there to keep a lid on this. Eventually, Rachel came through with another message to Nick and an image of the monolith. Together with actual footage from Mars that Khasimir had borrowed from IMTEC, the team went to work animating a video presentation around a single photograph.

As the presentation finished, Diablo calmly said, "There's another one on Mars."

The man stared at the screen in stunned silence.

Diablo remained at the cafe after his contact had left. He had notified his team that the transaction had concluded and they had been well compensated for their work. The money was great. It paid for the expensive tools of the trade, the travel, and the fees he had to pay to grease a few hands. He sipped his coffee slowly and smiled. The video they had rendered

around a single picture of the monolith from Rachel was spectacular. He pondered the two alien objects he and his team
had been consumed by for over a year. Regardless of what else
they discovered, he felt vindicated. He had known in his gut
some advanced alien race had been there on Earth. He and his
team had shown the world the truth. Yet there were still unan-
swered questions. Questions he and the guys had rehashed
countless times. Were the objects weapons? That didn't seem
likely, given how long the one had been on Earth. Khasimir
thought they might be part of some early planetary experiment, pushing the continents apart, forcing life to evolve. *That
would be a big ass experiment,* Diablo mused. *And evidently it
didn't work out so well for the Martians.* They were convinced
an alien race had placed the two in our galaxy. Or sent them
here. They just couldn't come up with a reason why.

TWENTY-NINE

At heart, Robert Van Der Berg was a scientist and adventurer, curious about other life in the universe and seduced by the growth in the space industry. He had spent the bulk of his career in space, wondering, and always opting for more missions in lieu of a life on Earth. Yet he had encountered nothing alien. Now, not one but two alien creations had been uncovered.

He was now running the preeminent space agency on the planet. With a bit of string-pulling and a light push to reclassify the Earth discovery as alien, Van Der Berg had broadened IMTEC's reach to now oversee all research on the object in Antarctica. He then folded Arnaud and his team into IMTEC. The world needed answers, and he was going to step up and provide them.

After clearing security at the IMTEC facility in Geneva, Jonathan, Ellie, and Nick entered the transparent dome covering the compound. A protective shield of connected forms flowed high over the buildings, trees, and manicured gardens. The entire campus was a prototype city for testing off-world construction techniques and self-sustainment technologies. Their vehicle followed a path and pulled up in front of the entrance of the building in the center of the compound.

Van Der Berg held out his hand to Jonathan as he climbed out of the vehicle. "Mr. De Clare, pleasure to meet you and your team of explorers here." He then shook Ellie's and Nick's hands. "I believe you all dug up what is possibly the most extraordinary discovery in the history of humanity."

"Oh? You think so?" replied Jonathan.

"Quite possibly," replied Van Der Berg. "Thank you for coming. I am sure you won't be disappointed. Dr. Davesne's team and our other scientists are eager to get started. Let's get you through security. We can talk more while we walk."

The tall doors swung open as they approached. Above the entrance, large gold-highlighted lettering engraved in the glass facade read, *LEADING HUMAN EXPANSION INTO SPACE AND BEYOND.*

The conference room rested on top of the building. Van Der Berg sat at the head of the table and gestured for everyone to take a seat. He then cued the room operators. The two assistants closed the four doors as they exited. Van Der Berg waited until the doors clicked shut before pressing a few buttons on the controls in front of him. The room darkened and the long curved wall behind him brightened. The left half showed a large crater with a tall monolithic object standing erect in the center. The right half displayed a map of Mars with bases and land markers identified.

"The image you see on the left is what you are all now aware of," said Van Der Berg, pointing to the screen. "It's a live video stream of a discovery on Mars. We call it C330. It was uncovered near Chronos, one of our secondary stations. The map on the right shows markers indicating all stations and the location where C330 was discovered."

He paused to observe Jonathan, Nick and Ellie taking in the display. "Some time ago, the scanning technology we employ flagged this object as an anomaly, meaning its material structure wasn't recognized. It was logged into a database of other *unknowns* and things to be researched like all such discoveries on Mars. However, this little finding was different. I remember seeing the scanning report come across my desk. There was a note that suggested it had a similar signature to a discovery in Antarctica. At the time, we dismissed it as a coincidence or a bug in the system." He leaned forward, resting his arms on the table. "Turns out it wasn't a coincidence, or a bug. As everyone can see, we have indeed found what appears to be a twin to what the Endurance team discovered in Antarctica.

Van Der Berg turned to another screen and activated it. It displayed stories and headlines from around the world. "We've all seen these in the media," he pointed out in a serious tone. "Tensions are growing. Government leaders want to know what these objects are. Scientists want to study them but, as Dr. Davesne and his team can attest, experimenting on them can be dangerous. I've moved the government research group into IMTEC and I've invited you, the Endurance team, here because you have the most hands-on experience with these things. Even though you are not a government group, your experience with the object in Antarctica will be invaluable. Between you, Dr. Davesne's team, and our other experts, I believe we can provide the world some direction as to what these are and how we should deal with them."

Ellie, Jonathan, and Nick looked at the different camera angles showing all sides of the monolith. There was no mistaking what stood there on Mars.

"Maybe the two communicate in some way?" offered an older IMTEC scientist, fiddling with his pipe. "Two of these, in the same star system, and relatively close to each other. It almost seems intentional. We could start monitoring all energy bands around both of them."

"At the same time, maybe they're monitoring things in our galaxy," replied a female scientist with a heavy French accent. "Like satellites and probes we send out into space."

There was a pause in the room.

"But monitoring what exactly?" asked Van Der Berg.

"Maybe it's not about *what*, but more about *why*?" offered Ellie. "What if they are watching all life, but not as a scientist driven by curiosity? Instead, they're more like guards. You know, like a sentinel. They monitor for potential threatening life forms. Like an early warning system. Just like the protective ring of satellites we have out in deep orbit around Earth."

"But buried in Antarctica seems so remote from life on Earth," replied Van Der Berg.

"That's true," replied Ellie. "But we know it has been there for a very long time. Maybe since Antarctica was a part of Gondwana. The reason we chose that location for the Endurance Project was because that northern part of the continent once joined with eastern Africa, once a wellspring of early life. If you had visited Earth a hundred and sixty million years ago, looking for life to monitor, that location where we found the object was near the epicenter of life. You would have had the best seat in the house to watch the show."

Van Der Berg smiled. It was a perspective his physicists and other scientists would not have conjured up. It had merit.

Arnaud looked at Ellie, then around at the group. "Let's assume for a moment, these ideas are true. These machines are communicating with each other, and they are monitoring life. Maybe they are looking for potentially threatening life. Then the question I have is, are they more than just monitors? Are they equipped with the power to act? Possibly. We've seen they can defend themselves. What else can they do?" He paused for a moment. "That's the question that keeps me awake at night and has for many nights since the incident. Could the one in Antarctica cause catastrophic damage to Earth? That ten... or sixty-million-year-old object is a very sophisticated, intelligent machine that is cognizant of its surroundings. It reacts to humans. It anticipated our actions when we attempted to pierce its surface. Anticipation denotes high intelligence." Arnaud glanced at the image of the monolith on Mars again, while reflecting on the one in Antarctica. "Even after being buried in Antarctica for an eternity, it is very awake and very capable. Before the incident, the object would revert to a steady state when humans left the chamber. Its surface temperature would drop and then oscillate slowly in a sine wave pattern. Since the incident, it has not returned to that state. Its temperature signal has remained elevated and undergoes periods of erratic, slightly turbulent, behavior. Maybe this *sentinel*, as Dr. Mayfield called it, is now standing at attention."

The room was quiet for a while.

"Maybe you should consider moving all further research and experimentation to Mars," suggested Ellie. "It's more remote than Antarctica."

"I think that's an excellent idea," said Van Der Berg.

Arnaud looked at the map of Mars and thought for a moment. "How close are the stations to the anomaly site?" he asked.

"Chronos is three-hundred and thirty kilometers away," replied a Mars expert sitting with the IMTEC team. "It's not continuously occupied. Athena is two thousand kilometers to the East and is the main station. All planet wide operations run out of there."

"And how many people are on Mars now?"

"Two-hundred and forty currently," replied Van Der Berg. "It varies with the research and missions."

"We do need to establish that the two are the same," said Arnaud. "Run a baseline test. I know the two objects look identical, and the measurements support that as well, but we need to be sure."

"What type of test do you have in mind?" asked Van Der Berg.

"I am sure your team there has a high-energy pulsing cutter to support all the mining work. Can they try to pierce its surface?

Run the same test we did on the one here? From a much greater distance, of course. Preferably via remote. The response they get would tell us whether we're dealing with the same type of machine."

Later that day, Van Der Berg wrote up his report. He detailed the next steps IMTEC planned to take. All future testing would move to Mars. They would begin by first establishing whether the two machines were the same. Next, they would amp up their tests to pierce the surface of the monolith on Mars. All coordination of testing procedures and analysis of results would be carried out by his team on Earth. *This was a good start,* he thought.

Once the report had made its way through his media team, where it would be transformed into a masterful presentation, it would be shared with all IMTEC stakeholders. Van Der Berg thought about the government partners. Most had been in contact with him, requesting details of the object on Mars. But the most powerful partner had been unusually quiet.

THIRTY

Station Athena, Mars

Station Orion had been under development for five years. Transparent panels for the protective dome had been formed, prefabricated buildings had been designed and constructed, power systems had been engineered, and water reclamation machines had been created. The Station had been fully constructed, tested, and debugged on Earth. Over two years, it was all disassembled, packaged up, sent to space, loaded onto many transporters, and shipped to Mars. On Mars, the civil engineering and construction crews assembled the new station, piece by piece.

Gabriele walked through the hangar bay door with her overnight bag in one hand and tablet in the other.

"Commander Rousseau." The pilot shook her hand. "We are almost ready. Two more from engineering are on their way."

Gabriele boarded and eyed who was already in the cabin. She walked between the seats, talked with the crew, and then shook hands with the lead engineer as she took a seat.

"Commander, glad you could make this trip," the man said with a smile.

"I haven't been to Orion in a while," Gabriele admitted. "I'm excited to see the progress. Drone footage is fine, but nothing like seeing it with my own eyes."

"That's right, Ma'am. It's a decent size project. Hard to take it all in on a little screen. Wait till you see the progress we've made. It's really taking shape now."

"Indoor swimming pool?"

The engineer grinned. "I believe that's phase two, Ma'am."

Gabriele smiled. She thought about what was happening on Earth and there on Mars. Van Der Berg said he had been in many meetings with government leaders around the world to discuss the monolith on Mars. Since seeing the power the object in Antarctica possessed and understanding it was now in some elevated state, many were looking for a solution to remove the one from Earth. Others feared rogue governments getting their hands on the technology. Van Der Berg saw Mars as the solution to all the challenges and issues surrounding Antarctica. Mars was to become the test site.

IMTEC had sent detailed plans of the first experiments along with adjusted project schedules to accommodate the additional workload. After returning from Orion, they would carry out the first test. IMTEC had titled it *Base Line*.

Gabriele studied the terrain out of the side window. East of Athena, the flat, rocky surface gradually turned to hills and caverns. Shortly before reaching Orion, the topography flattened out again. One hour into the flight, she saw it in the distance. Sunlight glistened off the plates of the half-submerged geodesic dome, nestled between two rugged hills. As the transporter approached the future base, it slowly banked and circled the construction site.

"A beauty, isn't it?" said the lead engineer.

"Yes, it is," replied Gabriele.

Station Athena's Operations and Control Center was the brain center of all IMTEC activity on Mars. All communication and coordination with Mars Space Station, Earth Space Station, and IMTEC's command centers on Earth were managed there. Monitors covered the walls of the control center. Some were dedicated to weather and atmospheric data, some covered planetary metrics and seismic activity, and others monitored life conditions at each station and all planetary work being carried out by crews at different sites.

Gabriele and a small cadre of scientists and engineers gathered in the control center to watch the *Base Line* test. Overhead, satellites had been directed to monitor the site. Signals from drones and sensors, positioned in rings around the monolith, streamed into the control center, and were relayed on to IMTEC. The primary screen displayed an aerial view of the entire scene. Mounted on a rigid frame, a high-energy pulsing cutter had been set up in front of the monolith and secured to a stabilizer platform.

"Alright, team," said the engineer. "Everyone ready? The crew back at IMTEC are eager to see how this guy responds to a little poke." He looked down at the control panel and pressed the button.

Across the bottom of the primary screen on the main wall, the power meter of the cutter was displayed. *10%... 20%... 50%.*

The monolith-machine woke. The cross markings on its crest pushed into the center. A shimmering blue light poured out from the marking and cloaked the object. In the instant the cutter fired its pulse, the monolith released an energy wave that rattled the platform and everything secured to it. The video streams shook. Drones were thrown backwards, crashing to the ground. A moment later, the light shield vanished.

The entire crew in the control center were quiet for a while.

"I don't think the cutter even nicked it," said Gabriele with disappointment. "I wonder what they will have us try next."

THIRTY-ONE

Endurance Site, Antarctica

The alien machine, now remaining in an elevated state, absorbed the latest communication from its comrade on Mars. *More human activity, spreading out more, more digging and extracting, and a first act of aggression.* Its perspective on this Earth life form was changing. After a while, it assembled all the data and knowledge it had been accumulating for eons of time into a single message and transmitted the message to its creators. Then, the machine went back to work, observing.

THIRTY-TWO

Jonathan's aircraft followed the tight approach path along the Potomac through the cold early morning dew floating over the river. He peered out at the capital of the United States. The Washington Monument still stood taller than all other structures in the city. Moments later, they landed and parked at a private terminal.

Jonathan buttoned up his coat, exited his craft, and was escorted to a government aerial transporter awaiting his arrival. Robert Van Der Berg held out his hand as Jonathan climbed in and took a seat. "Pleasure to see you again, Jonathan. And thanks for adjusting your schedule, I know you're a busy man."

Jonathan shook his hand. "Couldn't skip out on an invitation from the President of the U.S, could I?"

Jonathan occasionally visited the U.S. capital on business, meeting with government lawyers and negotiating mining rights in U.S. territories. He had never been to the White House though and had welcomed the chance to negotiate with the Americans, to persuade them to do something with this alien object. And if they wouldn't remove it from his site, maybe another country would.

Ten minutes later, they were setting down on the back lawn of the White House.

After going through the necessary VIP security checks, they were escorted into the Oval Office. The President, Secretary of Defense, and Director of National Intelligence were actively discussing something, though the conversation ceased the second the doors opened.

The President rose, met eyes with Jonathan, and shook his hand firmly. "Mr. De Clare, pleasure to meet you and thank you for coming on such short notice. Your little discovery in Antarctica has grabbed the world's attention."

"Mr. President, pleasure to meet you as well," replied Jonathan. "And, if you're that interested, it's for sale at a very fair price."

The President chuckled. "Well, Mr. De Clare, thank you. Let's just keep that option on the table, shall we?" He turned and shook Van Der Berg's hand before sitting back in his chair. "Gentlemen, I have to admit, I believe this just might be the first time a conversation on this topic has taken place in this office. This is a bit of history in the making."

Jonathan thought little of the President's statement. He knew his presence there was more a courtesy than anything else—a gesture—to get him to play nicely with the government team and Van Der Berg who was now running the research on the alien machine at Endurance.

The President looked at Jonathan and Van Der Berg. "I guess the first question to get out of the way here is, have we found any more of these alien objects?"

"Just the two," replied Van Der Berg. "But since we uncovered C330—that's what we call the one on Mars—I've met with many of our partners in IMTEC." His deep voice resonated around the room. "They also want details. To ensure information is being shared, I've folded the research group that had been formed to analyze the one in Antarctica into IMTEC. I've also put our top physicists and space scientists in the group. This team will coordinate all research we do on Mars."

The Director of Intelligence, seated across from Van Der berg, cleared her throat and leaned forward slightly. "We read your report, Dr. Van Der Berg. It was impressive. The actions your team are taking seem focused on getting answers as quickly as possible. I liked the idea of extracting the one from Antarctica and taking it somewhere to study. I think you suggested off Earth?"

"That's an excellent idea," said Jonathan. "And, as I said, I am open to help in any way I can." He had suggested extracting it to Van Der Berg after their last meeting. He had even offered to do the extraction if someone would take it off his hands.

"Unfortunately, Mr. De Clare, there are other things brewing around the world that can't wait for science to find an *off* switch on these things so we can extract it without pissing it off," replied the Director lightheartedly. "I think you will better understand once you've seen what we are about to show you." She pressed a button on the control panel lying on the table between them. One of the curved walls of the oval room slid sideways, revealing a wall sized screen containing electronic messages. She turned her chair slightly. "We intercepted these communications recently. They originated out of covert operating centers in AsiaPac and EasternEuro regions."

Jonathan read the reports slowly. The beginnings of what he had foreseen were on the screen right before his eyes. "This does complicate things," he said. "However, I can only imagine you would have expected this from these countries."

"Yes, it does complicate matters," replied the President. "And in more ways than one." He looked back at the Director.

"We did anticipate this, Mr. De Clare. And we believe one of these countries, or even another more rogue-type government, will stage an operation in Antarctica in an attempt to gain control of your site. Whatever actions such a group might take could spur that machine to retaliate in some way, possibly destroy lives. Or worse," she emphasized. "The risks are unquantifiable because we have no idea what power these things possess."

It was now the Secretary of Defense's turn. "Gentlemen, there's an entirely separate issue we also have to face." He looked at Jonathan. "When your team uncovered the one in Antarctica, most of us thought there was only that one. Now that the IMTEC team found a second one on Mars, we have to conclude there could be more. Perhaps on Earth or other planets. Given the power they've demonstrated, we need to know whether or not we can contain these things. Destroy them if we need to."

The Secretary paused for a moment to think through all the briefings he had attended recently. "Nothing we've seen indicates they are alive, right?" asked the Secretary, looking around at the group. "Rather, they are simply advanced machines. Destroying one would be akin to taking out some advanced weaponry one of our foes develops that we would rather not be on the other end of."

The Secretary's move was clear to Jonathan. By classifying these alien objects as weapons, he changed the play. The defense arm of a great world power just stepped on the stage. Other countries will quickly follow. The game just ratcheted up a level. As the power meeting unfolded, Jonathan started to see the path they were methodically following.

"Dr. Van Der Berg," said the President. "We need to run a containment exercise on the one on Mars. We need to do this so we are confident we can neutralize these machines in the event we need to do so here on Earth. And for any future encounters the world's space industry might have to face out there."

The corner of Jonathan's mouth turned up as he cracked a half smile. *That's what they want to do*, he thought. *Clever*. And, given they were likely the largest partner in IMTEC, that sounded more like marching orders to Van Der Berg than a nice request.

"What did you have in mind?" asked Van Der Berg.

"We have some ideas," replied the President as he motioned towards his Secretary of Defense. "Our defense arm will coordinate with you on the details."

The President adjusted himself in his chair and cleared his throat. "There's something else, gentlemen. We need to discourage rogue groups from attempting anything stupid at Mr. De Clare's site. We're going to blanket that region with surveillance. And to send a signal that we mean business, one of our orbiting response systems will be on alert, monitoring that area as well. Everyone will then get the picture. The Director here will work with you, Mr. De Clare, on ground level security."

"You're wanting to militarize my site?"

"In a very light-handed way, Mr. De Clare," replied the President.

"Then I take it you're not interested in extracting it?"

"Not at this point," the President said with a hint of a smile.

"Then what's your plan for the object at my site? Militarizing and controlling Endurance helps me in no way."

The President took a slow breath and glanced at his team before turning back to Jonathan.

"Mr. De Clare, assume every defense agency on Earth, all their little weapons scientists, and every rogue faction on this planet, is now aware of these machines. Assume they've seen everything you've seen. You know how the world works. We just showed you hard evidence that a power grab is starting to germinate. Everyone will begin to believe these machines hold great powers. Everyone will want them for their own benefit. No one will want anyone else to have them. If we extract that object from Antarctica—a neutral territory—where are we going to take it? Even if we could get it to space it would take a year, maybe two, to get a plan going. You see the challenges? This situation will most assuredly escalate. Our interests are in heading it off before it gets out of hand. And, more importantly, to know we can contain that uninvited visitor in Antarctica should we need to."

Jonathan understood the logistical challenges better than anyone. And he was now clear on their direction. One of the world's great powers feared the wrong group getting their hands on this technology and was willing to go at risk to discourage any actions to that end. He was sure they were equally as interested in the potential technology these things held. But, for now, they were playing their noble cards.

The meeting soon ended and the doors to the Oval Office opened.

As Jonathan turned towards the security escorts, the President spoke up. "Oh, I almost forgot. Mr. De Clare, please pass along our intentions to the Kremlin. We have no other interest in your discovery other than to protect the world from the potential threat it poses."

Jonathan's prized aircraft accelerated towards the south end of the runway, lifted its nose, climbed through the gray rain clouds covering the sky, and banked north on a flight path back to Europe. After it reached smooth air, he slid the cabin transparency control all the way up, leaned back and instructed the craft's virtual assistant to get Aleksander on the line.

A minute later, the assistant announced, "Jonathan, Aleksander is waiting. Shall I put him on cabin audio?"

"Yes. Aleksander? Are you there?"

"I'm here, Jonathan. I assume your meeting in Washington has concluded."

"It has."

"You don't sound pleased. Not the deal you wanted?"

"No."

"Well, we have the next meeting in two days."

"That's why I called. I want you to call it off."

"Oh?"

"They knew about it, Aleksander."

"They knew about what?"

"Our meeting. They knew about the meeting. The Americans are way ahead of everyone else on this."

Aleksander chuckled. "Corporate spies, government spies. No secrets are safe anymore. You should still hear them out, Jonathan."

Jonathan paused and looked out of his aircraft to the rolling desert of gray clouds below him. "It won't change anything. The Americans shared some intelligence. Every country that has any weight to throw around has their eyes on my project... this fucking anomaly I've been cursed with. I don't want to be in the middle of a war, but right now Endurance is at the epicenter of a global political problem bubbling up to the surface."

"Alright," Aleksander sighed. "I'll call off the meeting. So, what are the Americans planning?"

"I don't know exactly. The world has seen a taste of the powers this alien object possesses. They want to know what else it can do. They're genuinely concerned with some overly ambitious group staging an attempt to get control of it. And they didn't just tell me that. They showed me some proof."

"I see."

"They want to plant security at Endurance. Military. And to really send a signal to everyone interested, they're repositioning one of their space-based security systems to cover our site."

"So, they mean business."

Jonathan took a drink and set his glass down. "They are not playing around. They believe this is a very serious matter."

"If they don't want to extract it, then what?"

Jonathan paused for a moment. "Control is their aim at this stage. My guess is they either want to blow it up to keep the playing field level, or maybe just bury it."

"Blowing it up would surely, how do you say, ruffle a few feathers?"

"Yes, it would," replied Jonathan. "And I have no interest in being in the middle." He rubbed his forehead. "Hell, maybe I'll just extract it myself and drag it out to the ocean."

Aleksander laughed. "Not a bad idea."

Jonathan smiled at the thought. But he knew Endurance was now being watched by every spy satellite system orbiting the planet. He wouldn't get very far before someone stepped in.

"My friend," he exhaled as he stood to go make another drink, "Our path forward is the new Endurance site. It's the only way. This situation is only going to get worse. And as fascinating as that alien machine is, we have to distance ourselves from it. We're in Antarctica to chart a path to the buried resources that the world's markets are hungry for and to avoid political entanglements along the way." It was now clear to Jonathan. It was only a matter of time before Endurance would be fully taken over by these guys. And if not them, some radical group no one saw coming.

"So," Aleksander said. "Catch me up on the new site."

"Nick's plan is to have the structures, like the main station and the warehouse, moved in ninety days. Then they will start on the elevator shaft. In eighteen months, we'll be operating again."

"Sounds promising," replied Aleksander.

After their call, Jonathan sat back in his chair with his drink and thought more about the meeting with the Americans. He started to see a bigger picture. The wheels of expansion, probably more than anything else, were driving all the efforts to deal with these alien machines. Anything that got in the way had to be removed. He was on the side of expansion with all the world's governments and so moving Endurance was the right plan. *Let them take care of any big obstacles in our path,* he thought. *We uncovered a big one in Antarctica, and now we're going to step out of the way and let them deal with it.*

THIRTY-THREE

Winter in the Southern Hemisphere was slowly fading, giving way to warmer days. Months had passed since Jonathan had decided to move the Endurance site. Ellie wound down her work there and had ramped up projects in South Africa. She and her team of doctoral students were back exploring one of the oldest and highest yielding sites for hominid fossils in the Gauteng Province, a cave forty-one kilometers west of Johannesburg where many early human fossils and evidence of bone tools had been discovered.

It was Midday when Ellie took a break from the cave work and ventured off with Beau on a walk along a nearby creek. Beau ran ahead of her, chasing motion in the water. Ellie pondered on the things that had happened over the past year, her mind flashing through images of the monolith on Mars and pictures Rachel had sent her of the new base there. Jonathan once explained how the push into space had grown the demand for metals and rare elements and the demands increased every year. Resources on other continents were getting harder to extract.

She reflected on Endurance, a project essentially conceived as a first mover, to begin mining efforts on the last untapped spot on Earth. *What if these monoliths are monitoring us?* she asked herself again. It was a question she had begun to consider more often since the meeting at IMTEC. She knew about ancient civilizations that monitored less sophisticated neighboring societies. It's what intelligent creatures did once they have a quality of life they want to protect. *But how would we ever know?* she thought. *How could we possibly understand?*

She and Beau retraced their normal path along the water's edge and up across the rocky terrain, following the trail that circled back to their work tents and campsite. A student was outside the main tent, hovering over an old tree branch. Ellie followed Beau up to him. When she saw the log and the driver-ant colony, she knew what he was doing.

"Hi, Professor," he said as he bent down to pet Beau.

"Are we having an ant issue again?"

"Oh, god yes. They're aggressive little beasts, all in our food and my favorite snacks again. It's time to get rid of this colony."

Ellie stared at the student for a moment, not really looking at him but processing what he had said. She turned her gaze and squatted to study the tiny ants. *They don't know,* she thought. She frowned while watching them work. *They know we're here, but they don't know where the line is. They will never know... until it's too late.* She didn't feel sad for the ants. It was simply necessary so her team could carry on with their work. After a moment, she stood up. She realized it was impossible for them to know. The reality of the truth became clear in her mind. It would be impossible for *us* to know until it was too late.

Ellie finished her run, turned up into the Witwatersrand campus, and slowed to a fast walk in the direction of her office in the social sciences building. Inside, she paced up and down the long hall on the second floor, cooling down and thinking while she prepared for her call with Arnaud. She had to talk with him. Someone. Anyone who would listen. She hadn't slept well since returning from the field work. She didn't know exactly what they were doing on Mars, but she was confident she could guess.

Inside her office, she sat on a stool in front of the screen on the wall and called Arnaud. He appeared after a few chimes.

"Hi Arnaud," said Ellie, concentrating on her thoughts. "Thanks for taking the time. I wanted to talk to you more about Mars and the object there."

He raised an eyebrow. "The two things I can't stop thinking about."

"Do you remember the meeting at IMTEC?" she asked. "We discussed purposes, and possible reasons why these objects are here in our solar system?"

"Of course," he replied "I've lost a lot of sleep trying to come up with an answer. Do you have an idea?"

"I have an idea," she replied, "but I don't know if it's right. You have to start thinking about how intelligent life behaves once they start understanding nature and the universe we live in. I mentioned in the meeting at IMTEC these machines could be monitoring all life forms on Earth, watching for development of any intelligent life that could potentially become a threat to whoever or whatever created them."

"I remember. It was the idea that had some potential." Arnaud saw her pacing. "You're wrestling with this, aren't you?"

Ellie stopped. "Arnaud, I've learned a lot about the evolution of creatures on Earth. I've learned, the universe is indifferent to life. I've learned life forms that have advantages over others always seek to benefit from their supremacy. Advanced life forms always protect their ways of life." She looked intently at Arnaud. "These machines we discovered could simply be standing guard. Monitoring to see if any life on Earth develops into a potentially threatening contagion. You know, this is classic superior-race-monitoring-lesser-race thinking. Humans have done this to each other and to any threatening species since as far back as we can see. It is what intelligent races do to each other."

Arnaud reclined back in his chair and replied slowly, "That is a possibility."

"They watch for a life form that consumes everything as it expands out into the universe, and, if not contained, could become a threat to their creators," continued Ellie. "It makes sense why they have done nothing, at least not yet. We're not yet there. At *the* line."

"Let's assume for a moment this is true," replied Arnaud. "That some other very advanced civilization had placed these *sentinels* on Earth and Mars to monitor us. To make sure we don't become a threat to them or their quality of life. What then should we do? How do we know they wouldn't consider us a *contagion*? How would we know where the line is that we shouldn't cross?"

"That's the problem, Arnaud. We wouldn't know. How could we ever know? How could we figure it out?"

"Ellie, I don't know that we could figure it out. If these machines were made millions of years ago, you and I know their creators are so far ahead of us we would have no chance of comprehending them, much less understanding how they think. I guess the question is, if this were true, what do we do?"

"We should leave them alone," replied Ellie quickly. "Threatening them will cause a response, which you and your team have already witnessed. A bigger threat will likely bring a more severe response. It would be like a growing clan of small primates threatening us. They just wouldn't stand a chance. We would wipe them out and not look back. Their best option would be to not provoke us. Arnaud, you know far better than I do that no technology we have could stand up to such advanced life forms. Why would we even attempt it?"

Arnaud looked at the other monitor on his desk, at the monolith on Mars. He knew it would be impossible to get IMTEC to change course. The decision had taken months to come together and was supported by every major government. The plan was in motion. He looked back at Ellie and sighed. "Ellie, how could we prove doing nothing would be a better path?"

She gazed at her screen, at Arnaud, with no answer. She sighed softly, "I guess it's an incalculable risk either way."

THIRTY-FOUR

Inside the IMTEC virtual meeting, Robert Van Der Berg sat at the head of the round table and admired the map of Mars floating over the center between all the members of the leadership council. Three bases along the equator and Orion under construction. Small reactors and dense banks of solar arrays powering each station. Productive mining sites. Indoor farming facilities. Decades of work. *It's slowly becoming our first stepping stone*, he thought.

A month after the meeting with the U.S. President, a plan was on the table. He understood the idea that the United States and other leading governments were now backing: Vaporize the one on Mars successfully. If all goes well, then they know they could do the same with the one on Earth if they need to. *Or any others we might encounter in space*, he thought. The bottom line was, for the safety of the world, the controlling powers must know they can manage the potential threat of the object on Earth before anyone attempted anything else with it.

The United States had offered up a new device they were sure would do the job. The weapons engineering team who developed the technology were confident it would blow right through the alien machine's force field and render it to dust.

Van Der Berg gazed at the floating map of Mars, at Station Athena. He had seen footage of the device in action— completely vaporizing dense metal structures the size of modern buildings. There was no doubting its power. Yet, in the back of his thoughts, the questions still lingered. *What if it doesn't work? What if this device just doesn't faze that monolith on Mars? Will it retaliate?* He concluded there was just no way to know. He agreed with the plan and knew it was necessary. Given these other-worldly creations had shown them power that the world still did not possess was all the justification the plan warranted. They had to establish they could destroy these things if needed.

Representatives from each of the member countries of IMTEC took part in the secure virtual meeting from their own facilities. Input from all partners was considered at the table, however, the final decisions tended to go the way of those who held the majority equity positions in the venture.

He looked around at his colleagues in *this*, the world's greatest space organization. Van Der Berg was ready to put it to a vote, even though he knew the top members had long decided which way the decision was going.

Endurance Site, Antarctica

Nick stood inside the observation deck on top of the main station with binoculars held up to his eyes. Behind the glass dome, he panned slowly from west to east, taking stock of the military teams around Endurance. He stopped. A new group further to the East was setting up shop. He zoomed in on the small compound to check out their gear. *Four environmental pods,* he noted. *Enough for twenty troops. Long-range, High-speed snow crawlers. A small fleet of armor-protected snow-mobiles.*

He thought about what had happened at Endurance since Jonathan met with the US President and his team. Jonathan was right. It didn't take long for the Americans to coordinate with their allies and to deploy a ground presence around Endurance. He wondered what military gear was in orbit over-head, watching that region of Antarctica, ready to act if needed.

Troops rotated in and out. After a while, with the bits of infor-mation he accumulated from them—combined with what he read in the media, what Jonathan shared, and with what Rachel wrote in her messages—a picture started to come together. Since the world had learned of a second alien machine on Mars, countries had grown more interested in the one in Antarctica. After the one on Earth and then the one on Mars had shown the world their defensive energy fields, concern inside world governments peaked. Some more ambi-tious countries, and radical groups, who learned of the Mars events, became more captivated by their power.

Inside the subway station's dressing room, Sergey sat on a bench and cinched his boots tight. He stood up, grabbed his helmet, and headed towards the elevators. For the past week, he had noted each one of the IMTEC guys' daily patterns. At this time of day, they were either eating or in their own quarters.

"Hey, where are you headed?"

Startled, Sergey turned around quickly.

Nick grinned. "You're going to T11, aren't you?"

"Yes. I want to see with my own eyes what these new guys are up to."

"I'm coming with you. Go get the lift." Nick jumped into his suit, grabbed his other gear, and caught up with Sergey. Inside the elevator, they secured their helmets and finished tightening up their gloves and boots.

Months earlier, they would have met transporters carrying rubble from Atlas digging a new tunnel and would have heard rovers steadily scanning walls, floors, and ceilings of the tunnel. Now, since Jonathan had decided to move Endurance, all digging and scanning had stopped. The tunnels were empty.

It was the quietest quiet, thought Nick.

Fifteen minutes after they had set foot on the bedrock level, they reached the mouth of T11 and turned into the tunnel. The downward sloping grade was steeper than the main line and curved more, slowing their pace. Nick remembered telling Rachel they could be descending into what was once a valley in that region of Antarctica, once lush with tall trees and thick green plants—food for dinosaurs that roamed the territory. Nearing the end, Nick's thoughts circled back to the ancient machine from another world that had somehow been buried there, possibly as far back as when those dinosaurs had roamed those lands.

The two stood at the mouth of the chamber as the overhead lights turned on in succession. They each looked around for a moment. Neither one had stepped foot in the chamber for some time. The alien monolith was now encircled with scaffolding. Hundreds of devices attached to the framework watched, measured, and sensed any little change in the object's surface.

Near the bottom of the entrance ramp, they saw the newly installed device. Through Sergey's spy drones, they had watched the scientists pack up all the other gear then unpack this device. Now mounted on a flat platform in front of the giant monolith, the shiny metal obelisk looked almost like a toy.

"What do you think it is?" asked Nick curiously as they walked down the ramp.

"I suspect that's what was in the large container we saw them transport down here."

"Think it's some type of weapon?"

"That's exactly what I think it is," replied Sergey as he stepped around the platform, studying the device.

Nick left Sergey with analyzing the new device while he walked around the mysterious anomaly they had stumbled upon almost two years earlier. He rubbed his hand slowly along its surface. Once it was thought to be a meteorite, now it was an enigma at the center of the world's attention. He thought about Davesne's analysis, and his reports of the machine's awareness. *Why do you react to humans, but not machines?* he pondered. His hand balled up to a fist as he meandered along, tapping the hard surface.

"It's just the strangest fucking thing, Sergey," he mumbled into his mic, looking up at the stone-hard mass. "What a mystery. One here and one on Mars."

"There could be more, you know."

"There could be."

"Hopefully, we don't run into another one at the new site."

"Let's hope not," chuckled Nick.

"I found no markings on it," said Sergey as he stood up from inspecting the weapon. "Nothing. No control panels. Just this slot which must be to activate a first stage. From there, I am sure it would be remotely controlled."

"No weapons company logo?"

"No, not a mark. You told me Dr. Davesne spoke of tests at the meeting at IMTEC and how the twin monolith on Mars gave them options to carry out tests."

"That's right."

"Maybe they sent one of these to Mars. If they successfully destroy that alien object, and there are no serious side effects, then I think they plan to do the same thing here. I think this device is something they believe can destroy these alien objects. If they need to."

"This is why they've increased the military security," said Nick. "They also don't want this device getting in the wrong hands."

"Yes, that sounds right. I think this is a special device, capable of significant destruction. Hence the site evacuation they've imposed. Sounds to me like they plan on testing out this device."

Nick thought for a moment. "I don't know. Maybe it's here just in case they need to use it. A safety precaution. If that device has the power to destroy this thing, then it will take out all our tunnels as well, and maybe more."

Sergey turned and looked at Nick. "It's time to go, my friend. Time to leave this site and finish building up the new one. Let's not be a casualty of a mistake, like those scientists who did that last test."

Sergey's right, thought Nick. The signs are all too obvious. It was time to complete the move to the new site and put some distance between them and this alien machine, and this weapon. They had no role to play there any longer.

The men walked back up the main ramp, turned around, and looked back at the chamber and the otherworldly object they had dug up.

Nick stared at the round crest on its face and the three sword-looking cross marks. He remembered the shimmering energy field that nearly killed the scientists and wondered what power it possessed. He turned towards Sergey. "I just wonder what that mean machine might do if that little weapon doesn't do its job?"

THIRTY-FIVE

Mars

Forty-one days after departing Earth, the transporter slowed its approach and began its lateral movement to pair up with the dock extending from the Mars Space Station. Sensors in the dock and on the exterior of the spaceship communicated with the ship's navigation system. Small jets that lined the port side of the craft fired in pulses, nudging it slowly into its resting position. Aside from the piloting crew, and the passengers arriving for their rotation on the planet, this EMT carried one additional passenger: a new military device.

IMTEC's plan covered every detail. There were no big decisions for Gabriele to make. Just execute, continue work on Orion, bring all work at stations Leto and Chronos to a close, evacuate those stations, set up the device near the object, then detonate it from Station Athena.

A week passed after the arrival of the device before optimal weather arrived. The atmosphere outside was still.

Enrico walked through the bay door.

"Enrico." The pilot shook his hand.

"Cargo loaded, Captain?"

"Cargo is loaded. We'll depart here shortly."

There were three others already on board. Enrico patted Jordan on the shoulder as he walked between the seats. "I needed an expert operator with a steady hand." He then took a seat and pulled down his restrainer.

The flight from station Athena to the excavation site of the monolith was smooth as calm water. Enrico looked out the side window at the alien monolith as the air transporter circled the giant crater he and his team had dug months earlier. Studying the object, he noted how perfectly vertical it rose from the surface. *You look like you're here for a purpose*, he thought.

Eyeing a landing area a distance from the crater, the pilot banked and circled the site before lowering the craft to the surface. Its extended legs compressed, gently setting its underside down. The crew suited up and waited for the dust clouds to settle.

"Enrico, do we know anything about this device?" asked an engineer, sitting in a side seat with his helmet in his hands.

Enrico looked over at the young man. "We do," he replied confidently. "It's a very high energy weapon, engineered to incinerate everything within a close proximity. Once we have it set up and mounted, I'll insert this." He dangled a small, solid object in the air. "This is used to turn on its remote operation system. After that, we'll control it from Athena. Sound like a plan?"

The engineer nodded his head and smiled.

"Since IMTEC wanted us to evacuate back to Athena, it must be a serious weapon," said Jordan.

"It's the residual radiation," said Enrico reassuringly. "We'll have to keep our distance from this area for a while."

Enrico stood in the crater and gazed up into the engraved marking on the object's face. He remembered seeing the images of the one on Earth in the briefings but never really understood until that moment, standing there face-to-face with it, just how menacing it looked. *Why are you here on this desolate, lifeless planet?* he wondered. *Did you try to spawn life here and give up after a while? Or, did you somehow wipe Mars clean of life?* Enrico felt ground vibrations and knew it was the manned robot walking down the ramp behind him. "Okay, time to see what you're made of," he said, stepping to the side of the platform.

Jordan was inside the robot, maneuvering the arms and legs like they were her own. She walked down the ramp to the bottom and towards him, carrying the device with the machine hands. Standing in front of the platform, she rotated the shiny metal obelisk to a vertical position and lowered it into the footing brace. The engineer clipped the anchors tight around the base of the device and then secured the lateral braces. Its polished metallic surface glistened. It bore no markings, no signs of who made it or where *it* came from. The only markings were two recessed light bands around the top and one slot on its face.

"Looks like a modern monolith and an ancient monolith in a standoff," said Jordan into her mic.

"Yes, it does," replied Enrico. He backed up and took in the scene for a moment. After the engineer finished securing the device, he walked up to the face of the weapon and inserted the remote activator into the slot. A minute later, the top light band brightened with a soft white glow. It then dimmed and brightened in a recurring pulse. Enrico looked up and around the top of the crater and spoke into his mic. "Team, we're done here. Let's pack it up."

Rachel was sitting behind a pair of large screens with her headphones on, working on a new piece of code for ADESA when a message from Nick appeared. She grinned as she stretched her arms above her head and yawned. She looked back at her code for a moment and realized it was going to take longer than she cared to sit there. *Time for a break,* she decided. She grabbed her tablet and headed out to her favorite spot in Athena, the observation deck on top of the station. With a drink in one hand and her tablet in the other, she walked into the glass-domed room and shut the door. The sun was at eleven o'clock above the horizon, half the size as it looked from Earth and about as bright as a hazy day. Down on the surface, towards the East, a rover was returning to the station. A trail of dust stretched out behind it in the direction of one of the reactors.

Rachel set her things down on a small table, lifted her headphones up from around her neck, and played the message from Nick. His smiling face instantly filled the screen of her tablet.

"Hey, there!" he said, his eyes lit with excitement. "I have something to show you." Standing inside the main station, looking out through a glass wall, he panned his camera around slowly showing the warehouse at the new site, and what looked like a robotic crane. "That hole over there, near the crane, is where the elevator will be installed. We've started digging and it's going well." Nick's arm extended out in front of the camera and pointed. "That demolition robot standing on the platform is Hammer, another one of Sergey's creations that helped us dig the first elevator shaft. That's a killer machine. I love it! Sergey's working on a second one we'll need here with the glacier being deeper than the last site."

Nick turned the camera back on himself and sat down. "You know, this new site is a long way from the last one. And with a giant mountain range between us we can work here and not think about what's happening there." He smiled. "That's a relief. Anyway, I just wanted to show you how far we've come here at Endurance number two and to tell you, even with all the work, I still miss you."

After finishing the message, and watching it again, Rachel was happy that they had moved the Endurance site. A small, lingering concern for Nick faded away. She laid her tablet down on the table and looked around the red-orange terrain beyond the windows. It was hard to believe almost a year had passed by since she arrived on the planet. The initial awe of being on Mars had long worn off. She was now ready to be back on Earth and had started counting down the days.

———

Exiting Athena through one of the hangar bay doors and heading east, Gabriele set out early on a walkabout. She was feeling good after sending Van Der Berg the report he had requested—details on the top projects on IMTEC's radar. She thought about Rachel and how she had become a shining star on her command record. Since arriving on Mars, Rachel had worked tirelessly on ADESA and the scanning gear. Performance was now on par with ADESA projects on Earth. Installation of the shield panels over Orion were progressing according to schedule. Together with uncovering the first alien discovery on Mars, Gabriele's career at IMTEC was cruising along well. A kilometer down the trail, she picked up her pace.

She thought about Michael and told her virtual assistant to record a message.

"Recording," announced the soft voice.

"Hi," she breathed out. "I was just thinking about you while on a walk." She glanced up and to the right to make sure the recording timer was ticking away. "I'm headed east on the main trail and then plan to take the mountain loop back." She smiled. "You know, it's more like a small hill, not a mountain like we're used to." She glanced ahead at the terrain and the small incline where the path forked. "Today is the big day here. The big test. Then we pack up in ten days for the return trip to Earth. This one will be longer. Forty two days. Quite a long ride this time." She rubbed her wrist to feel under her suit. "So, I've worn the bracelet every day. I love it, Michael." She felt herself getting emotional. "I wanted to tell you... I..." She took a slow breath. "I love your proposal, and I can't imagine sharing my life with anyone else." She climbed the short path up and then took the south turn. Her suit sensed her elevated bio metrics and adjusted her oxygen content to match. "These alien discoveries are going to change our world, Michael. I don't know how, but you and I know they will. They already have, to some degree. Anyway, I think my work here will grow. And yet, I love the thought of a life together with you." She smiled. "We'll have a lot to talk about when I get back this time."

After finishing the message to Michael, she realized it was harder than she had thought it would be. She found herself choking up at times and then having to exercise the breathing training used to steady your emotions when outside in a space suit. It was tough with him and her career, both pulling her in opposite directions. But having both seemed like an impossible balance.

As she continued along the path, her thoughts found their way back to the alien objects she couldn't stop thinking about. The conversation with Michael on his boat began to mix in with her thoughts. *Some life form created these advanced machines, millions of years ago, and had somehow buried one on Earth and one on Mars. Their creators now know where humans are. They'd watched us grow and become an intelligent race. Yet, we know absolutely nothing about them. But why the two?* The answer was just not there.

Gabriele glanced up at the Mars sky as she paced along. She wondered if she was being watched at that moment.

At a quarter till the hour, all work at Station Athena came to a halt. Teams gathered in front of displays around the station to watch the event. All preparation work was complete. The device would be detonated at eleven-hundred hours—Universal Time.

Gabriele walked into the control center and stood in the back, out of the way. Inside the heart of all operations on Mars, she felt the usual energy level from the engineers and controllers moving about, managing every project on the planet. It was a busy operation, running twenty-four-seven. For the event of the day, monitoring-satellites had been repositioned over the quadrant and were streaming onto overhead screens. After detonation, banks of drones positioned outside of the blast radius would be deployed to the site to relay live video and sensor data back to Athena. A countdown on the large display in the front of the room overlaid the live stream from the site. Fourteen minutes and twenty-three seconds to go.

Enrico saw Gabriele and walked to the back of the center and joined her.

"Everything ready to go as planned?" asked Gabriele.

"We're all set. Just need you to do the honors at the top of the hour."

Gabriele's expression turned quizzical.

"Press the detonator button."

She smiled. "That I can do."

After a while, Gabriele's attention moved to the main display. She thought about the small range of outcroppings and hills west of Athena, sitting between them and Chronos. Two-thousand kilometers on the other side, deep in a crater, stood that giant alien object where it had rested for eons of time.

The countdown displayed 5:41.

She turned and smiled at Enrico. "That's quite a crater you and your team dug. I don't think I ever congratulated you on pulling that off so efficiently."

"Thanks, Commander," he replied with a wink.

"What did you think when you stood next to it?"

Enrico thought for a moment. "To be honest, my first reaction was to cover it back up."

"Oh?"

"But I understand why we're doing this. I get it. We have to make sure we can protect ourselves."

"That is the reason. If this one on Mars were the only one, then our whole approach would be different."

Enrico turned and looked at Gabriele. "What if it doesn't work?"

Gabriele hesitated for a second, then replied firmly, "It will. I've seen a demonstration of those devices totally incinerate solid blocks of metal larger than that monolith."

"Commander?" called an operator. "It's time."

After studying Enrico's concern for a moment, she turned and walked to the front row of control desks, to the one in the center. The Duty Chief inserted a flat key into a slot in the top of the desk causing the left quarter surface to slide forward, exposing a bank of buttons and a keypad. The countdown on the main screen read *1:05*.

"Once the countdown completes, we activate the detonator," said the Chief. He then pointed to the screen on the desk. "I will first key in the sequence there on the left and then press this button. After that light activates, you will key in the next sequence, and then press that button."

"That's a bit more than just pressing *a* button," said Gabriele, light-heartedly.

"Exactly," he replied, cracking a half smile.

Gabriele looked up at the countdown. 5... 4... 3... 2... 1....

"Okay, here we go," said the Chief.

All conversations in the center stopped.

A moment later, after Gabriele keyed in the sequence and pressed the last button, she turned her eyes up to the main display.

The pyramid-shaped metallic device looked puny compared to the top half of the monolith jutting up out of the Mars surface. The light ring around the head of the weapon device lit up and began to strobe. At first it was slow. Then the strobing sped up. At that moment, the monolith awoke. The three engraved cross marks on its face moved inwards and locked in the center of the ring. The full crest cast out a blue light that flowed over its head and down, like water being poured over it, encasing the machine in a shield.

Gabriele's eyes squinted in anticipation. A second later, the weapon detonated. A radiating energy wave blasted outwards in all directions, filling the screen with a burst of bright light for a second. A thick cloud of dust permeated the air for kilometers around the site. Nothing on the ground was visible.

Moments later, banks of drones in the quadrant received instructions, exited their charging facility, and headed to the site. Secondary screens on the main wall came to life with video from the drones as they flew across the Mars surface from three different directions.

Gabriele couldn't imagine anything still standing, but she wanted to see it with her own eyes. She waited, studying the screen, eager to see if anything remained.

After what felt like an eternity later, the cloud of dust thinned out. The first drones arrived to air glowing like light in a fog. Little by little, as the fine particles settled back to the Mars surface, the object could be seen standing erect, encased in a faint blue light radiating from its crest, staring out from the super crater. In an instant, the crest turned dark. The dome of light faded. The cross markings pushed outwards, locking perfectly in their original positions.

THIRTY-SIX

Given the current distance to Mars, the video signal would reach Earth in eighteen minutes and fifty-four seconds. Whatever it relayed, would have already happened.

Arnaud, Van Der Berg, and the entire research team watched from a control room inside an IMTEC facility. The primary screen in the room played the live feed from Mars. A countdown to the event had crossed zero, turned around, and began counting back up.

"Dr. Davesne?" came a voice. "Dr. Davesne? Sir, you need to see this."

Arnaud walked over to the analyst and peered over her shoulder. She was watching the video feed of the object's chamber in Antarctica.

"When did the surface temperature start increasing?"

"Just seconds ago."

"Do you think they're communicating?" asked Van Der Berg calmly, walking up to the side.

Arnaud thought for a moment while watching the sensor data. "Given what we just did to its comrade on Mars, I don't think we can rule it out."

"And we've detected no signal coming from either monolith?"

"Correct," replied Arnaud nervously, still eyeing the data from the Endurance site. "And we've never seen these sensor readings move this much either."

Everyone in the room was now standing, watching Mars as the time counter approached 18:54.

The two men turned their attention back to the screen on the main viewing wall.

The engraved crest on the monolith's face began to morph.

"It's anticipating," said Arnaud alarmingly.

Seconds later, the device detonated. The screen turned bright white from the explosion. A moment later, the signal from Mars switched to a satellite view showing a cloud of dust engulfing the site. Nothing was visible on the Mars surface. One by one, other screens on the main wall brightened and began to stream video signals from drones approaching the site. The room was silent, waiting for images to come into focus. Dust settled slowly, revealing the blue force field. The image of the monolith, still standing as erect as before, dominated all screens.

"It didn't faze it," mumbled Van Der Berg, standing next to Arnaud, his eyes locked on the staid monolith.

Arnaud was no longer looking at Mars. He was staring over the analyst's shoulder at her screen monitoring Antarctica. The video image shook. All sensor readings died. A moment later, the screen went blank. "It's waking up," said Arnaud, his voice quivering with angst. "The machine in Antarctica is reacting."

Van Der Berg turned to look. He explained to Arnaud the plan. What came next was a safety precaution. A second weapon device was installed at the Endurance site and activated after the area was evacuated. Inside a military control center somewhere, someone was watching the Endurance site during the exercise on Mars. If they saw movement in the object's chamber, their next step was to detonate the device and destroy the object there.

Arnaud's heart sank. "My god, what have we done?"

THIRTY-SEVEN

Endurance Site, Antarctica

Deep under the ice of the frozen continent, immersed out of sight under the earthen surface, the Sentinel had quietly stood guard for millions and millions of years—watching the evolution of life on Earth for its creators far off in the universe. Its creators sent it to Earth with a single purpose and had given it the technology and intelligence it needed to carry out that purpose on its own.

After traversing many folds of space, the Sentinel had arrived at Earth long before any spark of intelligent life had occurred. Its descent into its chosen perch went unnoticed by all life roaming Gondwana. As time passed, Antarctica separated and drifted to the South, then froze over, rendering the Sentinel virtually undetectable.

Eventually, humans emerged and began evolving, reproducing, expanding, and consuming. The Sentinel quietly took notes. It sensed the expansion and growth of humans. It sensed their usage of their home planet's resources. At some point, its intelligence system had flagged humans as a potential threat to its creators.

Having sensed the rapidly growing species, and after reaching an adequate understanding of it, the Sentinel had fulfilled the first part of its purpose. The second part was optional. It depended on the outcome of the first.

Intelligent civilizations who learn to overcome gravity and venture off their home planets always start by staying close to shore, in calm waters, developing their sea legs. With enough know-how and confidence, they set sail for the nearest planet. After reaching the planet, with that success under their belt, their confidence soars. Some civilizations then took a breather and tended to slow down their outward quests. While others, driven by their success, ventured out further and faster and in multiple directions. This created a potential containment problem. Aware of these types of behavior, the Creators gave their sentinel machines sophisticated algorithms to use when deciding a course of action.

Mars was the first real step for any intelligent life that might develop on Earth, so it became the observation point for the second sentinel. Resting quietly out of sight, it only had two simple tasks to occupy its time. First, notify its comrade if life forms from Earth ever showed up on Mars. Second, keep the Earth sentinel posted on the earthlings' progress if they did. The Earth sentinel would decide, if its comrade ever notified it, whether it would carry out the next stage of its purpose or not.

The Sentinel received the latest communication from its comrade. But the message was incomplete. The part it did receive simply notified the Sentinel of the aggressive force its comrade experienced from the Earth life form on Mars.

Sometime ago, The Sentinel had sent a compilation of its analysis of Earth and the planet's life forms to its creators. Even though it operated fully autonomously from its creators, it had waited for a response. None came. After the time it had allotted to receive a response had elapsed, the Sentinel made a decision.

Inside, its systems awoke from a very long slumber. Its surface temperature rose steadily as it shook off its hibernation. Once the Sentinel had reached a certain state, it yawned and released a low sonic wave. The ground all around the Endurance site rumbled like an earthquake. Sensing the elevated state of the device in its vicinity, the Sentinel shielded itself while it continued to power up its internals. The weapon device detonated. Its energy wave pulsed out in all directions, vaporizing everything in its path until it was completely spent. Moments later, the hollowed-out cavern it created collapsed.

Undeterred by the event, the Sentinel retracted its shield and continued its course. As its temperature continued to increase, slowly, the machine rose out of the earth. Its top pierced through the ice as it pushed upwards, the glacier shattering and rumbling like the continent was splitting apart.

The Sentinel emerged out from its cover, pushing a mountain of ice up into the air. Now, out of its resting place, it slowed its skyward ascent and gently hovered in the air, rotating, as if to reorient itself with the Earth and the universe. Awake, the

Sentinel now had work to do. It was time to complete its purpose.

THIRTY-EIGHT

New Endurance Site, Antarctica

Standing on the ice at the bottom of the shaft at the new Endurance site, Nick felt a rumble through his thermal boots. He quickly spun around and powered down the robot that was hammering away at the next layer of ice. "You guys feel that?" he said into the mic in his helmet.

The three men stood still and looked at each other, listening, feeling for vibration. A minute passed. Then another minute. Then a distant roll started and slowly grew.

"That's twice. Let's go!" ordered Nick.

The men stepped up on the lift platform, attached their secure lines, and held on. Nick pressed the high-speed button. The lift rattled on its way up. Small chunks of ice broke off from the sides of the shaft they were digging, hitting their helmets and thermal suits. They each looked up, each one counting down the meters to safety.

The lift jolted at the top, locking securely into position. They executed their safety drill like they had done it a thousand times. It was simple. Get inside the main station and into the emergency room. Nothing else mattered.

The ground shook and rumbled harder. The men fought their way across the shaking ice sheet to the underbelly of the station and stepped onto the entry lift. One of them punched the *Up* button. The platform rose into the station, screeching at the top as the air seals pressed tight against each other. They ran through the thermal lock and down the main corridor. Sergey was waiting for them in the emergency room, checking seismic activity in the area.

Nick popped his helmet release and looked out at the site. "Where's it coming from?"

Sergey was studying data on his tablet from sensors encircling their site. "Definitely south of here, toward the old site."

"Can you still access the site's surveillance?" asked Nick.

"Possibly. Give me a moment."

The station began to move more.

"It's getting stronger," said an engineer, pacing in the room.

"Strange," said Sergey.

"What'd you find?" Nick looked over his shoulder.

"Nothing."

"No activity there?" asked Nick.

"No. I am not getting any signal from the sensors."

"They should still be transmitting, right?"

"Yes, of course, but—"

The vibrations subsided. The crew stopped talking and just listened. Nick walked around the table and looked over the site again. He didn't see any apparent damage. The warehouse looked unfazed. Sergey laid his tablet down, breathed slowly, and waited. The crew sat quietly for a while. They had learned to give it time before claiming victory.

"I'm going up top to survey the area," said Nick as he ran to the observation deck. He gazed out of the glass dome around their new project site and looked for anything that had shifted or moved. *Everything looks well intact,* he thought. He took the binoculars and looked further afield in all directions, observing and noting the landmarks he had committed to memory. He began to relax.

"Well, comrades, that one wasn't too bad," said an engineer to the others.

"We've been through worse," said Sergey. He leaned forward and touched the room's control panel on the table, then activated the screen on the main wall and navigated to the station dashboard. He studied the data from all the site's sensors. "Looks like a six'er. And no reported structural issues. At least none yet."

"What's the transporter's ETA?" asked an engineer after noticing the flashing proximity alert.

Sergey checked the time. "Not for two hours, I thought. Call Nick. Maybe there was a change of plans." He then switched the screen to the perimeter cameras. Eight video streams appeared in a grid on the wall from cameras positioned five kilometers out from the main station.

"I don't see anything," said an engineer studying the video feeds.

"What are you looking for?" asked Nick, stepping back into the room.

"The perimeter sensors activated," said Sergey. "I didn't think they were due to arrive for another two hours."

"They're not," replied Nick. He saw something in the top left camera and squinted, trying to make it out. "Something's there... in the air. What direction is that?"

Nick's eyes widened. He backed up from the screen slowly, falling into a chair. "Jesus, it can't be." He stood up and bolted down the corridor and back up the stairs to the observation deck. Sergey and the other men followed.

Nick picked up the binoculars, turned towards the South and raised them to his eyes. He rotated slowly to the left, then back to the right, panning the horizon. He stopped. The object was dead center, slowly growing larger. Nick's pulse raced, seeing it move in the sky towards them. In that moment, he understood. He then knew why the ground had shaken. "Something bad has happened," he announced to the crew now with him. The object moved across the sky, accelerating as it passed. A low hum from the alien machine reverberated against the glass. Nick glimpsed the crest on its face. It was glowing. The alien obelisk continued on its lateral course, growing smaller and smaller until it vanished into the horizon.

Deep inside a cave in the Gauteng province of South Africa, a tiny drone navigated through a tight crevice. Ellie and her team watched the screen inside the work tent with anticipation. They had hoped there was an opening on the other side. A large chamber would be unbelievable. Ellie would settle for a small chamber. The drone's headlight illuminated the dark space as it squeezed through the opening. Minutes into its flight, it emerged into open space. Inside the area, it rotated three-hundred-sixty degrees to take room measurements. In their work tent, a computer received the drone's signals and translated the data into distances. Within seconds, a rendering of the small chamber appeared on their screen.

"That looks promising," said Ellie, peering over the teams' shoulders at the screen.

The crew cheered, elated to see the opening.

After a long day of careful excavation work to access the new chamber, Ellie and Beau started out on their routine afternoon walk beside the creek. Beau trotted along the bank, occasionally stopping to lap up a drink. Ellie meandered along behind him, looking for birds and other creatures. He continued on past their normal turn up point to circle back to their camp. Ellie didn't notice at first and pressed on in her thoughts. A few minutes further, he stopped. Ellie caught up. "What's wrong, boy?" she asked, squatting, and petting him. A lone bird on the other side of the creek flew off.

Beau looked around for a moment, then whimpered softly.

Ellie looked around longer, curious. She spotted nothing. "Something out there?" She listened. It was unusually quiet.

Beau laid down on the grassy bank and put his head down on his paws.

Ellie sat down beside him and petted his long fur. "It's okay, boy."

Beau looked up and barked.

Ellie glanced up and looked off in the distance towards the southeast. The horizon was glowing faintly blue, even though it was now early evening. The sun was at her back. She squinted and looked around, watching the blue light roll out in all directions and charge across the sky. As Ellie focused, she saw the source of the light trek northward. She knew what lay in that direction, where the light had started. In that instant, watching the Sentinel traverse through the air and its light energy intensify and permeate Earth's atmosphere, she knew. She knew what it was doing—its purpose. Her breath shortened. Her eyes grew wet with tears. *How would we know?* she thought. She felt the light's presence engulf her. A warm sensation. She couldn't look away. Darkness engulfed her vision. Her thoughts slowed for a moment, then ceased.

The Sun set. Night came. Stars off in distant galaxies painted the sky. It was warm out—unseasonably warm for winter in the southern hemisphere. Nocturnal critters chirped and sang their songs.

Beau laid beside Ellie and licked her face. She never woke up.

Standing inside the control room at IMTEC, fear grew in Arnaud's mind while he and Van Der Berg stared at the screen showing the dust settling on Mars. The alien monolith was standing erect, without even a scratch. He wondered what the object in Antarctica was doing. Had someone detonated the device there?

After the failed exercise on Mars, the control room cleared out. The tall windows around the room brightened as the environmental controls transitioned them from opaque to transparent. Sunlight filled the room.

Gazing out at the world through the windows, Arnaud noticed an unusual milky blue color shoot through the upper sky and then roll down across the IMTEC grounds. "What is that?" he shouted. He saw people outside suddenly fall over without warning. The room started to glow as the light permeated the walls and glass. He felt the floor shake, then turned and saw Van Der Berg sprawled out. His thoughts ran in all directions. "My god, she was right," he mumbled. His eyes closed as he hit the floor.

Hours later, Arnaud woke. The room was dark. After a while of fighting off the fog in his head, he sat up and looked around. Van Der Berg wasn't moving. He pushed the man. Nothing. He felt his wrist. It was cold. No pulse.

Jonathan looked up from his tablet when he heard the metal structures and machines behind him shift causing their restraining bands to creak. The cargo aircraft jostled up and down through air turbulence. He turned around to check on the gear for Endurance and then turned back and peered out of the side portal. Beyond the glass he saw nothing but clear sky and endless Southern Ocean below as they sped along at twelve thousand meters above the Earth en route to the new Endurance site, still two hours ahead.

"Mr. De Clare, can I bring you anything?" asked the co-pilot, strolling through the cabin.

Jonathan turned. "No. I'm fine for now. Thank you."

"The Captain is trying to find smoother air."

"Sounds good." Replied Jonathan. He continued reading the recent media article titled *Magnate Controller of World's Resources Discoverer of Alien Machine*. He found it amusing, the story a journalist could weave without ever having spoken to him. Of course, he rarely gave interviews, so the media had to find their details through other means, sometimes even pulling them from thin air. He was born into a working class family. That part was true. But the author's speculation on Jonathan's early life challenges as his motivations and drive in business were far from the truth. He looked up and towards the front of the craft, thinking, reflecting on the empire he controlled. All the mines, ships, smelters, refineries, machines, and technology he owned. The one hundred and fifty thousand plus people he employed. The craft he was flying in. The Endurance site. It was all because he loved the grit of the doing. The building. The digging in the Earth. Enabling human expansion. It was intoxicating work, and it felt like purpose. The more he did, the more content he felt with himself. Each success led to doing something bigger. Something bolder. The riches he had amassed had brought some pleasure, but they were not the end. To him, there was no material end. Only *the* end.

After reading the first part of the article about himself, he laid his tablet down. He knew the rest was nothing more than the author's take on all the alien object information now in the public sphere. He closed his eyes and folded his hands across his lap. Ellie came to mind. A small smile surfaced on his face. Jonathan had not seen her in a while. His mind drifted to the last time they spoke, to the conversation he couldn't get out of his head. She had seemed to grow more and more disturbed about the alien machines. Jonathan had listened to her theory about why they were here, on Earth and Mars. He remembered the conviction in her eyes and her tone. He didn't dismiss her idea out of hand. But in the end, it was simply too far out there for him to sink his teeth into, to entertain. Another life in the universe, millions of years ahead of humans, monitoring life on Earth, maybe even equipped to keep humans under control.

The turbulence eased up. The aircraft glided along through smooth air. Jonathan saw a glow through the slits in his eyes as he moved towards sleep. *The sun,* he thought.

Minutes later he heard, "Mr. De Clare!" The urgency in the pilot's voice jolted Jonathan. He opened his eyes quickly and saw the co-pilot whisk by. Jonathan popped the release on his restrainer and strode to the front.

"Look," shouted the Captain, pointing out of the front windshield.

Off in the distance Jonathan saw a blue light fuse through the atmosphere like ink in water and roll towards them.

"Should we turn around?" asked the pilot.

Jonathan's eyes widened, watching the blue light rapidly approach the craft and jet out in all directions. "Yes. Turn!"

"Restrain yourself," said the pilot, disengaging the autopilot and grabbing the controls.

Jonathan turned around, returned to his seat, and locked his restrainer. The aircraft banked hard. He looked around the cabin and grew tense seeing the air inside the craft slowly begin to glow. Jonathan felt pressure push him into his seat. He sensed the nose of the craft turn downwards. Ahead in the cockpit, both pilot and co-pilot were slumped in their restrainers. Feeling a warmth surround him and seeing his vision fade, the urge to bolt to the cockpit withered and instead, Jonathan slowly closed his eyes. His thoughts slowed. A dark fog washed through his mind. The thought of Ellie being right turned into his last smile.

THIRTY-NINE

Station Athena, Mars

Inside the control center, while studying drone footage of the monolith from just minutes earlier, Gabriele heard a rumble. She looked outside and saw a dust cloud roll through the air.

"It must be the shock wave," said Enrico.

"It shouldn't have reached us," replied Gabriele confidently.

"Chief?" said a systems controller, looking up from her monitors.

The Duty Chief, standing beside Gabriele, turned. "Yes?"

"Sir, I'm seeing fluctuations in power from grid Paris-4."

Gabriele and the Chief walked over and studied the data on her screen.

"This is the energy flow from the grid. It's dropping rapidly," said the controller, pointing at the flow gauge on her screen.

"That's our main backup array," said the Chief.

"I've tried to reach the maintenance crew at the site. They're not responding."

"There's a crew there?" asked Gabriele.

"Yes," replied the Chief.

"Let's get some eyes on that area," said Gabriele.

The controller accessed the satellite array and directed the closest one to lock onto the site. She then routed the video signal to one of the main overheads. A moment later, a screen came to life. The flat terrain along the equator west of Athena, home to the second largest solar array on Mars, came into focus.

Attention in the room shifted to the scene on the main wall.

"Zoom in on their craft?" ordered Gabriele.

Objects on the screen grew larger and came into focus; a toppled transporter, damaged arrays. "The shock wave," she said. Glancing around the room she spotted Enrico. She knew she should send one of her senior leaders, but she felt responsible. She had to go. She then turned to the Chief. "Notify the emergency crew. Let them know I'm on my way."

Minutes later, Gabriele dashed through the entrance to the hangar. The engines of the emergency craft were warming. Responder crew were boarding. The co-pilot followed Gabriele's pace up the stairs to the entry hatch, entered the aircraft and sealed the door as the main pilot throttled the engines up and navigated out of the bay. Speeding across the Mars landscape, the pilot maneuvered the craft between mountains west of Athena and across the terrain, following the navigation system's optimal path to the site.

The control center had deployed drones to the Paris-4 power grid from a shielded recharging bay a few kilometers away. With sensor data and footage relayed from the site, they briefed Gabriele and the team of medics on the situation. The maintenance aircraft at the site was toppled on its side. Only a handful of solar arrays remained standing.

The aircraft squatted down hard and fast, then released the back loading door. Gabriele followed the team down the ramp and across the dusty surface of the planet. She glanced around the area, taking in the details, looking for hazards missed by the control center's site analysis; damaged machinery, unstable structures that could pose a danger to the responder crew.

She walked over to where the pilot lay, being tended to by a medic. He wasn't moving. After a few moments, the medic stopped what she was doing and looked up at Gabriele. "The shock wave must have thrown him against the aircraft. His neck is broken."

Gabriele turned and walked to the others. One man was sitting up slowly, his face contorted with pain. The medics were lifting him onto a carrier. He was the lucky one. A smashed helmet from a flying array had killed his co-worker.

The flight back to Athena was somber. Gabriele looked around at the medical crew; the one survivor with a busted leg and broken ribs, and then the two bodies in the aircraft's bay. This would be recorded as the worst incident yet on her watch. She was mad and frustrated. She knew IMTEC had run many simulations of the explosion, and they would have factored in every known variable to model the blast wave. It shouldn't have come close to this site. Obviously, they missed something. She knew the process that would ensue. IMTEC would analyze the accident down to every micro detail until they figured it out.

Gabriele looked towards the cockpit. The co-pilot was approaching.

"Control center is trying to reach you, Ma'am."

Gabriele raised an eyebrow and activated her headset. "Chief?"

"Commander."

Gabriele knew something was wrong.

"Commander. Something's happened. We've... we've lost contact with Earth."

"Temporarily?"

"No. No. The signal from Earth is there. It's strong. It's just... no one is responding. It's like—"

"Like what, Chief?"

"Like everyone's left for the day, Ma'am. It's not just IMTEC. We're not picking up any chatter from Earth. No noise. Nothing. Nothing in any languages."

"What do you mean, no chatter?"

"We monitor all signals of all types coming our way. One minute everything was fine. The next, all signals went flat."

Like monitoring radio waves when out sailing far offshore, she thought. It was comforting to know someone else was out there. When the chatter died out, you got anxious.

"I wanted to alert you to the situation, Commander, and let you know we're working to figure it out. We're now checking solar activity reports, looking for anything that might be the cause."

"Keep me posted, Chief." After signing off, Gabriele thought about the day. It had been one bad thing after another. She then looked up. Seeing the curiosity on some faces, she said, unemotionally, "Communication issues with Earth. They're just keeping me posted as they work to get it resolved."

Back at Athena, the crew unloaded the bodies and gear. Gabriele made her way through the station. As she walked through the entrance to the control center, she noticed tears on some faces. Other people just sat in shocked silence. She felt tension in the air. The Chief looked up from his pacing. "Commander. Something's changed."

Gabriele followed the Chief into a side room and closed the door—sensing the direction of the news. "What's happened?" she asked calmly.

The man sat down at the table and took a deep breath. "We're still not receiving any communications from Earth, but we are back in contact with Earth Space Station. They're reporting the same thing."

"No chatter? Nothing?"

"Nothing yet." Using the control panel laying on the table, the Chief activated the screen on the wall, then looked back at

Gabriele. "Decades ago, we put a surveillance satellite in place to do nothing more than stream out into space a continuous video signal of Earth. All our ships and bases receive the signal. It's kind of a beacon, really. But given our modern technology, we have no real need for it. Well, one of the crew suggested we tap into it and take a look. You know, roll back the video stream and watch Earth around the time we lost communications. This is what we found." He pressed *Play*.

Gabriele heard the quiver in the Chief's tone. She slowly looked over at the screen. A big Earth was in the center. A time marker ticked away at the bottom. Forty-three seconds later, a blue light enveloped the Earth. It remained for several minutes and then faded. She looked back at the Chief.

"After that," the Chief breathed out and looked down at the table, "no more signal chatter from Earth. No more communications." He looked up at Gabriele. "Jesus, Ma'am. What's happened today?"

Gabriele gazed at the shaken man. Her mind on the numbing events of the day, the detonation of the device, the standing monolith, two dead colleagues, and now this. She rubbed her temples slowly, then ran her fingers through her hair and pressed on the back of her neck to ease the tension. It all started feeling like a nightmare. *What has happened?* she asked whoever was listening to her thoughts, begging someone to give her an answer. *What has happened on Earth?*

She looked at the Chief. The man was glancing around, hands shakily fiddling with the controls. The dead silence between the two was crushing as both struggled for answers. Gabriele forced a sincere smile, then grabbed the Chief's hands and squeezed firmly. "Keep talking with ESS. I am confident everyone at IMTEC is working to re-establish communications. We'll figure this out, Chief. In the meantime, we need to get engineers and maintenance crews out to the array site to bring it back online."

The Chief shook his head slowly, welcoming the directions. "Yes, of course. I'm on it, Commander."

"By the way," asked Gabriele, turning as they exited the briefing room. "What's the status of the inbound EMT?"

"It's ten days out."

"And the one after that?"

"Forty-one days. It just departed ESS."

Gabriele left the control center and went to her office. After pacing for a while and thinking, she sat down at her computer and checked messages. Nothing from Van Der Berg. Nothing from Michael. Nothing from anyone. It had now been nearly eight hours and still nothing from Earth. "Fuck," she said to her screen. Her stomach wrenched. *Keep it together*, she commanded herself. *Lead.* She turned her gaze out the window, searching for something, anything. Deep inside, she knew something bad had happened. *There was some connection in all of it*, she thought. *But what? What has happened on Earth?*

She calmed herself and began to think. The news from the control center and of losing two comrades would spread quickly. She needed to brief everyone, to head off rumors, and to bring everyone onto the same page. *Now*, she told herself. *This can't wait.*

The mood in the meeting hall was sober, unsmiling. The conversations were few. Crews drifted in from different sections of the station. Others out at the remote sites tuned in. Gabriele paced slowly, never imagining she would be in this moment, having to deliver the heavy news she was about to pour into everyone's minds. She looked around the room and saw somber faces and questioning eyes in place of happy scientists. *They all know,* she thought. Her mouth was dry. She made herself breathe deeply, calmly. Nearly ten hours and still nothing from Earth. It was serious.

The talk quieted down. She stopped pacing and looked up from the floor. "As most of you know by now, earlier today we detonated the weapon device in an attempt to destroy the monolith object. The explosive wave it created in the atmosphere killed two of our colleagues and damaged a backup power grid." She heard crying. She looked around slowly. "Something had been missed in the simulations of the weapon." She paused and shifted her gaze around the room. She knew there would be time for grieving later, but now she had to keep going. "Something else has happened, team. Sometime after that event, we lost communications with Earth."

"All communications?"

Gabriele recognized the voice. She turned and saw Rachel. "Yes, but we are still receiving some passive signals."

"What about ESS?" asked an engineer.

"They've lost communication with Earth as well."

"Something must have knocked out all terrestrial systems," said another engineer. "That's the only way all comms would drop."

"I agree," replied Gabriele. "And I am sure ground crews there are working hard to bring everything back online." She had to get out the last piece of information. She turned to the wall behind her and activated the screen. "What I am about to show you is footage of Earth captured by a legacy satellite system earlier today." She hesitated a moment, took a breath, then pressed *Play*. Forty-three seconds later, blue light flowed out from a point and shrouded Earth. Gabriele let the video play until the light faded. The room was silent. No one moved. "Since that time marker, all communications stopped. All chatter has stopped."

Eyes widened. Mouths moved as if to say, *what? What has happened?*

Now that all the data was out, she knew she needed to keep her crew focused. "Listen, everyone." She let the talk die back to silence. "You now know everything I know. There are no answers at this point, but they are coming. Control center is laser focused on this issue. The crew at ESS are working non-stop. The instant I know something more you will know as well. Let's let the crew in the control center do their work while we do ours. Time out here in space has not been without significant challenges. This is just another one. Together, we will get through this."

FORTY

Earth

The Sentinel's force targeted humans and was indiscriminate. It was also incomplete. Its force did not achieve the desired outcome to address the conclusions of its analysis. The laws of Nature had been at work inside the machine, and Nature's laws apply universally to all things. One of those laws is Entropy. Simply put, the second law of thermodynamics says, all things spread out over time. They break down. All materials, no matter how well engineered, will eventually, given enough time, break down and degrade.

Millions of years ago, it had lowered itself into its perch under the Earth's surface and over that span of time, the Sentinel's internal systems decayed slightly; just enough to reduce its abilities and to open up a slight vulnerability in its shield. However, slightly weakened, it had pressed on with its job.

The Sentinel's creators bore no malice towards mankind. It was designed to protect its creators from life forms that could eventually threaten them. Its algorithms analyzed humans over time and came to a conclusion. The Sentinel simply acted according to its program. The response was believed to have been painless, though the fraction who survived didn't understand why.

The Creators had devised models of how life forms in the universe would evolve and had used those models to program the sentinels. But the models were not perfect. A couple of life forms in other star systems, who had the real potential to become a threat to the Creators, had escaped their sentinel's wrath, while others who were highly unlikely to ever achieve that status did not escape. Still, given the number of races in the universe, the Creators considered the models' error rates to be insignificant. In a competitive universe, full of intelligent life, the sentinels erred on the side of their creators. They were the Creator's best method of risk mitigation.

FORTY-ONE

Mars

Latched onto one of the docking ports of the space station, the first transporter circled the small red planet while the ground and space-based crews prepared to depart. Gabriele had ordered an evacuation. All bases, all outposts, and the space station would be left in hibernation states. The first half of everyone on Mars and the space station would depart for Earth on this ship. The other half would leave on the inbound transporter, arriving in four weeks.

Days after the event, Mars had re-established communications with Earth. A skeleton team at IMTEC were doing everything they could to ensure Gabriele's crew—the last ones in space—could get back to Earth. The Mars crew learned many people had died, but no one knew how many. Nor did they know how it had happened.

During the long days that followed, the remaining crew on Mars and the ones en route to Earth began to piece together a picture of the world they were going back to. Automation systems the world had long adopted seemed to have held up, at least for a while. Aircrafts had piloted themselves to the ground, ships on the oceans had navigated themselves to their destinations. But everyone was in shock from the aftermath of the destruction of unimaginable proportions. In an instant, something had swept across the world, wiping out a large fraction of the human population. As each day brought new details, the picture of the Earth they were returning to turned grimmer.

On board the last transporter, Gabriele stood on the bridge and watched the departure events tick off one by one on an overhead screen. *Detach from MSS*, was next. The dock's latches released sequentially from around the exterior of the loading door. Moments later, the lateral propulsion jets fired, pushing the ship far clear of Mars Space Station and starting its slow rotation. A kilometer away, it had completed the maneuver and now faced the path towards Earth. Its rear propulsion engines ignited and started accelerating the ship away from the red planet. Gabriele watched the overhead screen showing Mars. It was like watching the planet disappear in her rear-view mirror. She knew she would not be back. Humans wouldn't be back for a long time.

The return voyage was almost unbearable. The extra days on Mars since the first transporter departed, compounded by a daily stream of distressing news from Earth, were spirit-crushing even for the strongest ones left at Athena. Now they had to endure the endless days in cold space.

Gabriele worried about her crew. She knew most of the remaining ones were seasoned astronauts and could handle the extra stress. Nevertheless, she engaged with everyone every waking hour of every day. She pushed everyone to maintain a daily regimen. She implemented and enforced systems to minimize alone time.

After long days, Gabriele retired to her quarters, drained. She checked for messages, hoping to see something from Michael. Nothing ever arrived.

"Have you heard from Michael?" asked Enrico, hesitating slightly as he set his coffee down on the table. He saw the fatigue in Gabriele's eyes. Eighteen days had passed since they shoved off from Mars. He was concerned for his friend.

Gabriele looked up from the meal she was picking at. "No. Nothing."

Enrico asked about others. Conversations around family and friends were hard, even with colleagues he had known for years. Where does he start? When did he stop asking?

Gabriele picked up her cup of coffee. "A new message came in this morning from IMTEC. A survivor has surfaced who was in the control room with Van Der Berg when they were monitoring the device detonation."

Enrico sat up and leaned forward. "Oh?"

"I read the transcript earlier. Evidently they were monitoring the object in Antarctica while watching the event on Mars."

"Did they send any footage?"

"No, not yet. But according to this survivor, the cameras died around the time of detonation. Maybe the one in Antarctica woke up and did something after we tried to destroy its comrade."

"Maybe," replied Enrico. "But there's a million reasons for those cameras dying."

"I just think it had something to do with what happened on Mars," said Gabriele, as she sipped her coffee.

"We never detected a signal coming from the monolith," replied Enrico.

"Maybe they communicate in some way we're not aware of. Given what we've seen, why not? Maybe the one on Earth kicked off some global chain reaction after hearing from its mate on Mars."

"Don't forget, it's buried under a mountain of ice. Hard to do anything from where it sits."

"You're assuming it's still there."

"They're solid masses," replied Enrico. "At least as far as we know."

"How did they get to where they are?" asked Gabriele. "How do they do what they do?"

Enrico nodded his head slightly.

They took their time finishing their post-workout breakfast, a morning routine they made themselves hold to for the journey back. Most mornings ended at the same point, discussing *what-ifs* and possible connections.

———

Days away from Earth, aboard the first transporter, Rachel laid in her bunk late into the night. She held out her tablet and stared at her messages. Nothing new had arrived. The dark, quiet wait was maddening. She sent message after message and then stared at the screen for hours, waiting for something to come back. She welled up inside again. It was just too much. She laid the tablet face down, closed her eyes, and slowly fell asleep.

Hours later, the tablet lit and shone into the bunk. Aroused from the dim light around its edges, Rachel rolled over and lifted the tablet. A message appeared. Nick's face slowly flashed. She began to cry again as she pressed *Play*.

"*Rachel...*" he choked. She had never seen this Nick before. She saw a large black bruise on his head. His eyes were sad and dark. She made out the background and knew he was in the control room of the main station.

"*I don't even know if you are there or if you will ever get this message.*" She had to pause it and clear her eyes. She looked up at the ceiling in her room and breathed in and then out, then started it again.

"*Something... something terrible has happened here. I don't know what. Something... some force, some... something has killed my team and many more. I don't know how many. If you are there, I know you are still in space somewhere. I hope you are okay. I hope whatever did this has spared you and everyone there with you.*" He looked up at the ceiling. After a while, he lowered his gaze back to the screen. "*My crew is dead. Sergey —*" He welled up again.

She started crying again.

Nick turned back to the screen. "*The transporter was on its way back with supplies. Jonathan was on board, coming to visit the new site.*" He paused. "*It never made it.*"

"*A few days ago, I started getting some news here. It's bad. Really bad. There's mass confusion. No one knows anything.*"

His voice calmed down. "*Listen, Rachel. I need to tell you everything. All the cameras here recorded what I am about to tell you. I am sending messages to others as well. Maybe others saw what I saw. I don't know, maybe not. I am the only one left here. I don't know why I was spared. Maybe I wasn't and somehow I am dreaming or something. It sure feels like it. Like I am in a bad nightmare and can't shake myself out of it.*"

He leaned forward slightly. "*Here's what we saw happen. We were working here. Excavating the elevator shaft for the new site...*"

Rachel listened to every detail as he recounted the events.

Nick squinted his eyes and shook his head slightly. "*It was the object. The anomaly we dug up. It... it was hovering in the air and moving towards us. That thing had to be what caused the ground to shake. It had to be. It busted up through the ice somehow.*"

He rubbed his eyes and his face slowly, as if he was still trying to wake himself. *"So, that thing hovered past us here. As it flew by, I saw the crest on its face. It was lit up. A very faint light kind of shimmered around it. We all watched it hover off towards the horizon."*

He rolled his shoulders and rubbed the back of his neck. *He's worn to a frazzle,* she thought.

"This is where it gets weird. Just after it vanished from our sight, it happened. I remember seeing a light on the horizon. A glowing light, that sort of flowed through the air. We watched it. It got really bright, and it was thick. I don't know how to explain it. It filled the air everywhere, flowing through everything. But it was light. A thick bright light. A bluish light. I remember it felt warm, Rachel." He paused as if he were stuck in a thought.

"Sometime later, I woke up. It was like an hour later. Maybe more. I had this." He touched his forehead. *"Sergey was laying there beside me. He never woke up. The other guys never woke up."* He slammed his fist on the table and then pushed his hair back over his shoulders.

She paused it again for a moment and dried her face on her pillow.

"Rachel, I have to leave here today." He mustered up a chuckle and smiled. *"I get to test my wilderness skills."*

"Oh, god," she cried.

"The transporter didn't make it so I have to set out across the tundra. I've mapped out my course to the next station. There I'll rest and then make my way to the next one. I am sure I will

find others along the way. I must go, Rachel. I can't sit here any longer. I have done what I needed to do here and now I want to get back to the world, to help out."

He then slowly opened his eyes wider, his cheeks raised as he smiled. *"I somehow feel you are out there, making your way back to Earth."* He leaned in towards the screen. *"That thought is my guiding star. I am on my way now. It might take a little while, but I'll find you."* He then winked and nodded. *"You know I will."*

Rachel looked at the bottom corner of the message at the date. It was from two weeks earlier.

"Where are you, Nick?" she whispered.

FORTY-TWO

Antarctica

Nick glanced down at his snow crawler's control panel and saw the charge meter tick down to zero just as the machine came to a stop. He knew, from that point, he had about fifteen minutes in residual juice to keep the heating going. Then, it would die too. He looked in his rearview mirror at the two crawlers he was pulling along on skids. On the bed of the last one, he had brought along two snowmobiles just in case. Out of the front windshield, he eyed the two scout drones hovering in place. They were his eyes on the road ahead, his ticket to navigating over the ice without falling into some endless cavern just waiting to swallow him and his entourage of snow crawlers. Nick picked up the control unit laying in the passenger seat and instructed the drones to dock and recharge. They turned around, flew overhead, and landed on the charging platform, mounted on the bed just behind him. Nick took a break, ate a sandwich from his supply, and rested as the sunlight streamed through onto his face. *Something to be thankful for,* he thought.

The trek was painfully slow going. The crawlers were slow, but that wasn't the problem, it was the scout drones that slowed him down to a snail's pace. But he knew he couldn't push them any faster without risking it all. Exhausted from having to focus and pay attention, he closed his eyes. He knew all it would take was one stupid mistake, one time of not watching the feedback from the drones, and he would die, right there, in the middle of nowhere.

An hour after the heat died, Nick came around. He opened his eyes, took a drink of water, and sat up. "Okay, time for you to go to the back of the line," he mumbled, patting the dashboard. In under an hour, he had detached the front crawler, pulled the rest of the train around front, attached the dead crawler on skids as the caboose, moved all his supplies over, and set off again.

Nearing the end of the fourth day, Nick spotted the outpost station and grinned. He knew this time of the year it wasn't occupied, but it was a place to rest and recharge and hopefully stock up.

That night, inside the station, Nick searched online for anything current. Very little was to be found. Most news feeds appeared to be lifeless. Through the scraps and tidbits of data he stumbled across, the picture of the world he was heading back to had become clearer. It was grim, sad, and confused. Many people had been wiped out. He found some news in foreign languages, ran them through online translators and discovered the same everywhere. It was like the trauma and result of a devastating plague or some dangerous virus. *But it seemed far worse,* he thought. As he grasped the immense impact on the world, he started to question why. He thought about Ellie and her ideas. *Did she survive?*

Eight and a half days after departing the new Endurance site, Nick reached his destination. He sat in the crawler at the top of the glacier and peered down at the coastal station below. The excitement of seeing the compound burned off the exhaustion that had built from another eighteen hour day. He knew from communicating with the station at least four men were there. One survivor from the station, one from another station, and two of the crew of Jonathan's ice breaker, docked at the port.

He spotted one man waving a flag and smiled, he hadn't seen another living human for weeks. He felt himself get emotional and tear up, then he wiped his eyes on his sleeve. He was ready for some companionship on what he knew would be a long voyage.

Of the two surviving sailors, neither was a captain, but they were engineers, and they knew how to power the ship. Navigation was their weakness. Automated guidance systems, reliant on a network of land and space-based communication programs, had become unreliable as systems began to shut down around the world. Someone had to have their hands on the wheel, and someone had to navigate through the ice by eye. The sailors knew the challenge they faced breaking free of Antarctica. They didn't fear ramming an iceberg. The ship could handle that at full throttle. They feared such an impact might kill two of them. Two down and they might not be able to man the ship.

After days of inching along, developing their skills through trial and error and learning to work as a team, they finally edged out of the sea of icebergs. As they worked the ship, rotating stations as a crew, they grew more confident in their skills and picked up the pace. They charted a course up the east coast of Africa, hoping to make it to the northernmost tip of the Gulf of Suez.

Day nineteen of their voyage, warm ocean air rolled in. Nick rotated from his shift manning the wheel to an hour break. He spent it on the upper deck, reclined in one of the chairs the crew had assembled for their occasional gatherings to hear Nick's stories of the alien machines. Under the midday sun, he closed his eyes and thought about his plans.

Nick had received a couple of Rachel's messages and knew she had received his. But then one day the messages stopped again. Others noticed the same. They assumed some land systems were shutting down and failing from lack of maintenance or power. If Rachel landed at their return destination, and if she stayed put, then she would be waiting at the IMTEC facility near Madrid, Spain. In his last message to her, he told her that's where he was headed. He just wasn't sure if she got that message. He tried to picture meeting Rachel again. The thought carved a smile across his face, now covered by a longer beard. He knew he would have to hold that image for a while, and she would have to wait.

He thought about seeing the Sentinel—the name Ellie had given it—move across the sky and remembered its shield flickering like its power was failing. He assumed the weapon device had been detonated and had damaged it in some way. *Its systems were sputtering*, he thought. He wondered if the damage had diminished the force it had released on the world. Staring out across the bow of the ship at the horizon, he remembered its trajectory. *It had to come down somewhere, and unless it had turned, its path was eastern Africa.*

Twenty-nine days at sea, the exhausted and weary crew couldn't take another. They needed to plant their feet back on land for a while before continuing further north. Anchored in deep water, off the coast of Africa, the men went ashore.

The small ocean village where they docked felt abandoned when they arrived. Stray animals lingered in the streets. The stench of death washed through the warm, humid air. Confusion was evident in the disordered array of the town. Some buildings were locked up, while doors to others were wide open.

After three days of the crew milling about, two lone fishermen on bicycles showed up at the docks. The crew learned the village had indeed been abandoned, and the two who remained did so simply to continue their basic way of life, fishing.

A few days on land, seeing the lack of life, and hearing the fishermen's stories hit the men hard with a reality they had evaded at sea. As the initial shock began to fade, the crew wanted desperately to continue on, to find the remains of their former lives. After hearing one of the fishermen tell them of a villager who had seen something in the sky, Nick realized his path lay on land, for he had picked up on the Sentinel's path.

The men parted ways like old friends. Shy one member, the crew returned to the ship and continued north up the Red

Sea. Based on the direction the fisherman had pointed, Nick strapped on his gear and headed northwest.

After hitting shore along the coast and traveling north, Nick started talking to everyone he could find. He knew there would be other survivors who would have seen the Sentinel in the sky. Trekking north, he caught rides with strangers, and stayed with ones who were fascinated with his stories of the machines.

Some power systems had shut down, forcing ones to migrate to towns where modern systems continued working. Along the way, he eventually caught a whiff of the Sentinel's trail. One survivor in a small town had seen it and was confident in the direction he pointed. Another day's journey, and Nick found another witness. Then another.

On the outskirts of Meroë, Sudan, near the east bank of the Nile, Nick and two nomads and their loaded camels set out from their tent camp and headed northeast across the Nubian Desert. No one else was around. They were alone in their hunt, guided only by what one man had glimpsed as he awoke after the event. An object had fallen from the sky. An obelisk wrapped in a faint, shimmering glow followed a straight northeast trajectory, angled towards the Earth. Having spent every day of his walking life navigating to all points surrounding that desert terrain, the man knew the exact direction of the path the falling object had taken. Intrigued by Nick's stories, the men bought into his quest to find the alien machine.

With the upper halves of their faces visible through their headscarves, the men set their sights on the red butte formation a day's walk into the desert. The glowing object had gone down beyond that point. From its speed and angle of descent, the navigator estimated it to be a two, maybe three days journey.

Nick's new nomad friends spoke little, their attention focused purely on what they were hunting. An evil had fallen over the world and taken many lives with it. Their friends. Their families. The nomads knew the stories buried in their religion and others that spoke of the end of days that would come. Somehow, the good would rid the world of evil and then eternal peace would ensue. This did not feel like those times. The nomadic hunters felt no peace, no tranquility. But they were curious. They wanted to see this evil that Nick was hunting with their own eyes.

The end of the first day with the nomads came with the sun setting slowly to the West, beyond the Nile. The men had reached the base of the tall butte and set about laying out their camp for the night. With light still covering the sky, their hunter instincts drove them to the top of the butte to survey the area and to try and spot the Sentinel.

The men sat peacefully on the edge of the cliff, facing north. After a moment of admiring the beauty of their world, one man extracted a binocular device from his pack. He switched on its power and then peered through the enhancing lenses. He panned the terrain patiently, systematically, west to east, near to far. Each object in his view was tagged with a marker and a distance measurement noted in a light red color. A minute into his searching, he stopped. "There. There it is," he breathed in his native tongue. The Sentinel lay half submerged in the desert sand, its faint, dimming glow giving away its location. He panned back east and then west, making a mental note of the markers that framed the object. He thought about the distance reading flashing next to it. "Two days," he mumbled in broken English. He then handed the device to his big, tattooed friend to make his own notes and distance judgements.

Early morning of the fourth day, the sentinel hunters quietly ate a light meal, then packed up their camp onto their camels and set out with a hint of daylight to the East. With the cooler morning air and desire to now see the dying object, the men's pace across the rolling dunes held steady. The older one in the lead peered ahead, studying the size of the two markers he had noted the first day from their lookout point. He eased their path a few degrees further to the East and continued on.

Two hours after breaking camp, as the top half of the sun rose above the horizon, the leader stopped on top of a dune and gazed ahead. Nick walked up on the right side and brought his camel up next to him. Their quest had reached its end. The Sentinel rested on a side, half buried in the deep trench it had dug before it had come to a halt.

The patient nomadic hunters studied it. Now seeing it with their own eyes, they wondered what power it might still possess. It didn't look mystical, or godlike in any way. Its appearance was more ancient looking than anything else they could conjure up.

Slowly, the men eased down the north face of the dune, then across the flat earthen surface towards the object, their camels encouraging more caution. Standing a hundred meters away, they felt waves of heat radiating from it. The leader studied the engraved crest on its face, still emanating a blue glow.

After walking around the object and investigating its smooth surfaces, they stopped on the west side. The older man studied the crest's simple design. He pointed with his walking stick. "It's a warning," he said firmly through his thick black beard. "Three swords. One pointing south, one east, one west. They protect their master sitting at the North."

Nick stared at the giant obelisk as he thought about what had happened to the world since they first uncovered that marking. Then he nodded slowly, agreeing. "Yes, it was definitely a warning." He now felt some small sense of contentment, having tracked it to its end, now knowing where it lay, and that it was dying.

Light of the early night faded. Nick rested with his new friends at their camp under trees in a small oasis, a short distance eastward. They watched the sky darken, and the sea of stars, planets, and man-made devices in the atmosphere come to life. Patiently studying the night sky and learning to recognize its known celestial bodies was the nomads' post-dinner entertainment, something they had practiced with their fathers and grandfathers, and then with their children.

This night, with the new knowledge from Nick, their thoughts and conversation expanded. The men's discussions explored new territory, new ideas, other things in the universe, even other life forms not from Earth.

As the night's conversation ended, the older man gazed back up at the sky. "It's not a sign," he said, unwavering. "It's not from god."

Nick nodded gently. "No. There's an enemy out there. An intelligent enemy. One with vast powers."

The elder thought about the dying object. "Something happened to it. It shouldn't have crashed and died."

"Something weakened it," said the younger man.

The older one looked at Nick, his beard parting as he cracked a slight smile. "We tracked the wounded beast to its end."

Nick smiled back with some slight sense of satisfaction.

Later, after the men retired, Nick's thoughts turned to Rachel and more importantly, how to get to Spain.

At the end of the last day with his nomad friends, Nick had realized where he was, relative to Spain. He was in the middle of the Nubian Desert, and he had to make a choice. Either go around the Med or across the upper lands of Africa. On advice from his friends, he chose the alternative route through Egypt, Turkey, Eastern Europe, and then across the regions on the southern side of the Alps. *A long journey indeed,* he thought.

Ninety-four days had passed since the event. Nick held his arm out the side window of the large transport rover and enjoyed the crisp early morning. He drew in a long breath and felt the cool air fill his lungs. In the darkness before sunrise, he gazed up at the few stars—still visible—and with a solemn look he tried to imagine what would create such machines and why.

The old man driving the rover manually said little. He enjoyed listening to Nick's stories of the alien machines and of Nick's journey from Antarctica to Spain to find his girlfriend. They talked about how Nick found the Sentinel in the desert, and the searing heat it was still putting off days after crashing to earth. The men shared with each other how they had felt waking up after seeing the blue light and then realizing they had survived a near-extinction event. They talked about how different life would now be.

After a long stretch of watching the road in quiet contemplation, the old man asked, "Why do you think this happened?"

"I don't know," exhaled Nick slowly. "I've asked myself that question a thousand times. We may never know."

The two men sat in silence and watched the changing landscape.

Seven hours after crossing the border from France into Spain and traveling cautiously along main roads filled with wreckage, they turned off onto an overpass and followed the signs to the IMTEC compound. The old man glanced casually at his new friend as he pulled off to the side of the road at the main gate and parked.

Nick swallowed hard. He looked over at the man and laughed once as he wiped his eyes and sighed. "It's been a year and half since I've seen her. She's in there somewhere, waiting."

"Well, son," the old man said firmly, "you're wasting time sitting here with me. Go find her."

Nick shook the man's hand, smiled, and said, "Thank you, my friend." He then grabbed his pack, opened the door, stepped down, and made his way to the gate.

The guard at the front shook Nick's hand warmly and welcomed him. He knew Rachel, and that she was hopeful for Nick's arrival soon. He pointed toward the housing quarters on the other side of the compound. Nick set out walking the path but then picked up his pace to a jog. Feeling alive and energetic, he sped up to a flat-out run. At the front door to the building, he stopped for a moment to compose himself. He slowed his breathing while looking at his reflection in the glass window of the door. Seeing a thinner, rougher face, he brushed his beard down with his hands and pulled his hair back into a hurried ponytail.

"Nick?" came a stunned voice from behind.

Still panting, he turned around. There she was, coming toward him from the neighboring building.

"Oh, my god," she cried, putting her hand on her chest.

Nick dropped his pack and ran to her, stopping just a breath away. He wrapped his arms around her and picked her up and held her tight, turning around. After a long while he let out, "Oh how I missed you."

"I missed you," sighed Rachel, tears streaming down her cheeks.

He set her down. Then he pushed her hair back behind her ears and held her close and kissed her. Rachel looked up and touched his windburned face and smiled.

The next evening, after a night and a day of reconnecting, the two sat alone under the night sky next to a fire Nick had built —a childhood pastime he loved when not in Antarctica. They talked and touched and tried to bring back some sense of the past—the way it was. But an unknown force had destroyed the past. That force had changed the world forever.

In the light of the flames, Nick saw Rachel's quizzical expression as they looked at each other. "What is it?" he asked.

"Something—" She squinted, studying his eyes. "Something's changed. The color. The pattern."

"Everything has changed." Nick replied, reaching over to hold Rachel's hand. "Everything."

EPILOGUE

Ten years later. The aircraft began its descent to the private runway of the Earth Space Institute. Gabriele peered out of the window and studied the terrain below. Her memories of what it had been like before the event mixed with what she saw now. Large cities contracted. Smaller ones completely shut down. Aside from the fringe communities—enclaves seeking to distance themselves from the technology-laden society that had brought this evil on the world—rural communities had all but disappeared. Large swaths of land had been given back to nature. Even after the years that had passed, it was still surreal to see with her own eyes.

After a smooth vertical landing, the aircraft taxied to its hangar and parked. Gabriele slung her bag over her shoulder, exited the machine, and set out towards the campus. At the gate to the high-security research building, she paused briefly for the scanner to complete its body sweep and give the guard a green light.

"Good morning, Commander."

"Morning," replied Gabriele, shaking the guard's hand then turning towards the stadium-sized building in the center of the campus. Inside the facility she passed rows of scientific gear, experimental devices, and racked computing machines lining the room. Everyone at that facility worked on the same project, with the same focus, and the same purpose. Understanding the alien machine that lay on the floor in the center of the building.

"Commander," came a familiar voice from behind while making her way to her office at the other end. She turned and smiled. "Enrico, morning."

"I wanted to introduce you to a new crew member. He transferred in from another facility."

Gabriele looked over and shook the gentleman's hand firmly. "Pleased to meet you."

"Thank you, Commander. It's a pleasure to meet you as well."

"I didn't catch your name."

"I prefer to be called Diablo, Ma'am."

"Well, Diablo. Do you know whose team you are on?"

"Dr. Dibaba's I hope."

"He said he knows Rachel, but she probably wouldn't know him," said Enrico.

"I know of her work," replied Diablo. "I'm a big fan. I finished my doctorate in astrophysics, got into AI, and then got fascinated with hunting for aliens, long before this thing showed up. I believe I can be of use on her team."

"She's away for a few days, but I am sure she will put you to work as soon as she returns. We're trying to assemble the best and the brightest here. We need everyone we can find. Glad to have you onboard, Diablo."

Turning to continue on her way, Gabriele spotted two scientists working with the experimental energy field generator. A glowing film of light flickered around a small model of a space transporter. She smiled. In the years since the event, scientists were just beginning to make progress. Slowly, different ways of thinking about matter, and the forces at work in the universe, arose from studying the Sentinel.

Gabriele entered her office, laid her bag down, grabbed her tablet, and sat on the small sofa to finish her morning reports. Two matching bracelets dangled from her wrist; the embedded stones clinked against the tablet. She looked at them and felt the feeling again. Her throat still tightened when she thought about Michael. She then stopped it and pushed it all back inside. She looked through the glass wall overlooking the research floor and the machine from another world laying there. Seeing it and realizing the unimaginable power it had unleashed on Earth still brought an icy chill to her. She tried to move past it, but it was hard. *Maybe we should have just left them alone,* she thought. Even though she had long concluded there was no way she could figure it out, she still couldn't erase the terrifying thought. Did their actions on Mars somehow trigger this thing on Earth?

Her hair was grayer now. Her face was harder. As Commander of Earth's new space program, she focused on leading a new era of exploration in a universe that now felt tougher, colder, and indifferent to life. Her thoughts of a simple life on Earth with Michael had quickly faded after returning from Mars and realizing he was gone. A simple life no longer fit the time nor the world. The lure of discovering who or what else was out there was too strong. It was also terrifying. But that was now part of the game.

Next encounter, we will be prepared, she silently affirmed to all.

Over time, the sentinels had set back other intelligent life in other star systems. On Earth, the setback was catastrophic but was far less than the machine had intended. The event taught the world there was at least one other life form in this competitive universe, and *that* life form had gotten a head start. Those who survived on Earth were now aware there was competition out there, and they were going to figure out how to compete.

———

Far off in deep space, light years away from Earth, while scanning galaxies for the signature blue light, a hunter probe caught a sliver of the light's frequency emanating from a tiny dot, a distant galaxy in a region of space unknown to its owners.

ABOUT THE AUTHOR

T. M. Haviland is a novelist with degrees in Physics and Finance and enjoys writing about his interests in the forces of nature and evolution of humankind.

For updates and new book releases:
www.tmhaviland.com

FIRST EDITION (1.0)

ISBN // 978-1-7375129-0-5 // E-BOOK

Made in the USA
Monee, IL
23 July 2022

10210924R00194